D0957874

St. Martin's Paperbacks Titles

by DD Barant

Dying Bites

Death Blows

KILLING ROCKS

BOOK THREE OF
THE BLOODHOUND FILES

DD Barant

St. Martin's Paperbacks

This is a work of fiction. All of the characters, organizations, and events portrayed in this novel are either products of the author's imagination or are used fictitiously.

KILLING ROCKS

Copyright © 2010 by DD Barant.

All rights reserved.

For information address St. Martin's Press, 175 Fifth Avenue, New York, NY 10010.

ISBN: 978-0-312-94260-1

Printed in the United States of America

St. Martin's Paperbacks edition / January 2011

St. Martin's Paperbacks are published by St. Martin's Press, 175 Fifth Avenue, New York, NY 10010.

10 9 8 7 6 5 4 3 2 1

KILLING ROCKS

ONE

I have this recurring dream where I've been ordered by a federal judge to join a support group.

"Hi," I say. I'm sitting on a folding chair, part of a circle of people. "My name is Jace, and I am a human being."

"Hi, Jace," everyone choruses.

"I've been a human being for—well, thirty-some-odd years. Actually, where I come from pretty much *everyone's* a human being."

A large woman in a floral-print housedress puts up her hand. "Don't use the people around you to justify your actions," she says primly.

"But it's true," I insist. "No vampires, no lycanthropes, no golems. And then I got shanghaied into this universe by a shaman named Ahaseurus—believe me, when I find that guy, we are going to have *words*—and now I'm trapped here until I catch a Free Human Resistance terrorist named Aristotle Stoker—"

A weaselly guy with a ridiculous mustache and a BELA LUGOSI FOR PRESIDENT T-shirt puts up his hand. "So none of this is your fault?"

"No! I'm telling you, I was kidnapped out of my own bedroom—"

"Why you?" he asks in a nasal voice. "Are you trying to say you're different from everyone else?"

"I *am* different. I'm a criminal profiler for the FBI, specializing in hunting down homicidal psychos—a job that doesn't seem to exist here. Pires and thropes and lems don't go crazy—well, they never used to, anyway—so they need me to hunt down Stoker, who's definitely out of his gourd—"

The woman in the flowery dress shakes her head. "I don't know what that means."

"Mentally unstable. Deranged. Squirrelly. Nuts. Wacko. Out to lunch—"

Nasally Mustache frowns. "You're no different from anyone else, Jace. You have to accept that before we can help you."

"—insane in the brain. Off his meds. Unable to locate his marbles. Needs to be fitted for a long-sleeved love-me jacket so he can hug himself all day long. Bats in the control center, long-term resident of a rubber room, lights are on but so is the VACANCY sign—"

The woman sighs. "Sounds to me like you're in denial, Jace." The rest of the group mutters and nods. "Normally we insist that members finish each step in the program before they go on to the next, but in your case I think we'll make an exception. You need to go right to Step Thirteen."

She gets to her feet. So does Nasally and everybody else.

"Being human doesn't have to be a life sentence," someone says. Coarse gray hair sprouts on the woman's face as it lengthens into a muzzle filled with long, sharp teeth. Nasally's teeth are getting longer, too, his eyes turning blood red.

"Fur or fangs?" he says as they all reach for me.

That's usually when I wake up.

At least they didn't threaten to turn me into a golem. Much as I care for my partner and official NSA enforcer, Charlie

Aleph, I really wouldn't want to go through life as a three-hundred-pound plastic-skinned mannequin filled with black sand. Not that he's ever been human himself—Charlie's body's animated by the life force of a long-dead *T. rex,* distilled through careful animistic magic by this world's shamans. It's something they do here a lot—though they usually use cattle or some other large animal to charge the lems' batteries—because golems make up something like 19 percent of the planet's population. Of the rest, 43 percent are lycanthropes, 37 vampires. One percent is all that's left of the human race.

Welcome to my life.

I've discovered that a few universal truths hold firm no matter what alternate world you're in; for instance, Mondays always suck. On a planet loaded with hemovores they tend to suck even more, in both volume and intensity.

"Morning," Charlie says in a deep-voiced rumble as I get on the elevator. He's his usual natty self, wearing a double-breasted dark green suit and matching fedora with a tan snakeskin hatband. His tie is black silk with an emerald stickpin, which compliments both the black chrome shininess of his plastic skin and his highly polished shoes.

"It is, isn't it?" I mutter. "AM. As in Awful and Malignant."

"Rough weekend?"

"No. Angels massaged my feet while I bathed in sunbeams and chocolate."

"Wouldn't that be messy?"

"It sounded better in my head." I take a long slug of coffee from the travel mug in my hand. "Will to live . . . returning," I say. "Damn. Thought I had it beat this time."

"The day's still young."

"Thanks for reminding me."

"Something's up." He glances at me and frowns. "Not

you, obviously. But Cassius wouldn't call us in this early unless it was important."

I give him a withering glare, which has about as much effect as a laser on a mirror. David Cassius is our boss, the head of the National Security Agency, which for some reason is based out of Seattle here. He's a very old, very powerful pire, and he looks like an eighteen-year-old Californian surfer boy—or at least he did until recently.

The elevator doors slide open and we step out into the NSA offices. It looks pretty much like the offices of any intelligence-gathering agency in my own world—lots of people in lots of cubicles, the murmur of voices and machines, people in suits and ties striding along clutching laptops or file folders or paper cups of hot blood.

Yeah.

See, that's the thing about this place. It does a real good job of seeming normal, at least on the surface—but then some little detail comes along and whacks you between the eyes. Cars look like cars until you notice how many of them have windows tinted so dark you can't see inside, even through the windshield. At Easter, the bunnies aren't made of chocolate—though there's still a hunt, and kids still stuff their faces. And during the full moon, every thrope beneath it participates in a massive, three-day party that makes Rio during Carnival look like a Mormon picnic. Okay, that last one isn't all that small, but at least I only have to deal with it once a month.

You can make up your own joke. I mentioned it's Monday, right?

We march through the room to Cassius's office, which has a large smoked-glass window beside the door. The other side is sometimes blocked by retractable wood paneling, depending on whether or not he feels like watching his people work. Mostly, just the fact that he might be looking makes them work harder.

Cassius's office looks more like a study—dim lighting, lots of books. He's sitting behind the desk, and of the four chairs in front of it two are occupied: one by Damon Eisfanger, a forensics shaman, and one by Gretchen Petra, one of our top intel experts.

Cassius is dressed in his usual dark blue suit, his short blond hair neatly combed, his hands clasped together on the desk like a high school student at his first interview.

"Hey, Damon," I say as Charlie and I sit down. "How's the baby, Gretch?"

"Growing at a prodigious rate." Gretch is British, sharper than a room full of razors and just as dangerous. She appears to be in her late thirties, wears her blond hair pulled back into a tight bun, and dresses like a librarian. She's a pire who recently had her first child, Anna—there's a spell here that allows that, as long as the parents are both willing to age six months for every year the child does. The kid becomes a full-fledged immortal when the spell is canceled, restopping the clock for the parents, too. That means Gretch is actually older than when we first met, though she doesn't look it—and so is Cassius.

Anna's father, Saladin Aquitaine, was murdered by a psychopath I helped catch. Cassius agreed to take on Aquitaine's time-debt, which otherwise would have fallen completely on Gretchen. My surfer-boy boss is growing up, after spending Lord-knows-how-many years with his internal stopwatch stuck at late puberty.

Damon Eisfanger just nods at me. He looks a little nervous, and I wonder why. Damon's a thrope, his bloodline descended from a pack of arctic wolves, which gives him his ice-blue eyes and snow-white crew cut. The wide, muscular build he gets from the other side of his family—sometime in the past a wolf-bitten pit bull chomped one of his ancestors, passing along the lycanthropy curse and adding a few additional canine genes at the same time.

Damon's a geek who looks like he lives in a gym, but he's also a friend who's slipped me information that could get him in trouble.

"Jace, Charlie," Cassius says. "Good morning to both of you. Sorry to get you out of bed so early—"

"Oh my God," I say. "You have a zit."

"Excuse me?"

"A zit. On your face. I realize you may not recognize it because the last time you needed skin care products they hadn't been invented yet, but that little yellow thing at the edge of your hairline wasn't there yesterday."

"I wouldn't know, Jace. I don't own a mirror."

"Point taken. Are you a squeezer or a grower? Because I really don't want to have to sit here and watch that thing expand every day—"

"Jace—"

"Hey, is your voice changing?"

Cassius sighs. "Are you done?"

"I've got more material, but not all of it's ready. Let me do a polish and get back to you."

Cassius taps his keyboard and a panel behind his head retracts, revealing a large flatscreen. The face on it drives a stake through the heart of the wisecrack I was about to make.

Aristotle Stoker.

"Do this right," Cassius says, "and you might not get the chance to perform any of it."

It's a shot of Stoker in a trench coat and sunglasses, walking down a city street. He's a big man, six foot ten or so, with the build of a linebacker. Good looking in that craggy, implacable way that speaks to the cave-woman genes—one look tells you this is a guy who'll bring you a saber-toothed rug and a stack of mastodon steaks on the first date.

Time-stamp on the photo is three days ago. "Where was this taken?" I ask.

"Brussels," says Cassius. "He was spotted coming out of a meeting with a representative of this man." The picture changes to a shot of a man sitting at sidewalk café, cup raised to his lips. His upturned collar and hat shade most of his face, but what I can see has an odd, shiny cast to it. "Is that a lem?" I ask.

"No," says Gretchen. "He's human. He goes by the name of Silver Blue, and he's an arms dealer. The color of his skin is a self-imposed condition known as argyntia, caused by consuming large amounts of colloidal silver. It makes him immune to lycanthropy, obviously—in fact, no thrope can even touch him without suffering severe burns. Silver, of course, isn't quite as deadly to hemovores—so he also consumes an entire bulb of garlic every day."

"Shiny *and* smelly."

"And dangerous," says Cassius. "Silver Blue supplies black-market weapons to anyone who can pay for them. That includes the Free Human Resistance, which is no doubt why Stoker was in touch. It appears that some sort of major deal is under way, and more than just the FHR are involved. Also present at the meeting was this individual."

The picture changes again, now showing me a golem dressed in a pair of cargo pants, steel-toed work boots, and nothing else. At first I think the picture's in black and white, but it's not; the golem's gray, not a variation I've seen before. Most lems are a sandy sort of yellow, though enforcers like Charlie are black.

"Tom Omicron," says Charlie. "Founder of the Mantle."

"The Mantle?"

"They're a radical golem rights group," says Gretchen. "Based out of Nevada. Much of the golem production in the country is centered there, due to the soil. The Mantle advocates civil disobedience, workplace sabotage, and criminal negligence as tools for social change. Essentially, members believe in isolationism; golems shouldn't even associate with the other races, let alone work for them. They've tried—unsuccessfully, thus far—to organize several general strikes of all lem workers. Considering how many golems are employed in essential support services, the consequences could have been disastrous."

Sure. Most lems were used as manual labor, but that included everything from forklift operators to construction crews—not to mention soldiers. If they all decided to put down their pallets, shovels, and crossbows at the same time, it would bring the world to a halt.

"There were four people at the meeting," says Cassius. "Silver Blue himself was not present, but he sent his top lieutenant. I'm afraid it's someone we're all familiar with."

The next picture is of Dr. Pete.

Except it's not Dr. Pete, not anymore. It's Tair. He still has Dr. Pete's boyish good looks, but there's a streak of gray dyed into his hair now, and his eyes have a glint of cruelty in them that Dr. Pete's never did.

Dr. Peter Adams was the man who looked after me when I first came here. He treated my RDT—Reality Dislocation Trauma—and saved my life when my heart stopped. He was a kind, gentle man with a large family that cared about him.

And now he's gone. Not dead—erased. In the kind of weird magic whammy that would be impossible on the world of my birth, Dr. Pete had his history rewritten, changing a vital decision in his past from a good choice into a bad one. It sent him down a very different, very dark path . . . and it's not that surprising to see where he's wound up.

"I'm sorry, Jace," says Cassius. "We all cared about him. But this is not the man we knew. He's not just smart, he's ruthless and ambitious. He's become Blue's right-hand man in a very short period of time for a reason."

"The last time we saw Tair," I say, "he'd just stolen two very powerful artifacts."

"The Midnight Sword and the Balancer gem," says Cassius. "The first can cut through time itself; the second is able to manipulate and meld large amounts of magical energy. Sheldon Vincent not only managed to mystically unlock both items—making them usable by anyone—he bonded them together. We believe Tair offered this weapon to Silver Blue in return for employment."

"But that's not all he's done to prove himself," says Gretchen. Her voice is firm. If circumstances had unfolded differently, Dr. Pete would have been the one to deliver her baby. "He's demonstrated both ruthlessness and loyalty. He's killed his own kind, Jace—more than once."

"I guess he'd have to," I say. "Blue doesn't sound like he would trust a thrope or a pire to work for him unless they did." I try to keep my voice as neutral as Gretch's; I am a professional, after all. Two major shocks in as many minutes don't faze me, including the fact that someone I once considered a trusted friend is now a murderer.

Then Cassius hits me with shock number three.

I recognize the new face on the flatscreen, too. It's the bony, hawk-nosed profile of the shaman who brought me to this world, a man I've only met in a half-waking dream. I'm not supposed to know who he is, but I've done a little digging on my own.

His name is Ahaseurus. He's a very old, very powerful sorcerer—in fact, he's the one who designed the spell that turns unliving dirt into walking, talking golems, centuries ago.

And he's the only one who can send me home.

Oh, sure, another shaman *could* do it—if I fulfill the terms of my contract and catch Stoker, that is—but cross-dimensional magic is tricky. Only Ahaseurus can put me back more or less where he took me from, a few minutes or hours from when I disappeared out of my own bed. This whole alternate-universe experience will become nothing more than a series of fading memories, made real only by the scars I've accumulated since I got here.

If anyone else tries to put me back, I'll lose decades, both personally and objectively—I'll arrive back home an old woman, in a world that's moved on without me.

"Well, well, well," I say. "You found that shaman you misplaced, huh? Where was he, behind the couch?"

"His name is Asher," says Cassius. "I see you remember him, Jace. He's an Agency asset that's gone rogue—we believe Silver Blue is brokering some sort of deal among him, the Mantle, and Stoker, though exactly what is on the block has not been determined. What we do know is that he doesn't seem to be representing any other organization; whatever his agenda is, it's personal."

Gretchen nods. "That suggests Asher has something to sell, and both Stoker and the Mantle want it." Eisfanger hasn't said anything the entire time, and all he does now is give me a quick, nervous glance. Cassius and Charlie just stare right at me.

"Right," I say. "Three of the four principals have connections to me, and the guy with something for sale is the same one who dragged my sorry ass across the cosmic divide. Gee, what do you think he's offering up for grabs?"

"It's not that simple," says Gretchen. "True, Asher does possess a certain mystic knowledge of you that no one else does—but we're really not sure how that would be valuable to anyone but yourself."

"Depends on what he can do with it," I say. "Can he use it to eavesdrop on me? Control me? Make my head explode?"

"Uh, no," says Eisfanger. "He can use it to locate you—

but I'm going to set you up with a masking spell that'll take care of that."

"And then what?" I ask. "You lock me away somewhere for safekeeping?"

"No," says Cassius. "I'm going to give you exactly what you want, Jace—the chance to go after both Stoker and Asher at the same time. You're going to spearhead the task force we're putting together to take them down."

I blink. I smile. I *grin*.

"Where and when?" I ask.

"The meet is sometime in the next few days," says Cassius. "I've assembled a strike team—you leave in two hours. You'll rendezvous with them on the ground, coordinate a tactical strategy and be in place when your targets congregate. After that—assuming you manage to take Asher alive and either kill or capture Stoker—you'll be going home."

Home. The word sounds strange in my ears. An obvious joke about Auntie Em burbles into my forebrain, but never makes it out into the air. There's this sudden stinging sensation in my eyes.

"Good God Almighty," Charlie says. "You actually made her shut up."

"Screw you, sandman," I say. I take a deep breath through my nose and pretend I don't hear a sniffle in it. "You know you're taking point, right? If I'm outta here, you're expendable anyway."

"Wouldn't have it any other way," he says. He puts just enough softness in his voice to make me want to punch him.

I can't believe it.

I might actually be going *home*.

I'm staring out the plane's window, thinking broody thoughts, when Charlie looks up from his magazine and says, "Don't worry. We'll get him."

"Sure. As long as Asher doesn't zap us all to the moon or something."

"That's what your shaman's for, to protect us from things like that. Wolosky, right? She knows her stuff."

"Good to hear." What I haven't told Charlie is that I have my own mystic ace-in-the-hole: a powerful magic relic that I inherited from Dr. Pete when he went rogue. Of course, I have no idea how to use it or what it can do, just that it's supposedly charged with eldritch energy. It's currently in my baggage, tucked between two pairs of pants. Maybe I can ask Wolosky for some advice on the proper use of an enchanted comic book.

"You know any of the others?" I ask.

"I did a tour with Brody—best thrope with a blade I know. Gunderson has a room full of trophies he won at ax-throwing competitions. Don't know Wilson."

"How about the lems?"

"You mean the ones on our side?"

I frown. "You know some of the ones working for Blue?"

"Not specifically. But I know lems with connections to the Mantle."

"The briefing was a little skimpy on them."

"I noticed. They're a touchy subject, especially in Washington."

"Yeah? Why's that?"

"Because some of what they're saying actually makes sense."

That makes me pause. Charlie's about as loyal—not to mention traditional—as they come. It's hard to see him endorsing the beliefs of any radical anti-human group. "You going anti-establishment on me, Charlie? Going to start showing up at demonstrations and yelling about Mineral Rights?"

"I didn't say I agree with everything they stand for. But they do make a few good points."

"I'm listening."

"For one thing, they think golems should be in charge of their own reproduction. Golems aren't allowed to own or even work in lem factories, did you know that?"

"No. Guess they're afraid you'll crank up production and flood the workplace. Golem inflation—now there's a scary thought."

"We're not a commodity, Jace." I can tell by his voice I've ticked him off—and not in the usual way. "We're people. We may not care about food or sex or any of the other ridiculously squishy things you're all addicted to, but that doesn't mean we don't care about anything."

"Hey, come on, I didn't mean it like that—"

"The thing is, *you need us more than we need you.* The one thing—the *only* thing—us lems really need from the other races is to be made in the first place. After that, we can do just fine on our own. That's the one basic right we demand—and it's the one you'll never give us."

I should have said, *Me? Don't rope me into this, Kemo Sabe—if I had my way, every lem would pop out of the mold with three hundred pounds of spare clay, a set of DIY blueprints, and an extra birth certificate.*

But I don't. Did I mention I have this bad habit of making jokes at inappropriate times?

Because what comes out of my mouth is, "Duct tape."

"What?"

"The right to reproduce, and access to unlimited duct tape. Those should really be the cornerstones of the golem constitution. You know how many times I've had to patch you up because you sprang a leak in some hard-to-reach place?"

He gives me a look even flatter than his usual stare.

"The one thing we do have in common with you organics," he says, "is a need for sleep. I think I'll get some right now."

He leans back in his seat, tilts his fedora down over his eyes, and proceeds to ignore me for the rest of the flight. Great start to the mission, Jace.

I spend the flight studying the files Gretch put together. They break down into two basic groups: my team and Tair's. Silver Blue's hired some of the best mercenaries in the business to provide muscle, while Cassius has done much the same by drawing on government assets. I feel a little bit like someone who's just bought an NFL franchise and needs to review the starting lineup. But while I don't know crap about football, I do understand the strategies and dynamics of a strike team.

I sigh, pull out my spray bottle of wolf pheromone, and spritz some more on. It's got an aroma like a sheepdog that's been rolling in a field of wet mushrooms, but rule number one when dealing with a pack is always to establish dominance. The pheromone makes me smell like an alpha female; that won't automatically make me top dog, but it'll get my foot—uh, paw—in the door. The rest is up to me.

Only three of my team are thropes, though—there are two lems and a pire, as well. I study each of their files in turn.

First up is Master Sergeant Otis Zayin, a lem who did three tours of duty in the first Persian Gulf War. Expert marksman with a compound bow, one of those complicated counterweighted deals with a pull like an anchor. I've seen a shaft from one punch through armor plate.

Next is Captain Caleb Epsilon, an NSA enforcer like Charlie. He's my heavy weapons man, which on this world means he throws javelins. Big steel ones, useful in case I need to take down a plane or helicopter. Charlie himself prefers silver-coated ball bearings, kept in a spring-loaded holster up each of his sleeves.

The pire is Jane Wolosky, one of the Baby Biter generation that sprouted up after World War II. She's my battlefield shaman, experienced in combat magic as well as being a specialist in the use of silver-nitrate-laced CS gas, aerosolized garlic, and a variety of acid sprays that'll melt a lem's plastic skin like a heat lamp on Frosty. They may not use bullets or explosives, but the supernatural races still know how to deal out industrial-strength death.

The three thropes are all NSA field agents, with a good sixty years of experience among them: Jake Wilson, Arnie Gunderson, and Joseph Brody. They'll be using body armor and bladed weapons—Gunderson's good with a throwing ax, Brody prefers a claymore, and Wilson likes a katana in one hand and a KA-BAR in the other. It goes without saying that all three can do major damage without any weapons except teeth and claws.

Plus, of course, Charlie and me. It's a good team, but leafing through their files is making the gnawing sensation in my belly get worse and worse. They're lethal, all right— but lethal is *not* what I need. I need Asher—or Ahaseurus, take your pick—alive.

My world has guns and bombs, while this one doesn't. Except for my own personal hand-cannon—a Ruger Super Redhawk Alaskan, sometimes used to hunt moose— nobody here uses firearms, or even knows what they are. This isn't a natural situation, either; it's the result of a spell that imposes a blind spot on the mind of every sentient being on the planet, one that's been in effect for centuries. This spell was cast right around the same time that the one animating golems was being disseminated, which is why lems have more or less taken the place of firearms in this world; given the power and accuracy with which they can hurl things, they're almost living guns themselves.

And the shaman who cast that spell is the same one I'm after.

What happens after I catch him is a big, scary blank; I have no idea how I'm supposed to coerce him into sending me home, or even if I can. And what if he decides to send me someplace even worse?

I stare out the window at the clouds below me and wonder just high up we are.

And what happens after we touch down.

TWO

The meeting's in Vegas.

Remember what I said about this world being the same on the surface but different underneath? Well, sometimes that just doesn't apply—there are places here that are just so mind-bogglingly different that they make me feel like I'm on a planet in a different galaxy as opposed to an alternate Earth. Places where everything's indoors, where everyone's a predator, where the action goes twenty-four seven and there are no clocks.

Oh, wait. That's Vegas on my world.

So, yeah, pretty much the same here. In fact, Vegas seems custom-made for pires and thropes; about the only major difference seems to be smaller salad bars at the buffets. Oh, and the Transylvanian Casino—impressive, especially the blood waterfall. Other than that, it's about as loud, tacky, sexy, and greedy as the Lost Wages I'm familiar with.

Maybe *familiar* isn't the right word. I've only been there once, and some of the memories I have are kind of blurry.

Not all of them, though.

It was right after I graduated from the Academy at Quantico. There were two other women in my class, and the three of us decided to celebrate in style. We booked a suite for the weekend, grabbed our highest heels and shortest skirts, and hit the town.

We had a blast. I'd tell you about it, but you know what they say about Vegas? It's true. History and Vegas have that in common; what happens in either place stays there. Well, except for tattoos and STDs, and we managed to avoid both.

It's funny how some of the most enjoyable experiences of your life can make you the saddest. I guess it's because the past is a country you can't ever go back to—once it's done, it's done. Your passport gets stamped by the clock, and the only thing you have left is something that's already fading. Memories are just postcards from a place you visited once.

I don't usually spend that much time thinking about the past, and I've done so even less since I got to this reality. You can't undo bad decisions or relive past glories; spending your time dwelling on either one will only lead to depression. Especially when you realize that the past contains more than just everything you've ever done; in my case it also holds the planet I was born on and every single person who lives there.

So, I don't think about the past. I don't think about the people I used to say hello to every day. I don't think about the corner store where I bought low-fat potato chips and 80 percent cocoa dark chocolate. I don't think about that pop song I used to hum on the way to work, or the secondhand store that I found my favorite blouse at.

But as the plane touches down, I find myself thinking about that weekend. Wondering what Stacy and Heather are up to these days. Haven't talked to either one in a long time—Stacy's working for the Bureau in Cleveland, while

Heather quit to be a stay-at-home mom. God, we had so much fun . . .

Maybe I should look them up, when I get back.

It's mid-afternoon when we land. Charlie and I take a cab from the airport to where we're staying—not one of the high-rise wonders, but a run-down little mom-and-pop motel in the wedding district north of the Strip. Gravel parking lot, neon sign with one of the letters burned out, peeling red and white paint on side-by-side crackerboxes. Charlie hauls our bags inside while I get us checked in.

The rest of the team is already here, each one in their own room. We've reserved a separate unit for our command center, the place we'll be meeting and planning.

I drop off the key with Charlie, then knock on the door to room thirteen. A pire in full daymask, gloves, and hood opens it—Jane Wolosky, I guess. I flash my ID, step inside, and close the door. The drapes on the window are pulled tight, and the bed's been flipped up and stacked against the wall, a flatscreen on a rolling table parked in front of it. An eight-foot-long table with folding legs now occupies the center of the room, with six chairs around it.

The pire pulls off her daymask and goggles, revealing a sharp-faced woman with short blond hair. "Jane Wolosky," she says, offering her hand.

I shake it. "Jace Valchek."

"I was the first one here—thought I'd get us set up."

"Good thinking. The others en route?"

"The lems just arrived, the thropes are freshening up in their rooms. We're all here."

"Okay. Get everyone together, all right? I want an ops briefing in twenty."

"You got it."

I go back to our room and find Charlie sitting on one of the twin beds patiently.

"All squared away?" I ask.

"Yeah. I took up most of the closet space, but the bathroom's yours."

I open the closet door and see at least half a dozen suits on the rack. "Jesus, we're only here for a couple of days. What are you planning on doing, changing your outfit for every meal?"

"Meal? I don't make a habit of cramming my body full of heated organic matter, thanks."

"Suit yourself. As many times as you can, apparently." I pause, then say, "Nice pinstripes."

"Thanks." He seems slightly less grumpy than he was on the plane, which I'm thankful for. Charlie isn't exactly thin-skinned, but I can piss off just about anyone—and the last person in the world I want mad at me is my partner. Though it is the second time in the last few hours he's used the word *organic* . . .

I take a few minutes to change clothes and clean up a little, and then Charlie and I head over to room thirteen.

They're sitting around the table, waiting for me. I don't waste any time; I walk to the head of the table, slap my files down and open them up. "Good afternoon. I know who all of you are, and I'm pretty sure you know who I am. Some of you know my enforcer, Charlie Aleph, as well. Any other introductions you can make among yourselves."

I pause, sizing them up. The lems look as impassive as statues, but that's pretty much the norm for them. Wolosky looks intent, focused. The three thropes, all in human form and seated on the same side of the table, look a little more skeptical; I think I know why.

I make a snap decision. "If you've heard of me, you know I'm human. The pheromone I'm wearing is cover for out in the field—I'm not a thrope and I'm not trying to pass for one."

Brody, a redhead with a wide face and a flat nose, chuckles. "Good thing, too. You smell like my aunt Irma."

"Well then, your aunt Irma must be a bitch from hell with a mean streak," I say pleasantly. "Because that's what I am. There's a reason they call me the Bloodhound, boys and girls, and it's not because I like to pee on fenceposts. I get who I'm after—no exceptions, no excuses. You work for me now, and I don't give a good goddamn what you think of me—I care about bringing down the target, and by that I mean bringing him down alive."

"I thought we had two targets," Caleb Epsilon says. He's the enforcer lem, same black sand interior Charlie has but a foot or so taller; he looks like he could throw a Buick through a second-floor window.

I'm already handing out information packets. "Our primary is this man, a shaman named Asher. Aristotle Stoker is secondary—we need him as well, but his survival isn't mandatory."

Wolosky studies the picture of Stoker she's pulled out of her packet. "The Impaler is our *secondary*? What did the other guy do, assassinate the pope?"

"We think he's trying to peddle something to an international arms dealer named Silver Blue. Stoker may be the one buying it, or he may be setting up an alliance with the Mantle. Whatever the reason, all these players are going to be in the same place at the same time—and we're going to take advantage of that."

Wilson grunts. He's a rangy-looking man with a shaved head and a Texas drawl. "What kinda resistance we lookin' at?"

I walk over to the flatscreen, slip a disk into the slot at the base, and grab the remote. "Give me a second and I'll show you."

I let them read while I get the menu sorted out and find

the files I need. I click on an option and a scowling, Teutonic face fills the screen.

"This is Heinrich Koltz," I say. "Professional thrope mercenary. He heads a paramilitary band called the Dobermans, for reasons you can probably guess. He favors a forward-curving, top-weighted blade called a *kukri,* a Gurkha weapon. He's been responsible for massacres in South Africa, Iran, the Philippines, and Bosnia. He's probably the most dangerous, so we need to remove him from the game as quickly as possible."

I switch to another file, and a photo of a grim-looking black woman. "Felicia Mbunte. Pire. Expert with a blowgun, which she likes to load with silver-tipped darts and neurotoxins cut with garlic and/or wolfsbane. Also extremely handy with a silver-titanium alloy garrotte. She's lethal as both an assassin and a sniper—used to work for the KGB. Careful with this one—she's a trained espionage agent, with skills that include disguise, surveillance, and sabotage."

I take them through the files one by one, detailing the strengths and proclivities of each professional killer. Wolosky takes notes, the thropes ask the occasional question, and the lems just stare at me without blinking.

And then I get to Tair.

"This is Silver Blue's top lieutenant," I say. "He goes by the name Tair. He's a biothaumaturge, a specialist in lem activation. Blue seems to trust him implicitly, and despite his lack of military training he's as ruthless as any of them—and extremely intelligent. Don't underestimate him."

I pause. What I really want to say is, *Don't kill him. He's a good man, or at least he used to be. He deserves a second chance.*

But I don't. In the field, giving the other side a second chance can cost the life of somebody on yours. You can't take that risk, not ever.

"We know where the meeting's going to be held, but not exactly when," I continue. "We'll be breaking into surveillance teams and keeping eyes on the spot from now until it happens. I've drawn up a tactical plan, but we'll need to remain adaptable; this situation is both volatile and fluid.

"Oh, and one more thing." I unholster my Ruger and hold it up for everyone to see. "This is my weapon. Believe it or not, it's enchanted with a spell that makes it seem ludicrous to anyone who lays eyes on it. It's not. It can kill a thrope, a pire, or a lem from a distance, just as effectively as a crossbow or a javelin. So swallow whatever wise-assed remark you're about to make—I've heard 'em all before. Besides, I've got plenty of my own."

"Where's the meet?" Master Sergeant Zayin asks.

"Right across the street," I say. "The Chapel of Saint Assisi, open twenty-four hours a day for your matrimonial needs. Also available for private events on extremely short notice, especially when you're willing to pay a hefty fee up front. Our intel says the meet will happen sometime in the next few days."

"I'll set up some shielded surveillance wards," Wolosky says.

"Good. Once those are in place, I want a physical recon of the place, inside and out," I say. "Wilson, you just got engaged."

"Gee, Agent, this is kinda sudden. Do I get a ring?"

"No, but I can promise you one helluva honeymoon. Zayin and Epsilon, you'll be in our support vehicle, the white panel van that's parked outside. I want both of you available for cover fire at a moment's notice—Epsilon, you'll be in charge of disabling any vehicle they might try to flee in."

"I could cover more area from a higher vantage point," Zayin says. "Maybe the roof of this place?"

"Too visible. The van will give you cover and has hinged panels that'll give you a wide field of fire. Sorry about the cramped quarters—hope you and Epsilon get along."

"We'll manage," says Zayin.

"Charlie and I will coordinate—he's my second in command. Any questions?"

There are, but only a few; these are professionals, and if they have a problem taking orders from a human they keep it to themselves. We work out a shift rotation, Wolosky digs out her field kit and starts muttering incantations, and Wilson changes into something appropriate for an eager husband-to-be.

And once everything's in place, we settle in to wait.

Wilson brings back a video he shot with a spycam concealed in his gimme cap. The chapel's laid out more like a strip joint than a church—small tables in the back, two obligatory pews up front with a wide aisle between them, and a small raised stage with a lectern. It does have a nice stained-glass window behind that, depicting what I guess is Saint Francis blessing the union of two thropes. Restrooms just off the entrance, and they've got a full bar with slot machines in the foyer. Classy.

Charlie peers over my shoulder; I'm sitting at the table in our improvised ops center. "Looks like there's a door beside the stage."

"Yeah. Private area, no doubt. I've got Wolosky working on it, but she says it's been magicked up with anti-surveillance. She's got eyes on the fire exit behind the building, though."

"Any word from Gretch?"

"Asher was spotted at an airport in Denver. Tair wasn't with him, but someone else was." I pull up the security video Gretchen sent me; it shows Asher, in a black business suit, crimson turban, and full beard, striding down the airport concourse with a woman keeping pace three steps behind him. At least I think it's a woman; she's wearing a full chador, every square inch of her except for a narrow band around her eyes covered in white cloth.

"Gretch is sure that's Asher, but has no idea who his friend is," I say. "Or where they went, for that matter. They didn't leave on any commercial flight, but they don't seem to be at the airport anymore, either."

"Doesn't matter. We know where they're going."

"We hope."

Charlie sits down across from me and pulls his sword out of the scabbard sewn into the lining of his jacket. It's a *gladius,* a double-edged Roman short sword with a triangular tip. He digs a whetstone out of a pocket and begins to sharpen it. "Any ideas on her identity?"

I shake my head. "No. Lover, bodyguard, human sacrifice . . . no idea. We'll just have to be ready for anything."

"You should get some sleep."

"Not likely—" I do my best to stifle a yawn.

"Try anyway," Charlie says. "Battlefield rules—grab your shuteye when it's available. You might not get another chance for a long, long time."

"Yeah, yeah," I say, getting to my feet. "Going to bed right now. Wake me when the apocalypse hits."

"If I remember."

I throw a halfhearted snarl his way and head for our room. It's only about 9:00 PM, but it's been a long day and I didn't get much more than three hours of sleep last night. Charlie's right—better to get some Z's while I can.

I pass out as soon as I hit the pillow. Some indefinite time later I'm woken up by the phone ringing. I grab it, thinking it must be the front desk—Gretchen or anyone on my team would have used my cell number. "Hello?"

"Special Agent Jace Valchek?" The voice is female, and not one I recognize.

"Speaking. Who is this?"

"My name is unimportant. You may be more familiar with my traveling companion—Mr. Asher. Or perhaps you know him as Ahaseurus?"

I have a flash of pure, unadulterated dread. Nobody in law enforcement likes to be caught exposed, and right at this second I feel like I'm standing naked on top of Mount Everest. This woman knows exactly who and where I am, and in a world full of sorcery that's like having a conversation with your head stuck in a noose. It takes a conscious effort not to throw the receiver across the room—I'm half convinced it's about to change into a snake and try to throttle me.

"Go on," I manage.

"I have no wish to be your enemy, Jace Valchek. In fact, I wish to be your friend. Let me prove it."

"How?"

"Meet with me. I will provide you with information no one else can possibly give you. It will enable you to accomplish your heart's desire."

I bite back a reply involving a school for male strippers and a gallon of tequila. "Fine. You obviously know where I am; come in and we'll talk."

"That wouldn't be a good idea. You and me, alone, in fifteen minutes. Don't tell your crew—if you're shadowed, I'll know."

I believe her. "Where?"

"The fountains in front of the Bellagio. That should be public enough for you if you're worried about an ambush. Come on foot—you won't be able to find parking."

"How do I know I can trust—"

She hangs up.

I put the phone down on the cradle slowly. No point in trying to do a trace—she's obviously not stupid.

The question is, am I?

The answer, apparently, is yes. Just *how* stupid is an answer yet to be reached.

If this mystery woman knows where I am, she must be using some sort of magic to keep tabs on me—guess the ritual Eisfanger performed on me before I left Seattle didn't work. Or maybe he's just outclassed.

Whatever the explanation, if I tell Charlie or anyone else, I'll get there and she'll never show. On the other hand, if it's true that somehow I'm the target of this little summit, then this is the perfect way to get me to step into a trap.

It boils down to two options: go, possibly get some inside information that could make the operation a slam-dunk and ensure the safety of my team; don't go, inform my team, and risk complete mission failure due to a no-show or a full-on battle. If I go, I'm only putting my own neck on the line—if I don't, I'm gambling with everyone's.

Still, it doesn't strike me as being that dangerous. I'll be out in the open, armed, and very alert. I've got Charlie on speed dial and I'll be holding my phone. And for added insurance, I write a quick note and stick it in my luggage—if I go missing, Charlie's sharp enough to search through my things.

I grab my weapons and head out the door. Charlie will probably figure I've just gone out to grab a coffee; he knows my habits all too well. He won't start to worry until I've been gone an hour or more—hopefully that'll be enough time to meet Ms. Chador and return.

The Bellagio is only about a ten-minute walk from here, straight down Las Vegas Boulevard; I can even enjoy a few of the sights along the way. Yeah, I think I've got everything pretty well figured.

Come on foot, she told me. And like an idiot, I did exactly that—giving her a ten-minute window when she knew not only exactly where I'd be, but that I'd be alone. If you were flying overhead, you could almost see a big dotted line connecting a giant cartoon A (the motel) with a giant cartoon B (the Bellagio fountains). That slow-moving X about a third of the way between the two? That's little old me.

Guess what happens next?

THREE

I don't remember getting jumped. Whatever she hit me with, it was powerful and very, very quick.

I come to with that slow, achy kind of sluggishness that's more like evolution than waking. First stage: shapeless prehistoric blob, swimming up from the inky depths. Second stage: vague awareness of gravity, light, limbs that don't quite work right on land. Third stage: primitive mammalian brain. Aware of immediate environment, limited understanding of same.

By stage four I can communicate with the members of my tribe through a system of grunts, whines, and barks. Unfortunately, none of my tribe seem to be present at the moment, so my eloquent if simple dissertation on my predicament goes unappreciated.

"Whuh?—Oh. Oooooh. Uff."

My eyes are open, but it takes me a second to identify what I'm looking at: stucco. Specifically, a stucco ceiling—the kind of bumpy plaster surface that for some reason people think looks really excellent overhead. Maybe it's some kind of caveman genetic memory.

I try to move, with limited results. That's because I'm

lying on a bed, with my hands tied to the bedposts on either side. In my underwear.

Stage five, cognitive thought—or what passes for it in my head, which I apparently use mostly for generating sarcasm and storing old TV theme songs—kicks in. It tells me I'm in a great deal of trouble. Maybe if I lie here for a while I'll evolve some actual intelligence and I can think my way out of this mess.

Nothing happens. I think stage five is about as far I'm going to get in this lifetime—and that's looking to be a lot shorter than I'd hoped.

I lift my head and look around. I'm in a hotel room, or what appears to be one. One double bed, with me the current occupant. Looks more upscale than my motel room—maybe something on the Strip?—but the drapes are closed so I can't tell for sure. Hell, I might not even be in Vegas anymore.

The bathroom door opens, and a woman walks out in a billowing cloud of smoke. No, wait—it's steam. She's dressed only in a towel, slung sari-style around her hips, and has an extremely contented look on her face.

"By the seven breasts of the Goddess of Wet-Nursing, I *love* hot showers," she says. She looks around my age, five foot two, tops, and maybe a hundred pounds if she drops the towel. Her hair is medium length and blond, her breasts impressive, her overall build that of an athlete. I've got better legs, but only because they're longer.

"Who the hell are you?" I snarl. I don't really expect an answer, but I really feel the need to snarl at *someone*.

"Name's Azura," she says. She smiles, which makes her look unbearably impish. Good Lord, I've been kidnapped by Tinker Bell. "Sorry about knocking you out like that, but you've got something I need and I didn't think you'd give it up willingly."

"I really hope you're not after one of my major organs.

My gallbladder or spleen I might be convinced to part with, but everything else is pretty much spoken for."

She laughs. "Don't worry, you're perfectly safe. What I need to borrow is your identity."

She drops the towel, then starts getting dressed.

In *my* clothes.

"You're about three sizes too tiny to wear those," I say. "Not that anyone's going to believe you're me, anyway—"

"Oh, you'd be surprised at what I can convince people of," she says. "Safety pins, safety pins . . ." She picks up a hotel sewing kit from the dresser, fishes one out, and pins the skirt into place. "There. Shouldn't fall off, anyway." She slips into my blouse, and then my jacket. She looks like an eight-year-old playing dress-up.

"Oh, very convincing. My own mother would swear we were twins."

She grins at me, then walks back into the bathroom. "Maybe a little makeup will help," she says. "You know, a bit of mascara, some eyeliner . . ."

"—steroids, plastic surgery, a pair of stilts," I snap.

She walks back into the room. She—

No. *I* look back at me.

She's a perfect duplicate. Hair, face, height, everything.

"How about now?" she asks, and her voice is mine, too. "Amazing what a little time in front of a mirror can do, huh?"

"I guess this is where I say, *You'll never get away with this*."

"Can we skip that part? Seems pointless."

"Agreed. Let me go and I won't beat you senseless with a random object."

"Can't." She shrugs with my shoulders. "I really don't have much of a choice, Jace. We're both after Ahaseurus, but what's at stake is a lot more important than whether or not you get to go home. If I had time—and thought you'd believe me—I'd stay and explain. But the meeting is happening in less than an hour, and I've got to go."

"Wait—I thought you were already close to him. Why do you need to pose as me?"

"Oh, I'm not who you think I am. Don't feel bad, though—I'm not who *most* people think I am."

"You're human."

"You're guessing."

"I'm not. Pires and thropes don't have that kind of skill with illusion glamours, and they don't shapeshift into forms other than hairy ones. You're Maureen Selkie's replacement, aren't you?" Selkie was the werewitch who used to work for Stoker—until I killed her.

"Don't know who that is. The only person I'm replacing is you, Jace—and just until I can get my hands on a certain shaman. Those bonds'll untie themselves in two hours. Just be patient."

She slides one of my scythes out of the holster tailored into my jacket. It's a modified *eskrima* stick: about two feet long, made of ironwood with a conical silver tip, holding a recessed foot-long blade that snaps into place at a forty-five-degree angle and turns it into a scythe. I carry two—one for each hand—and I'm trained in kali, the art of Philippine stick fighting. "These are nice," she says. "An old friend of mine would appreciate them. I'll try to get them back to you when I'm done."

"Don't bother," I say. "I'll come get them myself."

She sighs. "If you must. I'll try not to break them."

And with that, she leaves. No death threats, no warnings not to interfere, just the door closing behind her. Strange.

She leaves my gun on the nightstand.

That's not so strange. Due to the global spell, no one takes it seriously—it's a gimcrack, a cobbled-together piece of junk that will probably blow up in your hand. That's the kind of reaction I've come to expect—but even if Azura doesn't intend to use it, why not take it with her as part of her disguise?

I don't know, but I do know I have no intention of lying here while she screws up my op.

I consider my options. One, holler my lungs out; two, try to wriggle out of these ropes; three, try to get a hold of my gun.

I try the hollering option first. Five minutes of shouting my lungs out gets me a sore throat and nothing else; either Azura's got some kind of silencing spell on the room, or people in my immediate vicinity are even more blasé about what happens in Vegas than a high-roller on a heroin binge.

The second option actually makes the ropes tighten up. More magic, no doubt. That leaves choice number three.

Well, two years of yoga has its advantages, and my feet are bare. I'm limber enough to get them over my head and then around to the nightstand—do me a favor and don't try to picture it, all right? Then I get a toe in the trigger guard and haul the thing onto the bed.

Undoing the safety isn't hard. All I have to do then is aim at my own hand with my feet, and shoot the ropes without hitting my own limb. Or chest. Or head.

Did I mention that my gun is chambered with .454 rounds? True, the bullets themselves are hand-carved teak with silver tips, but the load is so powerful that even the gas that's ejected from the firing chamber is enough to sever a finger if you hold the thing wrong. And I'm going to aim with my *feet*? I'll only get one shot, too—the recoil will knock the gun across the room. I better make it count.

I spend the next few minutes trying to get the gun into the perfect position without accidentally setting it off. When I'm finally ready and looking down the barrel of the Redhawk, I stop for a second and take a deep breath. This is probably the craziest thing I've ever tried to do—even if it doesn't work, I'll probably lose a toe from the gas ejection—

Hey, moron, a little voice in my head says. *If it'll sever a finger or a toe, what do you think it would do to a rope?*

I relax my toe-grip and take a moment to realize how close I just came to probably blowing my own arm off. Then it's time to do some body contorting again . . . but this time I'm trying to get the gun into my right hand without dropping it.

I manage. The gas I want to employ is ejected sideways from the cylinder, so in order to use it I have to hold the Ruger parallel to the ropes. I can just barely bend my wrist enough to do that—but it means the barrel is now pointed, more or less, at my head.

I angle it down. Now it's aimed at my breasts. I lift up my chin, suck in my breath, and try to aim somewhere between. If this doesn't work, the bullet will go through my neck.

I pull the trigger.

The recoil almost snaps my wrist. I swear I feel the bullet graze my throat as the gun flies out of my hand.

But the ejected gas severs three-quarters of the rope. I yank on it with all my might—and it holds.

"No goddamn *way,*" I hiss, and then all rational planning and carefully executed maneuvers go out the window. I *haul* on that sucker, ignoring the pain of my wrist and cursing at the top of my lungs.

"You're *history,* you crappy little piece of string! You lousy, yarn-humping, thread-sucking—your mother had sex with *baling twine*! *Break, goddamn you!*"

It's a good thing my gun's now on the other side of the room. If it had been in reach when those last few strands *did* finally break, I'd probably have grabbed it and just shot the rope restraining my other wrist.

But it isn't and I don't. I untie my left hand, put on the

only piece of clothing I can find—a bathrobe—and tear out of the room.

I don't know how much time has passed since Azura left. I don't have a cell phone, or change for a pay phone. I can't even commandeer a car; I don't have a badge and I can't threaten anyone with a weapon they don't recognize. I doubt if a cab will stop for someone in a bathrobe, and when I get outside and try I see that I'm right.

I'm on the Strip, maybe a ten-minute walk from the motel.

So I run.

A woman wearing only a bathrobe and running down the sidewalk with a gun in her hand would get arrested pretty quick in my reality. Here, all I get is laughter and wise-cracks: "Hey, baby! Who set your tail on fire?"

"You just remember you left the bathtub filling up at home?"

"Slow down, you forgot to get dressed!"

I don't have the time or breath to reply. *Focus, Jace. Control your breathing. Long, even strides.*

Bitch even took my shoes.

I get to see a little more of Vegas, but not much detail. Don't see many thropes in were form, and the ones I do see are wearing a lot of jewelry. Guess that's how you indicate you're a high-roller without designer clothes.

It takes no more than five of the longest minutes of my life to get back to the motel. I'm on the last block when I see the crackle of high-powered magic flash into the sky, and know I'm too late.

I hit the parking lot of the chapel in time to see a thrope fly through a window backward and smash into the side of an SUV. Won't kill him, but the concussion's enough to knock him out; he reverts to human form at my feet. Gunderson.

"Charlie!" I yell. I barrel for the front door—and run smack into a body flying through it going the other way. And I do mean flying; it's about three feet off the floor and moving in a flat trajectory, slamming headfirst into my gut. We both go down hard, tumbling backward another ten feet or so in a tangle of limbs and curses. Okay, the cursing is just in my head; what little air I have left in my lungs after my mad dash is knocked out of me on impact. I gray out for a moment, and when my head clears I realize I've lost my gun.

I push myself off the ground, get to my knees. And look straight into my own eyes—Azura's no more than three feet away, blood running down her face from a cut on her forehead. She's on her feet, but wobbly.

My gun is on the ground, halfway between us.

I dive for it. I don't make it, though—Azura points her hand at me and something shoots out of her sleeve and wraps around me at chest level, pinning both of my arms. It looks like the same thing she tied me up with: thin white rope with the reflexes of a bullwhip and the attitude of an anaconda.

"Stop," she gasps. It sounds more like a request than a demand, not that I have a choice. "You don't have a chance. He was ready for me—"

That's all she has time for. The roof of the chapel blows off in the kind of light show that would give George Lucas an orgasm. It's clearly a magical explosion—the sound it makes is more like a giant sneeze than a boom. Red slate roofing tiles shoot up a hundred feet or more into the air . . . and then start to come down.

I throw myself to the ground—which *hurts,* since I can't break my fall with my hands—and roll under the nearest vehicle. Unfortunately, Azura does pretty much the same thing with another vehicle.

"I am going to put a bullet in you for every one of my team who's hurt," I shout. "Count on it!"

She stares back at me from under the car she's under. "*Listen* to me," she says. "Your team is down, but nobody's dead. Not yet. Ahaseurus is after *me,* now—I'm the one who tried to ambush him. Do what I say and your team lives—"

She's interrupted by the crash of several hundred pounds of kiln-dried shrapnel smashing itself into smaller pieces all around us.

"—we have to draw him away!" she shouts. "That'll buy your team some time! If we don't, he'll kill *both* of us and them as well!"

I don't trust her. She's abducted me, stolen my face, and may have gotten my team hurt or worse—but the smartest thing for her to do right now is bolt and leave me behind to take the blame. She isn't doing that—and my only other option seems to be going head-to-head with a sorcerer who's way, *way* out of my league.

I roll out from under the truck. "Get this damn thing off me," I say. Azura crawls out and gestures; the rope unwinds, snakes across the ground, and slithers back up her sleeve. Nice trick.

I reach down and pick up my gun. She watches me but does nothing.

"Go," I say.

And then I'm running again, and Azura's right behind me.

I don't like running from a fight. Hell, I don't like running from *anything.* But I think I knew all along that our only chance of taking down the Big A was to catch him by surprise, and that ship has sailed. Didn't get very far, either.

I only hope Azura's telling the truth about Charlie and

the team still being alive. So far her track record on
honesty isn't exactly unblemished.

I've done my share of chasing suspects through back-
yards and alleys, over fences, and around every conceiv-
able obstacle. This is the first time I've been on the other
end of the pursuit—but at least I'm half dressed and bare-
foot. Oh, and waving a gun around—that's always good
for establishing a general mood.

We're ducking through a yard with a pool when Azura
hisses, "Stop!" She's staring at the water with an intent
expression on my face.

"What?"

"I know how we can lose him, but you have to trust
me."

"Lose who? I haven't spotted anyone on our trail—"

"He's coming." She's got a shut-up-and-listen-if-you-
want-to-survive-this tone in her voice, so I do. "Follow
me, don't let go of my hand, and keep *still*."

She grabs my hand—then jumps into the pool, pulling
me in with her.

I have enough time to suck in a lungful of air—two
would have been nice, but oh well—and then we're not just
in the water, we're *under* it. Azura's pulling me down to the
bottom, and when we get there she looks me straight in the
eye and expels all the air in her lungs in one big, bloopy
bubble.

That's your plan? Drowning? I scream inside my head.

But she isn't drowning. Her other fist is clenched tight,
and I can feel a pulse of *something* coming from it. Something that travels through her body and into mine at our
clasped hands.

She takes a deep lungful of water, driving the last few
silvery pearls of oxygen out her nose. She stares at me
calmly and nods.

I shake mine violently. *No goddamn way.* A hundred

thousand years of air-breathing DNA tell me that now is not a good time to give up my addiction. I'll quit tomorrow. Really.

Azura frowns—and then her features shift, losing my contours and regaining her own. Maybe it's supposed to make me trust her, but a little face-time is not enough to make me abruptly change a lifelong—not to mention life-*preserving*—habit. I don't care what kind of mojo she's working, I'm just not that interested in changing my name to Aquagirl—

And then a star appears over our heads.

I think it's the spotlight of a helicopter at first, sweeping over the pool. But it's not focused or moving in the right way—it's radiating in all directions from a single fixed point. Oh, and it's a bright, arterial red.

But not fixed, after all. The star is getting closer.

Azura flattens herself against the wall of the pool, and I do the same. The pool is filled with an unearthly blood-red light, but the angle leaves us in shadow. That'll change if the light moves over the pool itself, leaving us completely exposed.

It stops. We stare up at the light, which is pulsing in a way more organic than astronomical. Whatever—or whoever—is radiating it must be standing a few feet away from the pool's edge. All they have to do is take a step closer and peer down . . .

Right about then is when I realize I can't hold my breath any longer.

My lungs insist I head for the surface. My brain vetoes that idea, but rebellion is in the air. No, don't think about air . . . lovely, sweet, chest-filling air, lightly scented with the smell of freshly baked bread and mountain pine . . . okay, screw this, I'm going up.

It's not my will that breaks—it's sheer physiological override by my monkey hindbrain that makes me start to struggle upward, the same kind of panic response that makes a drowning person try to stand on the shoulders of her rescuer. Azura refuses to let go of my hand, so I try to pry her fingers off mine—

She punches me in the gut. Hard.

And that's it for what little oxygen is left in my lungs. It comes out in a silvery cloud of bubbles, and a second later I inhale out of reflex. Water rushes into my lungs with a horrible, heavy sensation, like having my chest filled up with concrete.

But I don't die. In fact, a second after it happens, my panic subsides, along with my overpowering need to breathe, because I *am* breathing. Water is flowing in and out of my lungs as easily and naturally as air usually does, despite being a lot more dense.

Azura pushes me back against the wall and flattens herself again. If the bubbles I released a moment ago caught the attention of Mr. Bright up there, we're dead.

We wait. I wonder if I'm going to die with the overpowering taste of chlorine in my mouth.

A few agonizing years pass. Finally, the crimson brilliance moves on—Azura must be masking us with more than just water, or maybe the occult senses our tracker is using don't work so well on the aquatic. We wait another century or so, and then Azura motions me that we're going topside.

She lets go of my hand as soon as we break the surface, and the first thing I do is my impression of a whale: I spew water from my blowhole, emptying my lungs so thoroughly they ache. She does the same.

"Whuh, whuh, what the *hell*," I manage, gasping. I swim over to the edge of the pool and haul myself out. Wearing a wet bathrobe makes me feel like someone turned up the gravity.

"Sorry," she gasps back. She pulls herself out and sits on

the edge, then shows me what was in her clenched fist: a small bone, probably from a fish. The magic in this world is based on animism, the idea that all things—animal, mineral, vegetable, other—have a spirit in them, and by talking to it you can cause different things to happen. Apparently we were just talking to the spirit of a flounder. "Didn't exactly have time to discuss it, did we?"

"No," I admit.

"We have to keep moving—doubling back on our trail will fool them, but not for long. We need to get someplace safe, where I can throw up a few wards and hide us."

"Sure," I say. "Throwing up—*urrk!*—sounds like a great idea." I get rid of the last of the water in my lungs.

I ditch the bathrobe; I'd rather be running around in my underwear than lugging an extra twenty pounds' worth of H_2O and dripping everywhere. Besides, my own clothes are right in front of me—and surprisingly, I don't even have to ask. Azura shucks out of them and hands them over without a word. I notice that while she might be at home underwater, she doesn't seem to believe in underwear. No sign of her pet rope, either.

"Thanks," I say. She grabs my soggy robe and holds it up in front of her as water cascades onto the pool deck, then swirls it around her like a cape and settles it on her shoulders—except by the time the fabric stops moving, it's completely dry and has changed into a lightweight wrap-around dress that fits her perfectly.

"Okay," I say. "Can I have my shoes back, too, or are you going to turn them into hooker boots?"

"Sorry." She kicks them off.

I'm still wet, but at least I'm dressed. I put my gun in its holster—funny that she took that and not the gun itself—and say, "Let's go. We need to see if anyone needs medical attention—"

"No," she says. "We can't."

"My partner—"

"Your partner's fine. We're the ones who aren't." She hesitates. "That light we saw? I was wrong, that wasn't Ahaseurus. That was one of your own team, and she was looking for you."

"So why did we hide?"

"Because she thinks you're a turncoat, Jace. She thinks I'm you—and I just tried to kill the target you were supposed to take alive."

"Which doesn't make sense, meaning they'll see through it pretty damn fast—"

"No, they won't. I'm not the kind of shaman you're used to dealing with, Jace. I'm—well, on my world they call me an Astonisher. And when I want to fool someone, they *stay* fooled."

My stomach is starting to do that sinking thing I'm way too familiar with. "*Your* world?"

"Yeah. I'm not from around here, either." She shrugs. "How about I buy you a drink and tell you about it? Or we could wait for you to be arrested . . . but then I'd have to abandon you, and I *hate* drinking alone."

I sigh. "You're buying."

My shoes squish as we walk away.

"Look, I'm telling you nobody on your team died," Azura says. "I'd be able to tell—I'm attuned to these things."

"That doesn't mean nobody got hurt," I growl.

She takes a long sip from her drink as an excuse not to answer. I knock back my own—tequila, or what passes for it—and signal the waiter for another.

We're in a back booth of a dive called Miss Pointy's, a strip club catering to pires. The air is smoky, the lighting is either red or blue depending upon the act on stage, and none of the clientele is looking in our direction. I guess that's a plus.

"Give me one good reason I shouldn't march your ass back to the motel at gunpoint and have you explain all this to my team," I say. "And make it convincing."

"I'll give you several good reasons. One, they won't believe you unless I confess, and I won't. Two, you've got a way, way better chance of taking Ahaseurus alive if we work together. And three, you'd have a hard time aiming your gun at me when you don't have it."

I grab for my Ruger. It's not there. Azura smiles, and it's suddenly in her hand. "Interesting weapon. Not the kind of thing we use where I come from—or here, apparently. What's it do?"

"It makes holes. Big, messy ones, usually in people. Don't point it at me, please."

She shrugs. "Look, I'm sorry you got caught in the middle of this, but it makes sense for us to work together."

I don't like it. I can't trust her. But my only alternative is going back and trying to assure everyone I haven't gone completely insane—which is a condition thropes and pires don't exactly understand in the first place. I could wind up incarcerated, all my friends shaking their heads sadly and saying, "But she seemed so *normal*—I guess it's just a human thing . . ."

"Look, there's something else you need to know," Azura says. "Ahaseurus has something big planned. I don't know exactly what it is, but I know it's going to happen soon. We have to stop him, and we have to do it *now*."

I study her for a long moment. Finally I say, "What's an Astonisher?"

She grins at me. Impishly. "An Astonisher is many things. We specialize in making the impossible possible, in dazzling the senses, in making things vanish and making things appear. We cannot be imprisoned, we cannot be predicted, we cannot be seen if we wish to remain hidden.

We are master tricksters and cunning thieves, well versed in the arts of disguise and subterfuge. We are—"

I groan. "Oh my God. You're a *magician*."

"Well, of course I'm a magician—"

"No, I mean you're a *magician*. Card tricks, pulling rabbits out of top hats, sawing assistants in half. I'm in Vegas and I'm working with David Copperfield in heels."

"We prefer the term *illusionist,* if you don't mind."

"So you're not even going to deny it?" The waiter arrives with my tequila and I grab it from him with a glare; the man must have turtle in his genes.

"Why should I? It's true that Astonishers hone their skills in the public eye when they start out; illusion and performance go hand in hand, after all. But that's only our apprenticeship—we go on to much more serious matters. Astonishers, as everyone knows, are the power *behind* the power—we advise rulers, collect secrets, create or cover up scandals. Appearance is everything in politics—and we can make things appear however we wish."

"Right. So you're a glorified spin doctor?"

"Most of my assignments are closer to espionage than public relations. Like trying to stop a rogue sorcerer who's jumped to another dimension."

"Wait—Ahaseurus is from *your* world?"

"That he is. From a land called Nightshadow, which is also *my* home." She shakes her head. "I've been here for a while, Jace, doing some investigating. I knew you were my best chance at getting close to Ahaseurus, and I blew it. But we still have one advantage; he doesn't know I'm here. He'll blame the attack on you."

"Yeah, you've really made me the most popular girl in school," I say. "I hope you've got a plan beyond sitting in this booth and soaking up cheap booze. We need a base of operations, for one thing."

"But we have one," she says. "Right here. I've got a room on the second floor, and no one will think of looking for an NSA agent—or an Astonisher—in a strip club."

"You don't think two women in a bar that caters mostly to men will stand out?"

"Not when one of them works there." She gives me a look with way too much mischief in it. "Now if you'll excuse me—I go on in a few minutes."

She gets up and struts toward the stage. Apparently my new partner is not only a magician, she's an extradimensional stripper.

I sigh, and order another shot of tequila.

FOUR

One nice thing about Vegas is that it's so arid, I dry off quickly. The air-conditioning helps, too, but I'm shivering before long. I'd like to go outside and warm up, but can't risk it. The tequila doesn't actually raise my body temperature, but makes it easier to ignore.

Azura, it turns out, is actually one helluva dancer. She works the guys in the front row like a pro, collects more than her share of tips, and does some acrobatics that would make a Romanian gymnast envious. I wonder if she comes by her talent naturally, or if she's using some kind of magic—channeling the spirit of a spider monkey, or maybe a boa constrictor. All the yoga classes in the world wouldn't give me the flexibility to wrap around a pole like that.

I'm only watching with one eye, though—the other's keeping a lookout for anyone coming through the door that might be trouble, or anyone already here who might be looking to start some. Two women in a strip club are friends out for some wrong-side-of-the-tracks fun; one woman is more conspicuous and more likely to attract drunks with mistaken ideas.

When trouble shows up, it's not what I expected.

Two thropes at a table between me and the stage are

signing to each other—a muzzle full of fangs is designed to tear into flesh, not conversation—and it's not hard to eavesdrop.

Hey, did you hear about the Flamingo?

I thought they were going to tear that place down.

No, not until next month—but it's already gone.

What, they moved up the demolition?

No, I mean it's gone. Disappeared. Some kind of new spell, I guess.

So what's there now? A big hole? A parking lot?

No, that's the weird thing. It's a totally different building instead. And the cops have the whole area cordoned off, not letting anyone in.

Sounds like somebody screwed up.

Yeah. The place was probably supposed to turn into dust or something, and they forget to dot an i or cross a t. Got a Kmart instead of a crater.

Typical.

That doesn't sound like any spell I've ever heard of; if it was that easy to just zap a building out of existence, the Free Human Resistance would have been nine-elevening half the federal structures in Washington. The kind of power needed to do anything like that is usually restricted to what's known as HPLC, High Power Level Craft, and only government agencies have access to it.

Or rogue sorcerers from another dimension.

Azura disappears into the back when she's done her set, but I'm not worried about her disappearing—she's made it clear she needs me, and I have the feeling that someone with her skill set could ditch me at any time if she really wants to, anyway. I figure she's probably just gone upstairs to freshen up.

Sure enough, she comes back a few minutes later wearing black yoga pants, a belly-baring halter top, and a pair of red cowboy boots. She's got a plate of onion rings with her, too, which she slaps down in front of me before sliding into the booth. "Grabbed something from the kitchen for you. It's about the only edible thing they make."

"Thanks."

I tell her about the building as I eat. "It's got to be Ahaseurus," I say. "Any idea what it means?"

She frowns. "Maybe. We need to check it out, that's for sure. So what did you think?"

"About what?"

"My set."

"Oh. You're, uh, limber. And . . . extroverted."

"It's how I broke in to the Astonishers' Guild."

"By taking your clothes off?"

"It's a competitive field, with not a lot of women; I figured I'd turn a negative into a plus by doing something no one else had done before—and my act featured a lot more than just showing some skin. But you've got to draw a crowd before you can astonish them, and striptease does that extremely well. Besides, you'd be amazed how well misdirection and exhibitionism go together."

"Palm one thing while you're flashing another?"

"Exactly."

I understood what it was like to hit the glass ceiling in a profession dominated by men—but at the FBI, at least I'd managed to do it without resorting to pasties and a G-string. "Kind of a cheap trick, if you ask me."

She raises an eyebrow, but the smile stays on her face. "There are no cheap tricks, Jace—just the ones that work and the ones that don't. Like getting an NSA agent to desert her post for a sketchy meeting."

"That was a *calculated risk*—"

"So I'm guessing math wasn't one of your stronger subjects?"

Now I'm the one who's smiling—and it's not a nice smile. "As a matter of fact, I did very well at math. And forensics. And ballistics. And criminal psychology—oh, wait, you probably don't even know what the last two *are,* do you? Though I'm sure you got high marks in bra tossing and putting your ankles behind your ears."

She meets my eyes levelly, two cats with twitching tails staring at each other on a fence and waiting for the other one to lose her nerve.

"You don't like me very much, do you?" she asks.

"I don't know you. From what I've seen so far, you're manipulative, flamboyant, overly cheerful, and cute as a kitten. No, I don't like you."

"Well, there's really only one way I can respond to that." She stands up. "Hot shower. Dry clothes. Twenty-year-old scotch. And if you can hold off on cutting my throat for a few minutes longer, freshly made espresso."

I blink. "You're not fooling me. You're *Satan,* with . . . with perky breasts."

She walks away, crooking her finger for me to follow. I wonder if I can glare at her hard enough to make her burst into flames—then I can just take the keys from her charred corpse and help myself.

That doesn't happen. I surrender to the inevitable, muttering all the way. I think I would have just shot her and called it a day if she hadn't offered me espresso . . .

The apartment Azura's staying in is tiny, but she's got a shower massager in her bathroom, a bottle of something called McBeastie with a kilt-wearing thrope howling at the moon on the label, and an honest-to-God espresso machine in her minuscule kitchen. It looks like she ripped out the microwave to make room for it.

I take her up on the shower and the caffeine, but pass on the scotch. It's not that I don't appreciate a nice single-malt, but the tequila is starting to wear off and it's giving me the kind of jagged clarity that a mild hangover induces—you know, when the world is turned up just a little too high? Uncomfortable, but it can be a useful tool. I discovered it by accident, working on a case in Georgia near the beginning of my career—the brutality of the crime scenes had me using whiskey to kill the nightmares, and the morning-after effects wound up helping me catch the killer.

Before I get in the shower, I pull out my cell phone. I don't care what Miss Voodoo Boobs says, I need to know if Charlie's all right. And of course, I discover that our little midnight dip has drowned the damn thing—I should have downloaded that waterproofing app Gretchen was talking about.

I sigh and clean up. There's sweatpants and a T-shirt that almost fits waiting for me when I'm done; Azura must have stuck them through the door while I was showering. I get dressed and rejoin her. She's got a double shot of espresso ready and waiting, which I grudgingly accept.

"When your clothes are dry, we'll head over to the Flamingo," she says.

I down the espresso and slap the cup down on the Formica countertop. "I'm good now. Besides, it'll take my shoes forever to dry out—I'll wear them as is."

She slips on an oversize zip-up black hoodie. "Ready when you are."

I strap on my gun, throw on my damp jacket, and we go outside and hail a cab. He can't get us any closer to the Flamingo than a block away—the police have it cordoned off.

We get out and join the crowd that's pressed up against the roadblocks, gawking. What I can see isn't all that impressive—just a big gray building, similar to a warehouse, maybe three stories high. Nobody seems to be going in or out.

"That's not a casino," Azura murmurs.

"Not unless gray and boring is the new neon."

"I think I know what it is, though. A morgoleum."

"Sounds like an ointment."

"It's where they store underdead workers between shifts." She shakes her head. "This isn't what I was expecting at all. Unless . . . no, that can't be it."

"What?"

"Never mind. We need to get inside."

"I've got an NSA badge and you can look like anyone. I don't think we'll have any problems. Uh—you can look like anyone, right? Not just me? Because I'd rather not do this as the Doublemint Twins."

"My repetoire isn't unlimited, but I'll manage. I'm going to stick with my real appearance for now, all right?"

"Yeah, sure. Just follow my lead, okay?"

We stride up to the bored-looking thrope guarding the barricade. I flash my badge.

"We need to get a closer look at the phenomenon," I say.

The thrope is a burly Latino guy. He's doing that thing some cops like to do—transforming just enough to make his eyes go yellow, his teeth and ears sharpen, and a three-day growth of stubble sprout on his chin. Back where I come from, they grow mustaches—same thing, really.

"Can I see that again?" he says. His voice is deep and guttural, but the effect is ruined by the slight lisp his deformed mouth is producing.

Uh-oh. Didn't think they'd have local law enforcement looking for me this fast.

Which is when Azura steps forward. Except she's not Azura anymore.

"Excuse me, pilgrim," John Wayne says. He's wearing a dark blue denim suit that would look ridiculous on anyone else, and his cowboy boots are now black. "I've got a fair bit of money tied up in that casino, and I'd really appreciate taking a closer look."

The thrope's eyes go wide. "I didn't know you owned the Flamingo, Mr. Wayne."

The Duke chuckles. "Oh, I wouldn't go *that* far. But I am *one* of the owners, and apparently I'm the only one in town. The other guys asked me to drop by, see what's going on. That all right with you, son?"

He hesitates, but there are stars in his eyes and one right in front of him. "Sure, Mr. Wayne. Absolutely."

"Thank you. You come on by the bar at the hotel when this is all straightened out, tell 'em the Duke said they owe you a drink."

"I'll do that!"

We hop the barricade and stride toward the building before he remembers that something about me was off.

"John Wayne?" I say once we're out of earshot.

"What, you don't like cowboys?"

"On my world, he's dead. Cancer. Caused, some people say, by nuclear tests done near here that fried his cells with radiation while he was shooting Westerns out in the desert."

"Radiation," she says. Her voice is hard, as opposed to questioning.

"You have that where you come from?"

"In a way. Ours is worse."

It's not just the casino that's missing, it's the entire patch of ground that the hotel and parking structure stood on. What's there now is just bare earth, the same kind of rocky terrain that surrounds Vegas. Azura goes down on one knee and scoops up a handful, rubs it between her fingers. "Interesting," she says.

"Why?"

"I'll tell you after we've looked inside."

"Fine." I draw my gun. "Let's do this."

We walk up to the front door, which is a big, barn-like affair with leather hinges. I grab the handle and ease it open. We peer inside.

It looks like a warehouse, row after row of shelves that go all the way up to the roof. Walkways line them at the first and second stories, and ladders provide access at the end of every row.

But this building isn't designed to store merchandise. What's on the shelves are bodies.

I can see the soles of their shoes, one pair at the open end of every single compartment. It's like looking at a Costco of corpses; the only thing missing is a few cashiers and some extra-large shopping carts.

Azura and I both step forward at the same time.

And everything goes black.

I haven't lost consciousness. What I *have* lost is everything else—sight, hearing, taste, smell, sense of touch. I'm awake, but with only my own thoughts for company; my voice, my body, my new stripper-slash-partner are all AWOL.

And then I hear the voice.

A long, long time ago, at the beginning of all things, there was Chaos. And Chaos gave birth to Order, for Chaos inevitably gives birth to all things. But Order was different, for Order resisted the destruction that Chaos also inevitably brings; and Order spread, until it was the equal of Chaos and could spread no more.

But time blurs borders, and so it was with the border between Chaos and Order. What began as a shifting battlefront expanded over billennia to be a realm of both and neither; a place where some things held true and others did not, of laws that could be bent and improbabilities that could be tamed.

This was Reality.

And Life arose within Reality, and so too did Death. And Life and Death and Chaos and Order were the Powers that governed all things.

But Chaos was not content, for Chaos demands change, always. And so Chaos visited Life herself, and crept into her blood while she slept; for Chaos is at his most powerful in those parts of Reality that are very, very small. And Life's blood boiled with chance and change, and she bore him many children.

The offspring of Life and Chaos was also very small but very numerous; and it spread from Life's blood to many living creatures. And those creatures that it came to rest within were transformed into beings with aspects both animal and human; and they were called Weres.

The Weres were cherished by their mother, for Life loves all that lives; and she saw the multiplicity of their forms and the cleverness of their minds, and was pleased.

When Order saw this he was most unhappy, for he knew the children of Chaos would only spread more uncertainty and change in the world. So he resolved to counter this development, in his own straightforward, unimaginative way.

He began to court Death.

He had an advantage in that Death was not used to being courted; indeed, in her entire existence few beings welcomed her approach, let alone sought her out. Perhaps another would have been dismayed, even offended by Order's offer, but Death was lonely; and so she accepted his proposed arrangement.

And thus the Underdead were created.

Not born, no; for they were made of human beings who had abandoned Life, and so were no longer under her sway. And Order decreed that they would be nourished by the decay of all living things, and would be linked to all of Reality by the fundamental forces that he embodied; and those forces were the things that kept the planets and the moons and the stars in their orbits, for Order is at his most powerful with things that are very, very big.

And thus the Underdead did not rot, as other dead things do. Nor did they think—at least, not as living beings do, for their minds had none of the freedom that Chaos brings. They could not dream, or imagine, or play. They were creatures of Death and Order, unchanging and unfeeling.

There was, on one shelf of Reality, a land called Nightshadow. Nightshadow was encircled by mountains on every side, and the sun, even in highest summer, never rose past their peaks; it crept behind them instead, making the mountaintops glow crimson and making even Nightshadow's brightest days those of twilight.

But it was not a cold place, oh no, for many hot springs bubbled and steamed in its valleys, and the air was warm and moist. And even without sunlight, plants grew lush and thick: mushrooms and toadstools and fungus, towering as high as any tree and in all the blazing colors of nature, from iridescent greens and sky blues to passionflower oranges and yellows and scarlets.

And this land called to the Weres and the Underdead and the mysterious Lyrastoi, for they were all creatures that loved the darkness and mistrusted the sun; the Underdead especially, for the rays of the sun turned them into cold, unmoving stone. And so Nightshadow filled with beings of every kind, from human to animal to Were to Underdead, and they lived in harmony side by side; for any human who felt the call of wildness in his blood could choose to become a Were, and those who did not were left in peace.

But Chaos saw this and was not content, for Chaos demands change in all things. And so he took upon himself a new and terrible form, born of the sun itself, that he called Fyre. And he swept down into the valleys of Nightshadow and brought destruction to Were and human and Underdead alike.

But the Lyrastoi were clever, and they devised a way

to drive Fyre from Nightshadow. They called upon the Underdead to counter Chaos, for were they not the children of Order? And the Underdead agreed to help for the good of all.

It took much time and much labor, but what is that to those with no desires, no hopes, no plans? The Underdead toiled, without complaint, without rest, from the deepest valleys of Nightshadow to the highest, rocky cliffs, planting and tending the crops that the Lyrastoi cultivated, and in time a vast web of roots underlay all the land; these roots, hidden beneath the soil, were safe from the depredations of Fyre, and the Lyrastoi charged them with a mighty enchantment that banished Fyre from Nightshadow forever.

And all those who lived there rejoiced, human and Were and Lyrastoi alike—but not the Underdead, for joy was something they could not feel. They had found their purpose in work, and now that purpose was done; and they were like seashells on a beach, filled with nothing. And so the people of Nightshadow promised to always find work to fill the endless hours of the Underdead, until the very end of time itself.

And so a race was enslaved, out of gratitude. They toil to this very day, and they have done so for a long, long time.

A long, long time.

A long, long time.

A long, long time ago, at the beginning of all things, there was Chaos. And Chaos gave birth to Order, for Chaos inevitably gives birth to all things. But Order was different, for Order resisted the destruction that Chaos also inevitably brings; and Order spread, until it was the equal of Chaos and could spread no more . . .

I don't know how many times I listened to it. I was in some kind of a zoned-out, bodiless daze—all I know for sure is that I found myself mumbling it in my sleep a week later.

I can't take any credit for snapping myself out of it, either—that was all Azura. She pulled some kind of mystical spell-breaker out of her bag of tricks and *bam!* we're back in the real world, just outside the threshold of the morgoleum door.

"You—you all right?" she gasps.

"He was most unhappy," I say groggily. "For he knew the children of Chaos would only spread more uncertainty and change in the world . . ."

"Jace?"

I put a hand to my forehead. "So he resolved to counter . . . to *counter*—Ah! *Counter my ass!*"

"Uh—"

"*Su*percali*frag*ilistic*exp*iali—*do—shus!*" I shake my head violently. "Damn it, I need the mental equivalent of mouthwash . . . that makes the worst earworm I ever got stuck in my head seem like twenty minutes of brilliant improvisational jazz. Eeny, meeny, miny mo . . . Peter Piper poked a pie of pickled pork . . ."

Azura looks a little dazed—and a lot less like John Wayne—but she's no doubt had more experience in this department. "What is that you're saying? Is that some kind of spell?"

"No, I'm just trying to get my brain onto another track—Fee, fi, fo fum, I smell the blood of somebody dumb . . ."

"Uh-oh," says Azura. She's looking back at the cop we fooled, and he's talking into his radio and not looking happy. "Time to exit, Agent. I don't think Mr. Wayne's fan club is too thrilled with us anymore."

We bolt. I'm humming "Itsy Bitsy Spider" under my breath as we run.

* * *

We manage to disappear inside a casino. They'll no doubt analyze images of us on the security feeds afterward, but that won't help them now unless they're a lot more organized than I think they are—which, if Gretch is anywhere near the operation, they might be.

"What the *hell* was that?" I hiss under my breath as we stride between rows of slot machines.

"A myth-spell."

"So, a *spelling* error yanked the two of us into storybook time?"

"*Myth*-spell. A powerful enchantment that channels the power of an ancient story. In this case it was a creation myth, dealing with the origin of—"

"I was there, I know what it dealt with. Here's the part where you explain to me what it means and why it's there."

"I . . . don't know."

I grab her arm and yank her to a halt. "No. You might not have all the answers, but you know *something* about what our little trip down fairy-tale lane means. Spill."

"All I know is that the morgoleum we stepped into was focusing the enchantment, and that it came from Nightshadow itself."

"The spell?"

"The building. It and the Flamingo were swapped, one for the other. The land around it is in a transitional state—here and there mixed together."

"Like Chaos and Order, in the myth. A borderland."

She nods, her face grim. "Both places have symbolic significance, too, with the morgoleum full of underdead representing Order—"

"And the Flamingo—or flaming O—Chaos, as in Fyre."

"Yes. A casino is a powerful mystic focus, anyway—it's where choice and chance come together, a man-made mix of elemental forces."

"So—does this mean a casino full of panicked thropes and pires are trapped in this Nightshadow?"

She starts walking again. "No. Underdead magic is all about keeping things exactly as they are—the whole morgoleum was saturated with it, which is what the spellcaster is using to keep the enchantment running in a loop. More than likely the Flamingo and everyone in it is stuck in the same kind of thing—maybe modernized into a more accessible form."

"So we got the oral tradition and they got what—a PBS special?" I had visions of Leonard Nimoy intoning, "And now, in search of . . . the Underdead."

"Maybe. I don't know. It all depends on what he's trying to accomplish."

"Ahaseurus."

"We should really stop using his name—he could use it to track us. Call him Asher."

"It's a little late for that," a voice growls behind us.

FIVE

We spin around.

Facing us are two of Stoker's mercenaries: Heinrich Koltz and one of Koltz's fellow Dobermans. Both Koltz and his comrade are in half-were form, meaning they're close to seven feet of wolf-headed, clawed, and fanged hairy muscle. Koltz holds a kukri, which looks like a malformed machete, and the other one has a thrope bow—it has a maximum pull close to three times that of a human bow, and thrope speed means he can notch another arrow before the first one hits its target. He's got a broadhead aimed straight at me.

Thropes sign when in were form, because their mouths aren't shaped right to talk. Which means that whoever spoke just now—

Wanted us to turn. And isn't there anymore.

I hit the floor. I hear a sharp puff of air and something slices through the spot my neck had been an instant ago. Not an arrow—the Doberman still hasn't released.

Azura snaps her fingers and the bowstring breaks. I yank my gun out of the holster and fire a round to my right, where the attack came from. The bullet slams into a slot machine with a noise almost as loud as the gunshot itself.

I catch a glimpse of Felicia Mbunte, the pire assassin, as she scrambles for better cover. She's got a blowgun in her hand and a dart clenched between her teeth. I fire another shot to keep her moving then swing back to cover the thropes.

Koltz leaps for Azura, his kukri poised to slash her in half. She jumps sideways, throwing a handful of glittery dust in the air as she leaves, does an elegant shoulder roll, and winds up in a battle-ready crouch. Koltz finds his blade passing through empty space, inhales a lungful of sparkles, and collapses to the casino floor in a spasm of retching.

I've got the other Doberman—who does, in fact, resemble one; he's got the black-and-tan coloration and a long, lean skull—dead to rights, but he doesn't know that. He's already yanking a sword out of a scabbard. I stop that by putting a silver-tipped teakwood round into his shoulder—it should have been his heart, but I haven't been on a firing range since I got here and I'm a little rushed.

That puts him on the ground, but I've lost Mbunte. Pires are fast, almost as fast as thropes, and with that blowgun she can take her time and pick me off as efficiently as any sniper.

"Guhh," Azura says.

I glance over. Azura's standing upright, but just barely. She's swaying from side to side, and the look on her face is one of confusion.

There's a clump of bright blue feathers sticking out of her neck.

She pulls the dart out and drops it, staggers down the aisle a few steps, leans drunkenly against a slot machine, and then begins to slide down its face. She never makes it to the floor; Felicia Mbunte steps out from behind it and grabs her by the hair, yanking her up and putting a knife to her throat.

"Stop," she says. "You're coming with us. Discard your weapon and your friend will live."

Damn it. A year ago I would have put a bullet right between her eyes, but I'm not nearly as sure of my aim now. Plus Mbunte's not stupid—she's shielding her body with Azura's.

"Not going to happen," I say. "Let her go or I'll execute both your friends." I swing my weapon around to cover them—Koltz is still on his knees coughing up blood, while the archer has made it back to his feet.

"With that? Don't make me laugh." Despite the fact that she's seen firsthand what my gun can do, despite the fact that she just ordered me to throw it away, on a very deep and magic-imposed level Mbunte just doesn't *believe* in the gun as a threat. She can't. I've been in similar situations and used that to my advantage, but I don't see how I can in this one.

"You're right, I'm bluffing," I say, lowering the Ruger. I hold it casually at my side. "It only works for three shots, anyway." Maybe I can get her to lower her guard . . .

"Suh-silver," Azura says. "Silver . . . tips."

"I'm surprised you're even conscious," Mbunte says. "Put enough neurotoxin in you to tranq an elephant."

"Your darts are silver-tipped," Azura says, her voice slow but steady. "So they'll penetrate thrope *or* pire skin."

"Ssssh, little human . . ."

"I wonder what six will do?" Azura says, and then she rams a handful of them into Mbunte's forearm, the one holding the knife. Clever hands, that girl.

I half expect Mbunte to slice open her throat, but that doesn't happen—instead, Azura slithers out of her reach, leaving a handful of hair in Mbunte's grip and a surprised expression on her face. I'd love to put a bullet in it, but both Koltz and his buddy seem to have recovered enough to advance on me, fangs bared. I shoot Koltz square in the chest, the impact throwing him backward a good six feet, and he goes down for good; his body reverts to human as he hits the floor. The other Doberman's been shot once already—spell or no spell, he knows enough to dive for cover. I get off one more shot, but miss.

I've got one bullet left, and no time to reload.

Mbunte collapses to the floor, holding her knife stiffly in front of her as if Azura were still a captive. Azura's having trouble standing, so I put an arm around her for support. I stagger backward, keeping my gun up. "Come after us and die," I say.

I hear a growl from behind a row of slots, but the last were keeps his head down. I can only hope he stays with his buddies and doesn't trail us.

We make it through the casino and into the adjoining mall. It's crowded and people seem to think we're just another couple of die-hard partiers supporting each other.

"That was stupid," I say. "Could have gotten your head cut off."

"Nah," she says sleepily. "Knew it had to be a fash-actin' paralyddic. Froze her arm. Nodda problem."

"Yeah? So why aren't you a human statue, instead of a surprisingly heavy sack of potatoes?"

"M'Astonisher. Poison expert. Gots all kinda immule—immoon—immunitable—"

"Immunities."

"Yesh."

Which is why she's currently a half-conscious Astonisher instead of a fully paralyzed one. Must have surprised the hell out of Mbunte, too.

Still no signs of pursuit, but Azura's fading fast. I have no idea if this means she's dying or just going into a coma, but I have to get as far away from here as possible. I leave the mall and flag down a cab.

"She ain't gonna puke, is she?" the driver, a lem in a plaid shirt, asks.

"If she does, you'll get one helluva tip, okay?"

I manage to get her inside and tell the driver to take us to Miss Pointy's. "Really? Y'ask me, she's had enough," he says.

"Oh, she'll be up and twirling her pasties in no time. This is just how she loosens up before a show." I hope it's true.

When we get there I half carry, half drag her upstairs, find her keys, and get her inside. I wonder how she managed when our roles were reversed and she had to get me into that hotel room; I mass considerably more than she does.

Sirens outside. I sneak a look out the window, but they're not coming here. Wherever they are going, though, they're doing it together and in a big hurry; I count at least a dozen radio cars roaring past at full speed.

Maybe another casino vanished. People in Vegas hate that.

I turn back to the couch where I dumped Azura. She's still out, but her breathing is strong and regular; I don't think she's going to die, but I'm neither a doctor nor a shaman. I should get her to a hospital.

Which means this partnership is over. She can't help me if she's unconscious—the smartest thing to do is to find Charlie, explain what's going on, and regroup.

Azura shifts and mutters something. I bend down and peer at her head; her hair is shorter now, but there's no bald patch. I don't know what she did to get free of Mbunte's grip, but it wasn't a wig the pire was left holding—it was as if Azura just told her hair to let go about six inches away from her skull and it did.

"I don't know much about magic," I murmur, "but you could make a killing as a hairdresser."

* * *

I can't just leave her there—if Stoker's mercenaries found us once they can do it again. Better to take her with me, stick her in a holding cell, and see if she'll cooperate when she wakes up.

I search her apartment, hoping to stumble across some vital piece of information she's been holding back, but come up empty. She does seem to have a thing for Ding Dongs, though.

No phone, either, so I have to haul her downstairs and try to flag down another cab. After fifteen minutes I'm almost ready to give up—no cabs are stopping. Neither are the police cars screaming past in both directions; I'm starting to get a really bad feeling about this.

I finally manage to get a taxi to stop. The driver, a thrope in dreadlocks, looks nervous. "Where to?"

I give him the address of the motel we were using as an ops center. "What's going on with all the cops?" I ask as I get Azura inside.

"I don't know," the driver says. "My dispatcher won't answer. The airwaves are all messed up, too—all I get is this." He turns a dial on his radio.

What comes out is a low, almost subsonic rumbling noise—not static, more like distant thunder. It starts and stops, almost sounding like language.

"Turn it off," I say. I don't know what it is, but it's worrying.

When we get to the motel, there are no police in sight. Plenty of debris in the parking lot of the chapel and all over the street, but no official presence at all—I expected the area to be sealed off with crime tape and Vegas cops, but there's nobody here except a few stunned-looking tourists studying the damage to their rental cars. A wisp of smoke rises from the large hole in the roof of the chapel, but if any fire trucks were here they didn't stick around.

I pay the cabbie, haul Azura to my room, and dump

her on the bed. No Charlie. I run over to the unit we were using as an ops center and knock—no answer. I use my key to let myself in.

It's more or less exactly the same as the last time I saw it. Coffee cups on the table, papers spread around, flatscreen TV turned off.

TV. I turn it on, have to fumble with connections for a minute to get it hooked up to the cable, then find a local news show.

"—do not attempt to leave Las Vegas by car. All roads into and out of the city have been blocked by LVPD police cars." The newscaster is a young, attractive Latino pire, and she looks like she's about to pass out or maybe start screaming. Her hands are shaking. "All flights to and from McCarran International Airport have been suspended. Do not attempt to approach Nellis Air Force Base, as this area has been declared off limits by . . . by the insurgents." She pauses, clearly trying to get herself under control. "If you're just joining us, this is what we know so far: the militant golem group known as the Mantle have—have *taken* Las Vegas. They are an occupying force. All golems in the city—this includes the majority of police and army personnel—have seemingly declared their allegiance to the Mantle. They have barricaded all access to the city. No demands have been made yet. Lycanthrope and hemovore law officers have reportedly been killed or imprisoned—"

"Hold it right there," a voice says.

I turn, slowly. Jake Wilson stands in the open door, a compound bow in his hands. He's got an arrow nocked, the bowstring drawn back. He doesn't look happy to see me.

"Wilson," I say. "Put the bow down. I can explain."

"Explain what? How you double-crossed us, or how much the lems paid you?"

"That wasn't me. That was a shaman named Azura using an illusion glamour—she's in my room, unconscious."

"Uh-huh. Unstrap your holster and kick it under the table. And don't touch your . . . magically goofy weapon while you're doing it."

I do so. "What happened to the team? Is everyone all right?"

"Well, let's see. Wolosky's in a coma, Brody and Gunderson are dead, every lem in the city's gone crazy—so no, everyone's not all right. Hope it was worth it."

Azura told me no one died and that Wolosky was hunting me. Did she lie? Or were the lems responsible for destroying my team? "Where's Charlie?"

"You tell me."

"Look, if I really did betray you like you think—why the hell would I come back here? And why would I be lugging a passed-out woman in red cowboy boots with me?"

He thinks about it. "I'll admit it don't exactly make sense." He lowers the point of the arrow to the floor, but keeps the tension on the string. "Let's go take a look at your friend. Maybe she can give me a better explanation than the one you just did."

I doubt that, but it's better than standing here and waiting for an arrow in the throat. "Okay, let's—"

A javelin erupts from his chest.

It soars right past me, spraying me with blood, and sticks into the far wall. My first thought is, *That's impossible. That thing's way too long, it would never have fit inside his chest in the first place—*

Wilson coughs once. Blood trickles out of the corner of his mouth. The arrow *thunks* into the floor, and he crumples to the ground.

I hear footsteps outside. Heavy footsteps.

I dive for my gun, but I kicked it harder than I thought and it's not under the table, it's on the other side of the room—

"Agent Valchek," a deep voice says. "Get to your feet, please. Slowly."

I stand up, cautiously.

Golem Master Sergeant Zayin stands over Wilson's body. He's got one of Gunderson's throwing axes in one hand, and it's got blood on it.

"Good to see you, Agent," Zayin says. "We were hoping you'd come back."

"You killed Wilson," I say. Stupid and obvious, yeah, but seeing another officer killed right in front of you is not the kind of thing that inspires witty remarks.

"Regrettable but necessary," he says. He doesn't sound crazy. "Things are not what they seem, Agent. We've got to get you someplace safe."

"We?"

"Captain Epsilon and myself." He strides over to the corner and picks up my gun and holster, turning them over curiously in his shiny black plastic hands.

"Sure," I say. "Can I have that back?"

"I think it might be better if I hang on to it for now," he says. "Follow me." He strides out of the room without looking back.

After a second, I follow him.

He leads me out to the white panel van we had set up as a support vehicle, opens the passenger door, and motions me inside. I get in. I might be able to outrun him, but I wouldn't take more than a few steps without a javelin in my back.

"Where's Epsilon?" I ask as he gets in the driver's side.

"Guarding the perimeter." He starts the van.

Of course—that's where the javelin came from. Zayin prefers the collapsible bow he has slung over his back. Must make it uncomfortable to drive, but lems aren't big on complaining.

I don't tell him about Azura.

He won't tell me what's going on, just that he's taking me someplace safe and that I'll get an explanation when we get there. There's comm gear in the van, and when it starts making that rumbling noise I heard in the cab he grabs the microphone and makes the same noise right back; I had no idea golems had their own language. It sounds like thunderstorms having a conversation, dipping down into the subsonic and making my back teeth vibrate.

We head north, toward downtown. The only people I see on the street now are lems, and every one of them seems to be armed: bows, axes, swords, even shovels and sledgehammers.

We pull into a police station, or—as they call them here—an area command. It's a low-slung southwestern-style building, made of concrete and painted a sandy color that almost fades into the background of the desert behind it. The place is practically empty—I guess all the action's someplace else. There's not a single pire or thrope in sight.

But there is a lem janitor in coveralls mopping up the blood on the floor.

Zayin takes me straight through processing and down to the cells. That's when I begin to understand why he brought me here.

Every cell holds a human being.

It's funny how you can just tell after a while. Thropes or pires both look human most of the time, but there are always subliminal clues that let me know when I'm looking at a member of my own species. There are both men and women here, and more than a few children. Most look terrified; a few look resigned.

Zayin takes me to a cell and motions me to step in. I haven't been searched and still have my scythes; I wonder for a second if I can take him, and if I should. But there's another guard with a nocked bow standing twenty feet away, and there's no chance of me getting out of here without being turned into shish kebab first. I step into the cell, and he locks it in my face.

"Okay, tell me what's going on," I say. "Why did you bring me here?"

"For the same reason we brought the rest of the humans here. To protect them."

"Protect them from what?"

Zayin shakes his head. "Vegas is too dangerous for all of you right now. Once things have settled down, you'll be freed. I promise, no one is going to harm you."

"Yeah? Who exactly are you protecting me *from,* Zayin?"

"The predators, of course. That's why I had to kill Wilson—he was going to devour you."

"Are you out of your *mind*? Wilson was a *federal agent*—it's against the law to even *bite* a human, let alone turn one into *lunch*—"

"He was a beast," Zayin says, his voice devoid of emotion. "As are they all."

And then he turns and stomps away, leaving me there with my jaw on the floor. I don't leave it there for long; the floor is filthy.

"What's going on out there?" a woman in the cell next to mine asks. She's in her fifties, looks like she should be parked in front of a slot machine feeding it nickels. "Do you know?"

"The golems seem to have overthrown Las Vegas. A group called the Mantle is claiming responsibility. Don't worry—I don't think they plan on hurting us. In fact, they seem to be going out of their way to do the opposite."

"This just doesn't make any sense," the woman says. "Lems are always so . . . so *hardworking*."

"Looks like they still are. They just found something else they'd rather work hard at . . ."

"Don't surprise me none," a raspy male voice calls out from farther down the cell block. "Lems, thropes, pires—they're all the same. Just want to get rid of us once and fer all."

I should know better than to get into an argument with someone like this—even though I can't see him, I'm sure this guy's neck is as red as the Devil's derriere—but it's not like I've got anything better to do. "Yeah, that's it, Einstein. They've locked us up because they fear our spooky human powers of super-complaining and invincible stupidity."

"They got them some nefarious plan—"

"Oh, shut up. You learned the word *nefarious* from Saturday-morning cartoons and you probably still don't know what it means."

There's a pause. "I do, too." He sounds hurt. "It means *dastardly*. Evil. Real, real, bad."

"Congratulations, you'll be getting your diploma in the mail. Now, unless you have an idea of how to get out of here, please keep your insightful comments to yourself—"

The door at the end of the corridor opens. I'd recognize that silhouette anywhere; the fedora helps.

"Charlie!" I say. "About goddamn time!"

He stalks up to my cell, stops in front of the bars, and stares in at me. "Jace. Mind explaining to me what, exactly, is going on?"

"It wasn't *me,* Charlie. A shaman—well, she calls herself an Astonisher, but that's a whole other deal—named Azura took my place. Glamour spell. Wolosky should have caught it—"

"Wolosky's in the hospital. In a coma."

"I heard. Gunderson and Brody are dead?"

"Yeah." He stares at me intently, then shakes his head. "You really didn't know, did you? That explains a lot."

He believes me. I shouldn't have doubted it—he's my

partner, I trust him with my life and he trusts me with his, but up until this moment I was deathly afraid that was all over. "Look, I got a call from someone who claimed to have the inside track on the deal. She wanted to meet with me, alone. I wasn't going to do it, I swear—just scope out the situation, see if I could catch her in a mistake."

"How'd that work out for you?"

"Just peachy. Next thing I know, I'm tied to a hotel bed in my undies and Azura's doing a Jace Valchek Vegas act. She planned to impersonate me and get close enough to kill Aha—Asher. I got loose and tried to stop it, but got there just as the roof blew off."

"It wasn't pretty, Jace. Both Asher and Stoker had shown, and you were nowhere to be found. Then you suddenly burst into the ops room and tell us to hit them, hard. When we did—well, they fought back. I saw you—Azura, I mean—get blown right through the chapel doors."

"Good job protecting me, pal."

"You were the one who got herself captured. Twice, apparently."

"I left behind a note in my luggage in case something happened to me—go check, it should still be there."

"Did you give yourself up, or was there a giant shoe box propped up with a stick?"

"I'm sorry, I was distracted by every member of your immediate family deciding to turn Vegas into Bedrock City—"

"If you *wanted* a white flag for your birthday, all you had to do was ask—"

We both stop. He stares at me levelly, and I sigh. "Okay, you win," I say. "I, after all, am the one behind bars. So get me out of here already."

"Yeah, about that . . ."

"What? Come on, Charlie. Fun's fun, you can rib me

about this for years, but I'm not going to do you a lot of good locked up."

"No, but you *are* safe. Well, saf*er*. Actually, I'd prefer to lock you up in Fort Knox with a tank battalion around the perimeter and a death ray satellite orbiting overhead, but you'd just get into trouble on the Internet."

"Charlie . . ."

"Here's the thing, Jace. There's a war going on. Not just an investigation, a *war*. You haven't seen war before, but I have. It's—" He looks away, his jaw set. "It's hard enough to survive when you have supernatural strength or invulnerability. You wouldn't stand a chance."

"I'm not planning on storming the front lines with a knife in my teeth, Charlie. Asher has to be involved in this somehow; I need to get out of here and find him."

"That's just not going to happen, Jace. I won't—I *can't*—allow it."

Something's wrong here. Charlie is pigheaded—well, *T.-rex*-headed, if you want to be accurate—but this level of protectiveness is out of character. Charlie and I put ourselves in harm's way on a regular basis, it's what we do. For him to be acting this way . . .

"Charlie," I say. "This war. Whose side are you on?"

He stares at me for a second, then turns and walks away.

The door at the end of the corridor clangs hollowly as it shuts.

SIX

I can't believe it.

Magic. It's got to be magic. Asher has somehow laid a whammy on every lem in the city, probably using that myth-spell Azura was talking about. That's why Charlie's acting the way he is.

Except—he didn't seem like he was under someone else's control.

He busted my chops, same way he always does. He wasn't irrational, either; Vegas is probably a very dangerous place to be in right now, no matter what species you belong to. And considering how often I put myself in situations hazardous to my health, maybe I should consider myself lucky he hasn't locked me up before this.

Sure. He's just trying to teach me a lesson. Let me stew in my own juices before he shows up with an extra-tall latte in one hand and a key in the other. Won't let me out until I promise to behave.

But I keep remembering the argument we had on the flight here, when we were talking about the Mantle. Charlie seemed to agree with some of their points, and he reacted badly when I made a joke. This is something he takes seriously—maybe more seriously than I thought.

I spend so much time dwelling on being one of the few human beings on this planet that it never occurred to me to think what it would be like to be a slave here.

Maybe *slave*'s a little strong. They have rights, they're legally people, they aren't anyone's property . . . are they?

Tough question. They're made, not born, and they pop into existence with an immediate debt to whichever company or government made them. Parents don't charge their children for creating them, so why should a parent corporation? And wasn't the right to procreate the most basic right there was? After survival itself, that is—and really, having children is just survival on another scale. Survival of the race as opposed to the individual.

Survival of the race. The pires of this world have already proven how far they were willing to go for that one—they sacrificed six million human lives to an eldritch God in exchange for the ability to have children, an act so monstrous I can't really fathom it. But in my world we were willing to use the atomic bomb to obliterate two cities' worth of civilians to end a war, and I can't honestly say that one atrocity is greater than the other. Both were monstrous, but both ultimately contributed to the side of life.

So which side were the golems contributing to?

People talk about the terrors of jail, about getting shanked for your pudding or raped in the shower, but the ultimate truth of life behind bars is very simple: It's *boring*.

I lie down on the bunk and think about the situation. That gets me nowhere—unless I can get out of here or contact someone, I'm pretty much stuck. I could lure a guard within range and use my *eskrima* sticks—but it's almost impossible to knock out a lem with brute force, and I don't want to kill anyone unless I have to. Besides, that'll get me about as far as the outside of this cell before I run into a wall of arrows.

This isn't my first time in jail. I've been in plenty in the course of my career, and even before that—though prior to joining the FBI, I was more likely to be enjoying the same view I am right now. Yes, that's right, I have been arrested. What, no gasps of shock?

The first time I was only sixteen. Okay, I shouldn't have been in that bar in the first place, but the other guy started the fight. Well, other *guys,* technically. Seems they couldn't believe they were getting their asses handed to them at eight-ball by a girl barely out of high school. And by "out of high school" I mean cutting classes to drink beer and raise hell.

Okay, maybe I exacerbated the situation a little. But there were only three of them and I had a pool stick in my hands, which to my mind made me a Jedi Knight facing three stormtroopers wearing gimme caps and drinking Coors Light.

Of course, pool sticks break whereas lightsabers don't—but that just gives you two sticks to play with, and I'm more comfortable with that than a sword, anyway. In hand-to-hand I prefer a weapon that lets me break bones as opposed to severing limbs—it gives you more options in the long run. I'd rather face a lawsuit for dental bills than one for amputation.

Anyway, I did that one guy a favor. His teeth were all bad to begin with—he looked much better with dentures. Well, marginally better.

I have to shake my head and grin. Haven't thought about that bar fight in years; I put all that behind me when I signed up for the Academy. Used to be I'd grab any excuse to get in a fight—an insult, a look, a careless remark—but since I joined law enforcement I've internalized most of that. I still get in fights, I just tend to attack verbally instead of physically. Wish I'd learned how to do that first, but better late than never.

I was never good with a snappy comeback as a kid. I was taller and heavier than most of the other girls my age, and when they teased me about it I just shut down and tried to ignore them. Bad idea—kids can't stand to be ignored, it just makes them try harder. So when they found out they couldn't make me mad with taunts, they kicked it up a notch. Vandalizing my locker, stealing my gym clothes, that sort of thing. Then one day they decided to see what would happen if they actually *hit* me.

What happened was I got yanked out of school for two weeks. Well, out of one school and into another one— two weeks isn't enough time to master a martial art, but it is long enough to learn how to beat the crap out of someone. Especially when you train eight hours a day for fourteen days in a row.

I was ten.

I guess you could make a case for child abuse, but that's not accurate. What happened was my parents— both of them—sat me down and said, "This has to stop. We have an idea. How would you feel about *this* . . ."

I love my folks. Both of them are gone now, but they gave me an approach to problem solving that's stuck with me: If somebody's pushing you around, push back. Hard.

Which, inevitably, led to me getting into bar fights when I was five years shy of legal drinking age, so maybe it wasn't exactly a flawless way to live life. Never got beat up again, though—and never beat up anyone who didn't have it coming, either. Including those snotty bitches who used to rag on me in that way only schoolgirls can—the subtle put-downs, the gossip, the sarcasm.

Yeah, you heard me. Sarcasm. Nasty little voices dripping with poison as they mocked my clothes, my body, my actions. You think I came by my ability naturally? Hell, no. I had to study at the feet of masters—it was like learning how to use the dark side of the Force from a bunch of elementary school Darth Vaders.

"In order to defeat your enemy," my old sensei Duane Dunn used to say, "you must master the same weapons."

"But isn't that like, well, turning evil yourself?" I'd asked him.

Duane was an ex-marine, an old friend of my father's, with a fringe of white hair around a bullet-shaped skull. He'd chuckled and said, "No. Weapons aren't evil—people are. And mastering a weapon doesn't mean you have to use it; it just means you understand it and can make it do what you want it to. It's up to you if and when to do that."

As it turns out, sarcasm is sometimes more appropriate than violence, though usually not as satisfying. Easier to practice in public, though, and Charlie's the whetstone I've gotten used to sharpening my skills on. What am I supposed to do now—mock my dog? He'd just do the same thing he always does, stare at me with undying devotion, love, and absolutely no understanding. What fun is that?

Thinking about Galahad depresses me further. There's something about jail that makes you ruminate on harmonica music and miss your dog. I miss his big slobbery kisses, the way he rests his head in my lap when I watch TV, the way he makes me coffee in the morning . . .

Galahad isn't your average St. Bernard cross. He's a dog were, a canine that's been bitten by a thrope and now has the same disease—some sort of cursed virus, apparently—coursing through his veins as human lycanthropes do. In the case of dogs, though, it doesn't confer any supernatural immunities or strength; it just means they transform into a human version of themselves when the sun goes down. Oh, and every full moon they get a little smarter for a few days—I swear I found Gally trying to surf the Internet once. He's one of the bright spots of being stranded in this reality; I'm going to miss him when I finally go home.

Whenever that is.

Aside from the whole locked-in-a-cage thing, the lems treat us well. They bring us food, make sure we're okay for bedding, even offer us reading material. And they firmly, absolutely, refuse to let us leave. "For your own good," they say.

I notice something when they bring us food: The last cell on the end, across the corridor from me, doesn't get any—but does get three paperbacks pushed through the bars. I don't have a good view of the interior, but unless this is the local branch of the lem library somebody must be in there. A pire, maybe?

"Hey," I ask a guard. "Who's in the last cell?"

He doesn't answer for a moment. "A traitor," he says at last, then stomps off with more than his usual grimness.

I press my face up against the bars and try to get a better look. I can only see one of the paperbacks—a Zane Grey Western, it looks like—the other two having landed far enough inside to be out of sight. I wish I had one of those little mirrors they're always using in prison movies to look around . . . and then I realize I've got something almost as good.

I take out one of my *eskrima* sticks and open the blade. Twelve inches of highly polished silver snap into position, turning it into a scythe. I hold it outside the cell and angle it to get a better view of the last cell.

I see a glint of bronze as a hand reaches down to pick up the book, and what looks like the edge of a battered straw cowboy hat.

I know who's in that cell—and more than likely, he knows who's in mine.

I pull back my arm, close the blade, and put the stick away. "Well, well, well," I say loudly. "What's the matter, Silverado—you not planning on saying hello?"

After a moment a familiar voice responds: "Hello, Jace." I wait, but that's all he apparently has to say at the moment— Silverado isn't a big talker.

He is, however, several other things: a bounty hunter, a lem, and a near-mythical figure once known as the Quick-silver Kid. He's the only lem in the world with mercury in his guts instead of soil, and with a brass exterior that makes him look more like a robot than a golem. Legend says he's animated by the spirits of a hundred rattlesnakes, and I can say from personal experience that his reflexes support that theory. He carries a bandolier of enchanted silver knives that can cut through damn near anything— including spells—though I would guess that his current situation means he doesn't have them in his possession at this particular moment.

"Didn't expect to run into you here," I say. "Why aren't you out there helping your brothers-in-arms overthrow the state?"

"They offered. I declined."

"Doesn't look like they agreed with your decision."

"You could say that."

So lems still had the ability to make their own deci- sions. The odds of Charlie coming back and letting me go didn't look so hot anymore. "Don't suppose you've got one of those magic knives hidden somewhere on your person, do you?"

"'Fraid not. Don't suppose your partner's gonna come back and unlock these cells?"

"Doesn't look that way."

He doesn't say anything else, but it's kind of hard to tell when Silverado's done speaking; an entire civilization could rise and fall during one of his pauses. I finally give up and say, "Last time I saw you, you were on Tair's trail. How'd that go?"

"Got close a couple times. Then he hooked up with an arms dealer, surrounded himself with a gang of mercenaries. Tracked him here. You?"

"Pretty much the same. He was supposed to be fronting a deal of some kind—the other players were Aristotle Stoker and a mage named Asher. Know anything about that?"

"Can't say that I do." He answers just a little too quickly, and my cop instincts tell me it's deliberate. Silverado knows something, but he doesn't want to talk here.

"Damn," he says. "I've read all three of these, 'bout a dozen times each. Nice of 'em to provide a so-called traitor with reading material at all, I guess—I must still have a little mojo with the locals."

"Wish I could say the same—"

"I was made around here, you know," he says, actually interrupting me. I get the hint, shut up, and listen.

"Little town called Wolf's Hollow. Founded by thropes, which I don't suppose comes as much of a surprise. What with the Mexican border being so close, they had more than a little trouble with thrope banditos, coyote-blood packs swooping in and taking whatever they wanted. Town had a sheriff, but he just rolled over and showed his throat at the first sign of trouble. They couldn't afford a regular shaman to build 'em a lem, but there was this crazy old Englishman living there who offered to make 'em one for free. Make a long story short, he made me. That was a long time ago."

He pauses, but this time I wait. After a moment, he continues. "I've been around quite a spell, and I've done my share of traveling. I've seen some mighty strange goings-on, but I've been *told* things that were even stranger. Learned to pay attention, too—someone tells you a tale, they generally got a reason to do so. Sometimes they're trying to hoodwink you, but sometimes they're trying to clear the scales from your eyes. Up to you to decide which . . .

"I was in a bar outside Flagstaff, hunting a bank robber who had jumped bail. Heard he might be found in this one particular watering hole, so I was waiting around and putting quarters in the jukebox to pass the time. This old Medicine Man, wrinkled and white-haired, walked up to my table and asked me to buy him a drink. I asked him why I should; he told me a wise lion feeds the crows by the water's edge, so as not to startle the deer. I got his meaning, bought him a shot of cheap whiskey, told him to keep his mouth shut.

"He took the whiskey happily enough, but I guess he figured I was good for more than one because he sat down at my table. He drank the shot real slow, making it last, and as he drank he told me this story.

A long time ago, in the land of my father's father's father, there was a shaman who had not yet chosen his Spirit Animal. In those days, a shaman could do such a thing, for the Earth was still young and Man was still powerful. To be the Spirit Animal of a human shaman was considered a great honor, and many beasts of the land, the sea, and the air vied with one another to be chosen.

"Choose me," said the Falcon, "for I can fly to the very tops of mountains and see all things no matter how small or far away."

"Choose me," said the Killer Whale, "for I can swim to the very depths of the ocean and guide you to the richest fishing grounds."

"Choose me," said the Mouse, "for I am clever and quick and wise in the ways of love; I will guarantee you many, many children."

But the shaman was not satisfied with any of these ani-

mals, for he wished to be the most powerful and feared shaman in all the land. "I choose the Wolf," he said, "for it is not only fast and clever and strong, but savage as well; and all those who see it are afraid."

And so Wolf was pleased, and guided the shaman when he traveled to the Spirit World in search of knowledge and power. But on his very first voyage, the shaman had gone no farther than the foothills of the Great Mountains when Wolf stopped. "I can go no farther," Wolf said.

"Why not?" asked the shaman.

"The Great Mountains are the dominion of Cougar, and should I trespass, he would fall upon me and rend me throat-to-belly."

This made the shaman very angry, but Wolf would not be dissuaded. So the shaman banished him, telling him he was no longer his Spirit Animal, and Wolf slunk away.

The shaman made a fire, and burned certain herbs that only grow in the Spirit World, and invited Cougar to visit him; and after a while Cougar came down from his home in the Great Mountains and approached the shaman's fire without fear.

"Wolf is afraid of you," said the shaman. "You are mightier than he, and so I choose you as my Spirit Animal." And Cougar accepted, for that was how things were done in those days.

Cougar took the shaman into the Great Mountains, and showed him many things, and the shaman was well pleased. But at length they came to the Great Forest, and Cougar would go no farther. "This is the domain of Bear," said Cougar. "If I should trespass, he would tear me asunder with his mighty claws."

The shaman was angry once more, and banished Cougar back whence he came; and he took out his drum and beat out a message that would reach the very deepest, *darkest parts of the Great Forest. And Bear heard the message, and he came.*

"You are surely the fiercest, most powerful of all creatures," said the shaman. "Even Wolf and Cougar are afraid of you. You will be my Spirit Animal, I will be the strongest of all shamans, and none will bar our way."

Bear thought about this, for he was indeed the mightiest animal in all the land, and feared nothing. "Very well," Bear said. "I can tell you will be a powerful shaman indeed, and so are deserving of my partnership." And he and the shaman entered the Great Forest, and Bear showed him many things.

"All was well, until winter came. Then one day the shaman summoned Bear and he did not appear. He searched the Spirit World until he found him, fast asleep in a cave, for Bear grew slow and tired when snow lay upon the ground, and would not be roused until spring had come.

This time, the shaman's fury was terrible to behold. "I have become the most powerful shaman in all the land," he shouted, "and yet my Spirit Animal slumbers away a third of the year? I will not have it!" And he called down a lightning bolt upon Bear's cave, and it turned his fur as white as snow. And Bear bellowed in pain and fear, and ran far, far away, and never came back; and to this day he will not sleep when there is snow on the ground.

Though he no longer had a Spirit Animal, the shaman had learned much from Wolf, Cougar, and Bear, and now he turned all his knowledge and power to the problem at hand: finding a beast so fierce, so strong, so hungry, that it would never be content, never be at rest. He went into the desert, where he drank certain potions and ate certain bitter roots; and after a timeless time, he had a vision that told him to dig at the base of a towering cliff, where he found a single tooth.

It was like no tooth he'd ever seen, even larger than

*that of Orca, the Killer Whale; and though it was made
of solid stone like something carved by man, the shaman
could tell it once belonged to a living thing—a creature
that had not been seen on the face of the Earth for millions of years, an animal no man had ever set eyes on.
And though this beast and all his kind had vanished long,
long ago, the shaman knew that its spirit still walked the
Spirit World, for spirits live forever.*

*So the shaman polished the stone tooth, and placed it
at the center of a web he had woven from dreams and
shadows; and he danced around it, calling upon the
spirit that once owned it. And deep beneath the surface
of the Spirit World, in the Black Pools of the Great Caverns, the spirit heard him. And it rose up from the thick,
dark deeps, climbed out into the Great Caverns, clawed its
way through the secret tunnels of the Underworld until
it reached the surface. It burst up through the earth
beneath the shaman's feet, knocking him to the ground;
and he gazed upon its terrible face as it looked down
upon him.*

*It was a great stone lizard, larger than a dozen bears,
with jaws like the mouth of a cave and teeth like spears.
"I AM THE DEVOURING GHOST," it said. "WHO
SEEKS THEIR DEATH?"*

*"I seek not death, but power," said the shaman. "I am
the mightiest shaman in all the land, and only the most
powerful creature will do as my Spirit Animal. That, it
would seem, is you."*

*The Devouring Ghost considered this. He was not used
to his food answering his question; they usually just died
of fear on the spot. "I HAVE BEEN ASLEEP FOR MANY
YEARS," he said. "WHY SHOULD I NOT CALL YOU
BREAKFAST?"*

*"Because," said the shaman, "all things change, even
the Spirit World. The animals that roam the plains, the*

mountains, and the forests of this place are not the same as when you fell into your slumber. I have much knowledge, and knowledge is power."

"NO," the Devouring Ghost said, "THIS *IS* POWER." And he reached down with his immense jaws and ate the shaman in one bite.

Or so he thought. But when he straightened up, the shaman still stood before him. "You are powerful, Devouring Ghost," the shaman said. "But you are still only a ghost, and I am a living shaman. You cannot harm me in the Spirit World, for I am protected by my magicks. Did you really think me so foolish, so unprepared? Am I nothing but a rabbit in the middle of a field, waving a greeting to the hawk circling above?"

The Devouring Ghost considered this. "WHAT," he replied, "IS A RABBIT? OR A HAWK?"

And the shaman smiled, for he knew that the Devouring Ghost would accept his offer.

Which he did. For powerful though the Ghost was, he found himself in a place very different from the land he'd once roamed, and the shaman's advice was useful to him. So the Devouring Ghost agreed to be the shaman's Spirit Animal, and the shaman agreed to teach the Ghost about this strange and new world.

But even though the Ghost knew none of the beasts that now filled the Hunting Grounds of the Spirit World, some things were still the same.

He was still very hungry. And they were still good to eat.

It wasn't too long before the shaman was visited by the spirit of one of his ancestors.

"Greetings, blood of my blood," his ancestor said.

"Greetings, Grandfather," said the shaman. "How are things in the Spirit World?"

"Terrible. There are no caribou, few elk, and hardly

any deer. At this rate, even the rabbits will soon all be gone."

"How can this be?" the shaman asked. "The bounty of the Hunting Grounds is endless."

"I'll tell you what's endless," his ancestor said. "The appetite of your Spirit Animal. He's eating everything on four legs, and I'm pretty sure that when they're gone he'll start on things with two. I have to tell you, we're starting to get nervous."

"I'll have a talk with him," the shaman said.

But the Devouring Ghost wouldn't listen. "TELL THE MEMBERS OF YOUR TRIBE TO KILL MORE GAME AND SEND MORE SPIRITS HERE," he said. "I JUST ATE THE LAST MOOSE, AND I'M STILL HUNGRY."

"You need to think about going on a diet," said the shaman. "You keep eating like this and you'll get fat and slow; then you won't be able to hunt at all."

The Devouring Ghost just laughed, a sound like thunder in a canyon. "HA HA HA! THAT WILL NEVER HAPPEN. NOW IF YOU'LL EXCUSE ME, I HAVE A CRAVING FOR—WHAT ARE THEY CALLED AGAIN? BAFFALO?"

And so the Devouring Ghost ate the Hunting Grounds bare of all game. And the shaman was secretly pleased, for now he was without doubt the most powerful shaman of all. Even when the Devouring Ghost turned on the spirits of his own ancestors, the shaman was not moved; for soon he and the Devouring Ghost would have the Spirit World all to themselves, and the Ghost could not devour him.

The people of his own tribe came to the shaman, saying that they had heard the screams of their ancestors in their dreams, but the shaman laughed and called them fearful children.

The day came when the Devouring Ghost appeared to

the shaman and said, "I HAVE EATEN ALL THERE IS
TO EAT. IT IS TIME FOR ME TO RETURN TO THE
BLACK POOLS, FOR OTHERWISE I WILL STARVE."

But the shaman refused to let him go. "You are bound
to me as my Spirit Animal. You will stay here and survive
on the spirits that trickle in, for animals die every day.
You will not be happy, but you will obey."

"I WILL NOT," growled the Ghost. "I AM A HUNTER,
AND EAT WHAT I MUST. YOU WILL NOT REDUCE
ME TO A PENNED ANIMAL FED ON SCRAPS."

"You have no choice," said the shaman. "You cannot
harm me, remember? And if you do not do as I say, I will
cast a curse on the living creatures of my land so that
when they die their taste will lie foul in your mouth."

But the Devouring Ghost was not so easily beaten, for
he had learned much from the shaman. That night he appeared to the people of the shaman's tribe, and told them
of the great evil their Medicine Man had wrought; and
though the men and the women of the tribe were terrified
of the shaman, they were even more afraid of what the
Devouring Ghost would do to their spirits once they left
the land of the living.

So they crept into the tent of the shaman as he slept,
and they killed him; for as mighty as he was, he was still
just a man.

When the shaman's spirit appeared in the Hunting
Grounds, the Devouring Ghost was waiting, and spoke
only two last words to his former master: "HELLO,
BREAKFAST."

Once he had consumed the shaman's spirit, the Devouring Ghost kept his promise to the tribe and left their
Hunting Grounds. Where he went is not known, but the
Spirit World is large; some say he found another hunting
ground, one with even more game, and will return when
he has eaten it all. Others say he went back to the depths

of the Black Pool, to slumber for another hundred million years.

The only thing the Devouring Ghost left behind was the stone tooth the shaman had dug up. They say that it is in a museum now, but nobody knows for sure.

I knew Silverado's story was over when the ritual tone left his voice. "Tried to buy the man another drink when he was done, but I guess I was wrong about his reasons for sitting down; told me he only allowed himself one while he was storytellin'—otherwise, he'd be drunk all day. Guess one was more important to him than the other."

"Yeah," I say. Not sure how to respond, but the redneck in one of the other cells does it for me.

"Hey! That was pretty damn good! Tell us another one!"

"Sorry," Silverado says. "That's the only one I know. Think I'll get me some shuteye now, if you don't mind. Revolutions always tire me out."

"Aww, come on! I already read the damn magazine they brought me, or leastways all the interesting parts— hey, I bet you know some good lem jokes, don'tcha? Or knock-knocks?"

He goes on for a while, but Silverado ignores him. Me, I lie down on my bunk and think about what I just heard.

Seems pretty clear to me that the hungry spirit in the story is a dinosaur. That's interesting, because while most lems are animated by the life force of a domesticated animal like a cow or a horse, enforcement lems—the ones who work for the military or the police—are powered by predators. Charlie, though, is a special case; his metaphysical engine is the spirit of a *Tyrannosaurus rex,* distilled by animist magic from crude oil. Black Pools of the Underworld, indeed.

But what does it *mean*?

Silverado said he'd tracked Tair until he joined Silver

Blue's band of mercenaries. The last time I'd seen Tair he'd had a powerful mystic artifact in his possession, a gem called the Balancer that had been bonded to a blade known as the Midnight Sword; apparently they were Tair's ticket into Blue's inner circle. Silverado didn't mention either one—not unless he'd made some sort of veiled reference to them in his story. Is that what the stone tooth represents? It's both a cutting implement and a rock, as well as being a magical focus . . .

That's about as far as I get, because that's when they bring Azura in.

SEVEN

A more accurate statement is that they carry Azura in.

At first I think she's still knocked out from whatever was in that blowgun dart, but she's a little more banged up than the last time I saw her: nasty bruise starting to form on her forehead, ugly gash on one arm. I hope it wasn't from a thrope claw.

The lem carrying her is Caleb Epsilon, the one Zayin left behind to "guard the perimeter." He puts her in the cell across from mine.

"Caleb," I say. "This is ridiculous. You've got to let me out of here—I'm your commanding officer, goddamn it!"

"I'm in a different army now," Caleb says, meeting my furious stare calmly. He walks away without looking back.

Great. I have to admit, until this moment I was entertaining certain hopes about Azura showing up—probably disguised as a lem—and breaking me out of here. Well, she showed up all right, but it doesn't do me much good when the cavalry arrives unconscious and slung over the backs of their own horses.

I hear a groan, and see Azura twitch.

"Hey!" I call. "Wake up! You're going to be late for the school bus!"

"Don' *wanna* go to school," she mutters, then opens her eyes and lifts her head groggily. "Jace?"

"Present. How's your head?"

She sits up slowly, wincing as she looks around. "Sore. I see my clever plan worked."

"If you mean getting knocked out and locked up, yeah, it's really chugging right along. Can't wait till we get to the part where we're stuffed in a sack and beaten with tire irons."

She sits on her bunk with her head in her hands for a moment. I almost feel sorry for her—whatever our differences, she's just trying to do her job, same as me. She's been blasted, beaten, drugged, and imprisoned; I wouldn't blame her for having a good cry right about now—

She lifts her head and turns to look at me.

And grins.

"*Your* problem," she says, "is that you're oversensitive to sarcasm."

"What?"

She gets to her feet—no, she *springs* to her feet. "When I said my clever plan worked, I was being factual. Are you ready to go, or would you like to use the facilities first?"

"*What?*"

She walks over to the door, squints at the lock, then sighs. "I was hoping for a challenge. Oh, well."

She tugs on her hair, and a tuft comes off in her hand. She rolls it between her fingers, whispers a few words, and suddenly it's a little piece of tightly braided wire. She inserts it into the lock.

"That's an electric lock, controlled from a master panel," I point out. "You're dealing with more than just pins and tumblers—"

The lock clicks loudly and she pulls the door open. "I know what I'm dealing with, thank you. No matter how sophisticated, a lock has to obey certain principles in order to do its job. Just like me."

She's about to start on my lock when I say, "Hold it. Free the lem in the last cell, first. You might be a whiz at getting out of cells, but as soon as a guard glances at a security camera we're going to be dealing with some very annoyed sandbags. We'll need backup to get out of here in one piece."

She hesitates— "A lem? But—"

"You know your job, I know mine. We don't have time to argue!"

And she doesn't—she sprints over to Silverado's cell instead. As she starts to work, the redneck calls out, "Hey! Don't forget about me, sweetcheeks!"

"I'm sure you're next on her list," I hiss. "Now *be quiet!*"

She gets Silverado's door open—just as the one at the end of the corridor clangs open, too.

"Stop! Go back to your cells!" the guard shouts. He's already got his bow in his hands, drawing back the bowstring. The arrowhead is a three-bladed razor designed to rotate in flight; it won't just punch into flesh, it'll bore a hole through it two inches wide.

Azura doesn't pause. She runs *toward* the guard—then stops in front of my cell and bends down to the lock. She's completely exposed.

I yank one of my scythes out of its holster, stick my arm through the bars, and throw it to Silverado. He grabs it out of the air as casually as if I'd just tossed him a beer—then staggers back as the arrow hits him full in the chest.

The noise it makes is loud, closer to a gunshot than an arrow striking home—but that's what happens when metal meets metal at those speeds. It puts a nasty dent in his chest, but doesn't penetrate. He throws the *eskrima* stick before the guard can nock another shaft.

Saying that lems are good at throwing things is like saying water's good at being wet. When Silverado was known as the Quicksilver Kid, he supposedly had the fastest and most accurate arm in the world; that was a long time ago, but it seems he's kept in practice. The stick whips past almost too fast to see, and hits directly between the guard's eyes. There's an explosion of sand and the guard drops to the floor with a boneless *thump.*

The lock *chunks* open and I shove the door aside. "Okay, we're out. Now what—we fight our way past every lem in the place?"

"No, now I escort my two *very* important prisoners to see the Mantle High Command," Azura says. She's already pulling off the guard's uniform.

Silverado strides up, moving with a clockwork precision. "Forgive me for saying so, Miss, but you don't exactly look like a lem guard."

"Give her a minute," I say.

Azura finishes pulling on the guard's pants, then does a little pirouette—and when she finishes her spin, she's a dead ringer for our jailer. She grabs his bow off the floor to complete the illusion.

"Hey!" the redneck says. I can see him now, his face pressed up against the bars of his cell: a short, potbellied guy with a scraggly beard and what I assume is a pathetic attempt at a mullet—short sparse hair on top, long greasy hair down the sides. "You gonna take us, too?"

"I hate to say it," I tell him, "but you're probably safer here than outside. Sit tight and we'll be back once we've got this whole mess sorted out—"

"Well, what if I don't *want* to sit tight?" the redneck says. "You better take me with you or maybe I'll just holler my lungs out that there's a jailbreak goin' on—"

I step up to the cell and lean in close. "You don't want to do that. And you know why not?"

" 'Cause it'll get you put right back in that cell?"

I meet his eyes and smile while slipping one arm—the one holding an *eskrima* stick—through the bars at waist level. He smiles back, with bad teeth.

"No," I say. I snap the scythe out behind his back and bring it up quickly, so his neck is trapped between the cutting edge of the blade and the bars. I pull just hard enough to let him know he shouldn't move. "Because I'd hate to have you get killed while trying to escape. Right?"

He sees what's in my eyes, starts to nod, then thinks better of it. "Y-yes, ma'am."

"Good. Stay here, keep your mouth shut, and you'll be fine."

I take the scythe away, close it, then slip it back in its holster. Silverado drags the unconscious lem into my cell and locks him in.

"Move it," Azura growls in a much deeper voice, gesturing with her bow. I sigh, and let her march us down the corridor.

Hard as it is to believe, nobody's missed the guard yet. We go out the door at the end of the corridor, past the guard's post, and out into the main area of the station without being stopped.

I'm a little nervous. There aren't that many lems in here—they're probably out helping secure the rest of the city—but there are enough to take the three of us down pretty damn fast. As long as we can just get out of here without being noticed—

"Hey," Azura calls out. She's trying to get the attention of one of the lems at a workstation, tapping away at a keyboard.

He looks up. "Yeah?"

"These two were brought in with weapons."

Shut up shut up shut up I think as loudly as I can.

"So?" the desk jockey says.

"So I'm supposed to bring them with me when I do the transfer," Azura says. "But nobody seems to know where they are."

Now the lem looks a little suspicious. Great. "They weren't signed in to evidence?"

"You'd think so, but—you mind checking for me?"

"Just a second." He taps a few keys, studies the screen, then says, "Well, they're down there now. Want them sent up?"

"Yeah, if you don't mind."

"Nah." He taps a few more keys. "Knives and some kind of metal device, right?"

"Right."

"Just hang on." He picks up a phone. Azura pulls two sets of iron manacles off her belt and chains Silverado and me to a heavy steel bar jutting from the wall while the other lem talks to someone in evidence.

During this ordeal—every second of which lasts a geologic era—Lem-Azura manages to look bored and slightly sleepy. Silverado stays impassive the whole time, but from my prior encounters with him I know that's pretty much how he always looks.

Fortunately, the desk jockey doesn't seem inclined to make small talk and goes back to work. A few minutes later another lem with two large plastic evidence bags and a clipboard shows up. He hands the bags to Azura and tells her to sign the release form. She does so, then picks her bow back up and asks the lem to unlock us from the wall.

"Can't be too careful," she says, training the bow and a notched arrow at us. "Wouldn't want 'em to rabbit on me."

We make it outside. "Now what?" I ask. "You just going to march us down the street?"

"My car's in the impound lot," says Silverado. "Get us in there and I'll take care of the rest."

The impound lot's around the back of the building, and we just walk right through the open gate. I've been locked up for nearly a full day; it's just after dark now, the lot illuminated by harsh security lights. Silverado spots his vehicle—a dusty black Mustang—in the back corner. He digs a spare key out of the wheel well and hands it to Azura. With a uniformed officer at the wheel, nobody tries to stop us from driving away, either.

"If they weren't so short-staffed that never would have worked," I say from the backseat.

Azura shrugs, her features shifting back to her regular look. "Hey, we need every asset we can get. Silverado got back the Seven Teeth of the Moon and you got your Booger-Hawk thing."

"Ruger. Super. Redhawk," I growl. "And how'd you know about Silverado's knives, anyway?"

"It was on the evidence form, along with his name. Impressive—even I've heard of them. The knives, I mean. Can they really cut through any spell?"

"I always thought so," says Silverado. "But it's startin' to look like I may have to rethink that a mite . . ."

He grabs the wheel, wrenching the car over to the side of the road, while stomping on Azura's foot and slamming on the brakes.

"What?" I say. "What's going on?"

"You are," Silverado says. "Without me." He pulls the keys out of the ignition with one hand—and a knife out of his bandolier with the other. "Get out."

"Look, I understand you like to work alone," I say. "But we all have a much better chance of surviving this if we work together—"

"Maybe that's true for you two. Not for me." He pokes Azura in the arm with the point of the blade. "Go on now."

Azura's studying him intently. "Let's go, Jace," she says

abruptly. She opens the door and gets out without another word.

I'm a little more stubborn. "I want an explanation first."

"Can't do that. You get that, Special Agent Valchek? I *cannot* give you one. What I can give you is eleven inches of enchanted silver across that pretty little jugular of yours, and I expect I may just have to. Real shame, too—bloodstains are a bitch to get out of upholstery."

I get out of the car.

He roars away, tires screeching and smoking on the asphalt. "Well, damn," I say. "I haven't been dumped like this since my ninth-grade prom."

"He didn't trust himself. Whatever's got lems in revolt, it's more than just political. He's resisted so far—probably with the help of those knives—but he doesn't know how long that'll last. My guess is he's hoping to break through the barricades, get himself out of range of whatever magic's being worked."

"He said he couldn't give me an explanation. The way he put it, it sounded as if he literally didn't have a choice." Then I remember the tale Silverado spun, and it starts to make a little more sense. "He was trying to tell me something while we were locked up. At the time I thought he was being careful because he thought somebody else was listening—but maybe that wasn't it. Maybe he *couldn't* just come right out and tell me. Is that possible?"

"A secrecy component to a spell? Sure. But there are always ways around such things. Stories want to be told, you know. That's why they created people . . . now, let's get off the street before we get picked up by a lem patrol."

We duck down a side street that seems completely deserted. The front door of every house stands wide open; Azura ducks into the nearest one, motioning me to follow.

"Everyone's gone," I say.

"Evacuated? Or rounded up and imprisoned like we were?"

"They wouldn't have the facilities. Not unless they're digging a really, really big grave somewhere."

"Or a bonfire," Azura says.

The idea's almost too grim to contemplate—except this wouldn't be the first time I've run across a situation like this. At the end of World War II, the Allies made a deal with an Elder God: the ability for pires to procreate on their own, in return for six million human souls. The victims were burned alive, the whole thing covered up by blaming a virulent plague.

That was how far pires were willing to go to be able to bear their own children. Would lems do the same?

I pick up the phone in the living room. No dial tone. My own phone died a watery death, but maybe the person who lived here left without grabbing their cell.

"What are you looking for?" Azura asks as I stride from room to room.

"A cell phone. I've got to get in touch with my boss, let him know what's going on."

To my surprise, she nods emphatically. "Yes. We need reinforcements—I'm sorry to tell you this, but it seems your team is now either compromised or dead." She looks grim. "And we've lost the element of surprise. Asher will have surrounded himself with an army of golems by now."

"He's not the only one with an army," I say.

We have to search four houses before we get lucky and find a mobile phone sitting upright in its charger. I just hope the lems haven't taken out all the cell phone towers . . .

Not yet, it seems. My call goes through, someone picking up on the third ring. "Hello?"

"Cassius?"

"Jace. Are you still in Vegas?"

I can't believe how relieved I am to hear his voice. "Yeah. On a real hot streak as far as luck goes, too."

"What's your situation?"

I fill him in as quickly and concisely as I can. "What's it look like from where you are?"

"Much the same. I'll fill you in when I get there." The phone goes dead in my hand—and I hear the screech of tires sliding to a halt outside.

Sure enough, Cassius walks through the door a second later. I half expect Azura to zap him with something, but she just studies him coolly.

"What the hell are you doing here?" I blurt. My relief's vanished—it was based on the idea that the person I was talking to was far away, completely safe, and able to call down vengeance in the form of fighter jets and National Guard units.

"I flew in to oversee your operation personally," he says. "I was in my hotel room when the revolt started. I've managed to avoid being captured, but lem battalions have forcibly evacuated all thropes and pires to the city limits."

"Yeah, we figured that out for ourselves," I say, sinking onto a nearby couch. "Not the humans, though—those they're rounding up and incarcerating, 'for their own good.'"

"Which means we're *not* very good, at all," says Azura.

Cassius's attention has been on me, but that doesn't mean he hasn't noticed Azura; Cassius notices everything. He turns to her, gives her one of his professional but guarded smiles, and says, "That depends on how you look at it. You've proven quite adept at destroying a carefully planned operation all by yourself."

Azura smiles back. "Your mission never had a chance."

"Why is that?"

"Because this was more than a simple weapons deal. It

was a summit—a meeting to discuss political power sharing. There were more players involved than either of us knew."

"The lems."

"Yes. Asher's behind this revolt—and it was *your* lems who tipped him to my assassination attempt."

"So we were hooped from the beginning," I say. "The question is, now that Asher has Las Vegas, what's he going to do with it?"

"I have at least a partial answer to that," says Cassius. "Several buildings—casinos, mainly—seem to have been transformed into other structures. It's happening all over the city—"

"Not transformed," says Azura. "Exchanged. They're being swapped for buildings from another city in another dimension. A city called Night's Shining Jewel."

"I thought you said it was called Nightshadow?" I say.

"Nightshadow is the country it's located in. Night's Shining Jewel is the capital—and, in many ways, it's like Vegas itself. It's surrounded by mountains, it's full of theaters and casinos, and it thrives when the sun is down."

"We've been to one of the switched sites," I say, and give him a brief rundown on the myth we encountered. It takes a considerable amount of willpower to not repeat the whole thing verbatim.

"Mythic magic," says Cassius, frowning. "Powerful stuff. With a natural predilection for cross-universe effects."

"Yes," says Azura. "But he's up to more than just juggling real estate."

"What else?"

"Can't say yet."

"Can't or won't?"

"Hey," I interject. "We've got a lem revolt and someone playing *Trading Spaces* with cities from two different realities. I think that's enough for now—"

A roar from overhead interrupts my interruption. I recognize the sound: fighter jets.

"Is that a good sound or a bad one?" I ask.

"It's not that sound we have to worry about," says Cassius. "It's the one that comes after it."

He goes outside and we both follow. This world doesn't have guns or bombs, so I've always been a little unclear on how they use aircraft for combat—guess I'm about to find out.

We stand on the front lawn and scan the sky. Three contrails to the north, over Nellis Air Force Base. The jets are visible in the distance, circling back around for another flyover.

"Those are N-17 Hellbats," says Cassius. "I don't think Nellis has any stationed there—they must have been scrambled from out of state."

"What do you think they'll do?" I ask.

"Hellbats carry Banshee missiles—they can scream for up to forty-eight hours after impact. Not fatal, but intensely painful. They'll probably use them to soften the lem forces up—"

Something arcs from the horizon into the sky, and suddenly one of the jets is a tumbling ball of fire. We can't see where it hits, but a moment after it falls out of sight a plume of dark, oily smoke rises to the east.

"What was that?" asks Azura.

"Anti-aircraft lem," says Cassius. "Probably a Grizzly 110. Nellis has a number of them in hibernation, but it's obvious they've been woken up."

I've seen Charlie throw an iron-cored, silver ball bearing hard enough to punch through armor plate—and he's just a cop. I shouldn't be surprised that a golem designed and built by the military would be capable of taking down a jet.

"They've taken the base, then," says Azura. "Which means they have a fair chance of holding the city."

"Not indefinitely," Cassius says.

"But probably long enough for what Asher's planning," says Azura. "And I think I know what that is. He's trying to create a permanent link between this world and mine."

"Why?"

"I'm not sure," she admits. "I need to visit another of these sites, see if I can learn the specifics of the enchantment being created."

"They're being guarded."

"I know. But the lems are going to have their hands full just defending their borders. Jace and I have infiltrated one already; we can do it again."

"Hold on!" I protest. "About the only thing we accomplished last time was having a bedtime story permanently engraved on our frontal lobes. You think repeating the experience is going to tell us anything useful?"

"We should discuss this further indoors," says Cassius, turning around and heading back to the house. Azura's right behind him. Glaring at their backs isn't going to get me anywhere, so after a moment I follow them inside.

We spend the next hour arguing. I want to go after Asher directly; he's not going to expect another attempt so soon after the first one, not when he's surrounded by an army. Okay, maybe it sounds a little foolhardy—but I can take out just about any lem from a distance with the Ruger, Azura can use her skills to get close, and Cassius can probably call in an airstrike as a diversion. As far as insane plans go, I think we have a pretty good shot at catching him unawares.

"And then what?" Cassius says. "We need to capture him, not kill him. How are we supposed to escape the city afterward?"

"Helicopter?" I suggest.

"We'd never get one inside city limits before it was shot down."

"So we steal one that's already here."

"Sure," says Azura. "We're already going to attack the most powerful shaman within a thousand miles. Let's break into an air force base full of renegade golems and steal one of their choppers, too."

I hate to admit it, but they're right. In the end, I can't come up with a plan to take Asher alive and get us out of the city in one piece. Azura, however, is pretty sure we can sneak into one of the swapped sites—there are four of them so far—and whether that turns out to be useful or not, at least it's doable.

I'm a little envious of how at ease she seems to be. I guess for an Astonisher this is all in a day's work—travel to another dimension, get caught in the middle of a war among three supernatural races, attempt the assassination of a powerful shaman. I didn't take things nearly so well when I first got here—but then, the only exposure I'd ever had to craziness was criminal psychosis, as opposed to an entire reality that seemed schizophrenic.

And to be honest, it bugs me a little how well she and Cassius are getting along. The first time I ever met Cassius, I shot him. Twice. Azura just bats her big Tinker Bell eyes and tells him how happy she is to finally have an *ally* in this world. One that hasn't gotten her drugged or beaten up yet, anyway.

I finally give up and try to find some coffee while they discuss which site we should choose and the best route to take to get there.

The cell phone I found earlier is lying on the kitchen counter. I pick it up. What I want to do right now, more than anything, is call Charlie. I need him here, I need him to watch my back; that's what a partner is for, after all. Cassius is my boss and I know he sticks by his people, but being in command brings with it a whole different set of priorities. If he has to sacrifice one mere human for the greater good, he'll do it—he's done it before. A few million times, in fact.

I stare at the phone for a long time. I think about the conversation Charlie and I had in the jail—and I think about Wilson, dying at my feet with a fist-size hole in his chest.

I put the phone down.

We head out at 3:00 AM. The site we've chosen was once the Sands, but now it appears to be a gaming house called the Singing Fortune Casino. Azura, it seems, knows the place well. "Spent more than one evening—and more than a few days' wages—playing Spear-and-Shield there. They used to have a great house band."

"I'm sure," I say. We're creeping along a side street, keeping an ear out for lem patrols. Cassius has stayed behind, our fallback in case we're captured; I've got his number on speed dial on the phone I lifted. "I'm surprised they'd let someone like you within sight of the place."

"Oh, I wasn't an Astonisher in those days—well, not a full-fledged one, anyway; the guild hadn't accepted me yet. All the gaming houses had very strict rules and magic detectors to keep us honest, in any case. If I'd ever done anything but lost money, they would have had my head cut off and mounted on the wall."

"If you weren't allowed to win, why'd you even bother?"

She flashes me a wicked grin. "Any number of reasons. Maybe that cute were jackal at the card table; maybe that fat diplomat drinking a little too heavily with important documents in his back pocket. Or maybe just the rush of playing, the thrill of watching your fortunes rise and fall with the tides of chance. Gambling's not called a vice because it's bad for you; it's because it feels so right to be doing something so wrong."

"Being bad feels pretty good?" I say. "Yeah, I saw *The*

Breakfast Club, too. But I still have no desire to date Judd Nelson or dance to eighties music in a school library." I pause. "Well, mostly."

We both hear it at the same time: a heavy, muted impact from the cross-street ahead of us. We fade back behind a low fence and crouch, ready to run if we have to.

Another impact, and another. It sounds kind of like a pile driver set on low, steady *thuds* evenly paced a few seconds apart. And getting closer.

And then it comes into view at the intersection, and I realize that what I'm hearing are footsteps.

It's a lem. I've been told that the first really effective military lems were built by the Chinese during the Song dynasty, made out of fired pottery filled with pebbles and standing around fifteen feet high. Those early models are to this monstrosity what a bicycle is to a Harley.

It stands at least thirty feet high, its metal skin painted in desert camouflage, sandy browns and tans in uneven streaks. Even though its face is covered by a metal grille, it reminds me more of a giant medieval knight than a robot. It's wearing an armored backpack, and has twin spotlights mounted on its shoulders. A bandolier of six-foot-long javelins is slung across its chest, and what looks like a belt made of bowling balls around its waist.

It stops in the middle of the intersection. The twin spotlights flare to life and swing our way.

EIGHT

We crouch, holding our breaths, field mice hiding from an owl.

The searchlights pass over us without pausing, and after a moment the lem continues on its way. It has to duck to get under the traffic light.

"Okay," I whisper. "That is obviously not someone we want to run into again. Unless you can turn *yourself* into—"

"Are you *kidding*?" She gives me an unbelieving look. "If I could do *that,* we could just stroll down Las Vegas Boulevard with you on my shoulder like a sarcastic parrot."

"Well, *I* don't know what your limits are."

"No, you don't. And we don't have time to discuss them, either." She straightens up and resumes walking.

We're lucky and don't run into any more patrols on our way to the Sands. Vegas is eerily deserted; garbage blows through the streets, but there are no vehicles moving, no drunken tourists stumbling down the sidewalk. The hotel and casino signs flash and flicker with the same Technicolor intensity, but there's nobody there to appreciate it but birds.

And us.

The spot where the Sands is supposed to be is now occupied by a large structure that resembles nothing so much as a mansion made of bamboo. It stands at least five stories high, and has an immense sign over the front door in a language I don't recognize. The sign seems to be made of vines that glow with bright yellow bioluminescence. It's being guarded by two gray-colored lems holding large battle-axes; the only clothes they're wearing are white armbands with some sort of chevrons on them.

We stay out of sight behind the corner of a building. "Those are members of the Mantle," I say in a low voice. "Why is it that every radical faction in this world feels the need to get naked as their first political act?"

"Clothing's a human invention. Rejecting it symbolizes a rejection of human culture and values."

Says the stripper. "So what does that make you?"

"Popular."

"I'll bet. How do you want to do this?"

"Without getting our heads cut off, preferably."

I glance around the corner, cautiously. "You say you're familiar with this place. There a back entrance?"

"Not as such—but as I recall, there is a fairly easy way up to the second floor."

We circle to the back. What looks like a smooth, high wall of vertical poles glued tightly together turns out to have a series of almost imperceptible handholds conveniently spaced all the way to the top. I let Azura go first, paying close attention to where she puts her feet and fingers, then follow her up. In a minute or two we're on a narrow ledge, just outside a shuttered, glassless window. Azura's already got the lock picked by the time I join her. She pushes the shutters inward, revealing a room that looks like it's used for storage; I see a broom, shelves lined with hollowed-out gourds, and more of the glowing vines strung along the ceiling—these give off more of a greenish light.

"Ready?" Azura says, already perched on the window-sill. "There's no telling what we'll encounter inside, but it could be another story."

"In that case, there'll be a *lot* of telling, won't there?"

I vault over the sill without waiting for her reply.

And find myself falling.

There's a split second of sheer panic, ending abruptly with me landing on something soft and springy. I didn't fall that far; it's like the building vanished and I dropped one story back to the ground.

But the ground is a lot spongier than a Nevada alley. In fact, I seem to be sprawled on a carpet of thick green moss—and a moment later Azura lands right beside me, with even less grace. She sits up and spits out a mouthful of moss.

"Well, this is an improvement," I say, looking around. "This must be the show part of show-and-tell."

We're at the edge of some kind of tropical jungle, the air warm and humid. The moss beneath us is part of a broad swath that extends in either direction, looking more or less like a green road. It's either twilight or predawn, judging by the quality of light, but the mist that hangs over us obscures the horizon; I can't even tell which way is east.

"Nightshadow," says Azura. She tilts her head back and takes a long, deep breath through her nose, her smile getting wider and wider. "Somewhere in the Edenheart Jungle, I'd say. But I know of no thoroughfare this wide outside the city—"

She breaks off, staring. I look in that direction and see a figure walking toward us out of the mist, down the mossy road. It's hooded, wearing a long, brown cloak, and holds a spear in one hand.

I tense up, but Azura puts a restraining hand on my shoulder.

"Wait. He may not be able to perceive us."

The figure gets closer. I can hear birds calling to one another, and the sound of rushing water somewhere nearby—there must be a river not too far off.

The figure stops about twenty feet away. I can't see its face.

"Hello?" says Azura. "Can you see us?"

"Of course I can see you," a male voice answers. "I'm standing right in front of you, aren't I?"

"I'm sorry, I just thought—"

"It's a bloody stereotype, you know that? 'Blind as a bat.' Just because they're nocturnal predators doesn't mean they don't have *eyes,* does it?"

"Well, no—"

"You don't see people saying 'blind as a cat,' or 'blind as an owl,' do you? Of course not. But they're both night hunters, too."

"I'm sorry if we offended you—"

The man throws back his hood. He's got a long, narrow face, jet-black hair that reaches to his shoulders, and very pale skin. A pire, I'd say—except pires' ears aren't usually that pointed.

"I'm not offended, merely disappointed," the pire says. "It's my belief that weres, trues, the Lyrastoi, and even the underdead should all be able to live together in peace and understanding. And possibly condos."

I frown at Azura. "Condos?"

"Ah, yes, of course," she says quickly. "We didn't mean to interrupt your—whatever you were doing. Just pretend we're not here."

The man studies us. "I am Baron Greystar. And you are?"

"Jacinda Valchek and Azura Splintertree, Your Lordship."

"Two trues, and lovely ones at that. Sourcelings?"

"Sadly, no," Azura says. "Humble performers, no more."

"Performers?" Greystar glances around him. "There's no one to perform for, out here. More's the pity—I could do with a good show. Something with a song, and maybe puppets. Do you do puppets?"

"I'm afraid not, my lord."

"Well, that's just a damn shame. Wouldn't it be nice if there was someplace you could go for a spot of entertainment now and then, instead of just waiting for minstrels to show up on your doorstep? See a play, have a nice meal, maybe enjoy a little gambling . . . all they do at the Keep is go hunting. That, and sit around talking about all the wild boar hunts they've been on, and how good that roast wild boar was, and the best weapon to use when you're chasing down a wild boar. Bit tedious after a while, believe me."

He almost seems to be talking to himself now, looking down and shaking his head. Azura takes a slow, careful step to the side, catches my eye, and puts a finger to her lips. She takes another step, and another, motioning me to follow her, until both of us are at the edge of the wide, mossy path. As soon as we step off it altogether, Baron Greystar flips his hood back up, as if to dismiss us.

"What's going on here?" I whisper.

"Cross-universe cultural contamination," she whispers back. "We've stumbled into a myth, but our presence— well, *your* presence, actually—is warping its presentation. The more we interact with it, the more anachronisms will pop up."

"But that's a good thing, right? It means we can disrupt whatever enchantment Asher's trying to work."

"Only the surface elements. It's more dangerous for us—we run the risk of being assimilated into the myth, becoming part of it. That's probably what's happening to all the people who were in the Sands when it disappeared."

Baron Greystar lifts his spear over his head, holding it in both hands. I notice it's tipped with a multifaceted black rock, probably obsidian. "This shall be the place," he intones. "Here, where the stormstalk roots converge, where the power of Life flows and protects. This shall become the Heart of the land, and all will be welcome here; and great joy will be our commerce, and song and laughter and drama our food and drink. This place will be a bright beacon in our eternal twilight, and no creature of the night will fear its warm and beckoning glow. All who live in Nightshadow will know this place . . . and it will be known as *Night's Shining Jewel*!"

He plunges the spear into the moss. It goes deep, around half its length, and quivers with the force of the impact.

The baron steps back. The spear keeps vibrating—in fact, the tremors are getting worse.

And then the wooden shaft begins to sprout twigs, branches, leaves. Whatever's in that moss must be the best plant food money can buy, because in a matter of seconds there's a tree, its trunk getting thicker by the moment. Not a normal tree, though; it's growing in a decidedly unnatural pattern, roots straight as arrows, branches forming right angles as neat as any carpenter's work. A building is growing in front of my eyes.

"Amazing," Azura murmurs. "The founding of Night's Shining Jewel, the birth of the Palace Verdant."

"So this is another creation myth?"

"I don't think so. It's just the prologue—the main event hasn't started yet."

We watch the castle take shape for a minute. It's really amazing, both beautiful and uncanny, like watching one of those time-lapse films of a skyscraper being built or a plant growing. Or both.

"Splintertree?" I say.

"It's a family name."

"Splinter? Tree? You come from a family of lumber-jacks or something?"

She gives me an annoyed look. "My father was a were rhino, all right?"

"Ah. That explains a lot."

And then everything jumps like a bad edit in a movie, and suddenly we're in the middle of a city. The Palace Verdant, now big as a castle, stands in front of us, the moss road running right up to its front gate. Structures line the thoroughfare, ranging from tents to huts to elaborate bamboo constructions like the one we encountered back in Vegas, and there are side streets branching off at regular intervals.

The people who stream along the road all seem the basic medieval peasant type—except that most of them are half human and half animal. I see weres of every kind, from elephant to badger, most of them roughly human-sized and shaped except for their heads. They pull carts, hawk wares from stands, eat at roadside stalls; some of them just stand around and stare like tourists. The glowing vines provide light in various shades and hues, giving the place more of a Christmassy than neon feel.

And then the wolves sweep in.

You don't see thropes in full-on were form all that much, at least not in downtown Seattle. They stick to human or half were, which leaves them with hands and makes their clothes fit better. When they do go all-out hairy, the result is usually something around the size of a large timber wolf, massing around 180 pounds and standing maybe three and a half feet at the shoulder.

These are much, much bigger.

Their fur is black, their eyes a gleaming gold. They're as big as small horses, massing at least double what the average thrope does. They're wearing leather harnesses strapped across their backs, with pouches or loops of rawhide dangling from them, and they run in formation; I have the eerie feeling I'm looking at the world's biggest dogsled team, and any second now the sled itself is going to come into view, being ridden by a crazed, fifty-foot-tall Paul Bunyan.

The street clears before them, everybody getting the hell out of the way. The furry horde races up to the palace and then cuts to the right, following the curving avenue that circles the building. When they've surrounded it entirely, they slow to a stop and then sit, facing outward.

"The arrival of the Wolf Nation," Azura says softly. "Every wolf-were in Nightshadow."

"Is it an invasion?"

"No. They were summoned by the king, Bloodsong the Second."

Reality jumps again, and now we're in what has to be the Royal Court, at the back of a cluster of nobles to one side of the royal carpet; the king sits on an ornately carved throne at its head. The carpet is the selfsame moss that runs up to the royal gates, and no doubt runs out the back gates of the palace as well.

A tall, bearded man, dressed only in a rough breechclout and a leather harness, stalks up the mossway and stops in front of the throne. The king, a pire with a definite resemblance to Baron Greystar, is dressed in vivid purple robes with elaborate fur trimmings, though his jeweled crown seems to be carved from wood.

"Your Highness," says the bearded man. "The Wolf Nation stands ready."

"My thanks, General. The people of Nightshadow respect and appreciate your loyalty." He pauses, his brow furrowed. "What news of the enemy?"

"They have a terrible new weapon, Sire." The general pulls an object layered in thick cloth from a pouch on his belt, and carefully unwraps it. It's a short dagger, dull with tarnish. "They call it *silver.*"

"We've seen metal weapons before," says the king. "Dangerous, yes, but obsidian or underdead-strengthened edges cut just as well—and the wounds of weres heal much faster than those of the invaders. Metal cannot even pierce the skin of the Lyrastoi."

"This metal can, Sire. Observe." The general runs one finger lightly along the edge of the blade, then holds up a bleeding hand. Smoke curls from the wound. "You see? Barely enough to draw blood, yet it bleeds still. Were-soldiers unlucky enough to take a serious blow die, even from wounds that crush instead of cut. The metal cuts Lyrastoi skin as easily as any other, with effects just as deadly."

The king considers this gravely. "And the passes?"

"They hold, for the moment. They cannot burn them, and their weapons are not as effective in a siege. They loose the odd arrow with a silvered head, when they feel confident of taking down one of our sentries. But they are building something, something we fear will turn the tide in their favor."

"Tell us."

"A vast disk, silvered on one side and sand on the other. The sand has been melted with flame, so that when it cools and hardens, it is as clear as water. They call this a mirror."

"For what purpose?"

"It creates a reflection, like that of a clear pool of water, only so sharp and clear it seems you are looking at a perfect duplicate of your own image. When light from the Poisoned Star strikes a mirror, the reflection is as bright as the Star itself, and can be directed by adjusting the mirror's angle."

"Surely our passes are deep enough in the mountains to be safe from such a device?"

"From one, yes. But they are constructing a series of these mirrors, from which they can direct sunlight the way a riverbed directs water. Such a river could reach the very walls of our passes."

"And undo the underdead enchantments strengthening them," the king murmurs. "Without those, they are merely bamboo and sporestalks, brittle and weak."

"Yes, Your Highness. Our one chance is to launch an assault in the dead of the night, before these mirrors are finished. Our enemy has committed all their forces; we must do the same. They must be destroyed, so thoroughly that it will be another generation before they can remount an attack. That will give us time to strengthen our fortifications so this will never happen again."

"I see." The king falls silent once more.

"Who's invading?" I whisper to Azura.

"The Pharjee," she whispers back. "They're a small but aggressive country to the east of the Clawrock Mountains. Evil sun-worshippers."

"They worship an evil sun?"

"It is to us. We're not big fans of daytime, as you might have noticed."

The king is speaking again. "—the ultimate commitment, then. Your people are prepared?"

The general lowers his head. "As I said when I entered, My King: Our lives are yours."

"Then the order is given. Let it be known throughout the land of Nightshadow that the Wolf Nation is willing to give everything they have to defend their home—and that, as our mightiest warriors, they shall not give their lives alone, or in vain. Their king shall fight alongside them."

The general raises his head in alarm. "Sire, is that wise? You are a ruler, not a soldier—you are versed in neither weapons or warcraft."

"That is true. Indeed, I own neither bow, blade, nor armor; but my ancestors did, and they passed those things on to me in another form. That, I still own; and it is both my spear *and* my shield."

"I know not of what you speak, Sire," said the general.

"Then you do not see what is before your eyes. For behold, it is all around you . . ."

And the throne begins to tremble.

"Find something to hang on to!" Azura says with a grin on her face. She's already grabbed some sort of ornamental bracket on the wall holding a shelf up. "This should be one hell of a ride!"

The floor lurches, like a ship in a rough sea. Nobles yelp and scramble for balance. The king grips the armrests of his throne tightly and lets out a loud, booming laugh. The general looks grim, but he manages to stay upright.

With a sound like a forest uprooting, the entire palace gets to its feet.

I've grabbed on to a window frame for stability, so I've got a pretty good view of what's going on outside. Just as that spear decided it would rather be a castle, the castle has now decided it would really rather be a giant wooden octopus, its foundations sporting massive, tentacle-like roots now free of the ground and boosting the structure into the air. It celebrates its momentous career shift by going for a walk, wolf-weres scattering in its wake like a pack of confused dogs confronted by a moving bus they'd been assured was a pet food store. Some of them start to howl.

"Onward!" shouts the king. "You take the southern pass, I'll take the northern! *We will crush them like bones in our teeth!*"

And abruptly, we're someplace else—not the whole palace, just Azura and I. We're perched on a rocky crag overlooking a narrow valley, with a tall bamboo wall stretching between the two cliffs on either side. A full moon rides low in the sky, providing the only light; and massed at the base of the wall is the same army of wolves I just saw surrounding the octo-castle. There's a raised, empty platform in front of them, beside an immense, closed gate in the barricade.

"They made good time," I say. "I guess this is the southern pass?"

"Yes." Azura's smile fades from her face. "At the northern pass, King Bloodsong catches them by surprise. The Palace Verdant is too large to pass through the gate, so he simply smashes through the wall. He's stopped to pick up soldiers along the way; they drop down on the enemy's head from above while the palace itself wreaks havoc."

"Good times, very mythical. So why are we here instead of there?"

"Because," a familiar voice says from just above us, "that was just a good story. What's about to happen *here* is history."

Azura and I spin around. Standing on a ledge around five feet above us is a man with a streak of gray running down the center of his skull.

Tair.

I have my gun out and aimed at his heart in a second.

He just grins. "Hey, take it easy, ladies. If I was looking for trouble I wouldn't have announced myself, would I?"

"Who are you?" Azura asks.

"Depends on who you ask," he answers. He leaps down from the ledge and lands beside us gracefully, but not so close as to be threatening. He's dressed in black jeans and a black sweater, with a long tan coat over that. He looks even more like a young Harrison Ford than when I first met him. "These days I go by Tair—though Jace might slip up and call me something else if she's . . . distracted." He meets my eyes and smiles, two old friends sharing a private joke.

I keep my gun on him. "There's all sorts of things I could call you, Tair. Don't think you'd like most of them. And if you get too close, every single one will be a variation on *deceased*."

He laughs. Hearing a close friend's laugh come out of the mouth of a stone-cold killer feels like coming home and finding out you've been robbed. "Only most of them? I must be growing on you, Valchek. Told you I would."

"If any part of you grows on me, I know where to get an *excellent* wart remover. Why are you here?"

"Same reason you are: to witness a legendary battle."

"You know what's about to happen?" Azura asks.

"I have a pretty good idea. It's a story that pops up in lycanthrope folklore more than once. In Russia they call it the Slaughter of the Dark; in France it's the Battle of Final Honor; in Germany, simply the Pact. All of them boil down to basically the same thing."

"Which is?" I say.

"You don't really want me to spoil it, do you?"

"It's starting," Azura says.

We shut up and pay attention to what's going on below us. It's not a conscious decision—we're here to observe, and the power of the myth compels us to do exactly that.

The wolf-were general mounts the platform and regards his troops. "Warriors of the Wolf Nation," he says, his booming voice echoing off the valley's walls, "We are here today to prove what we have always boasted: that there are none so brave, none so fierce, none so loyal. We shall go forth as a mighty wave, sweeping all before us, and we shall be united as never before. Our very souls shall be as one, for our king has granted to us a powerful enchantment. Just as the stormstalk roots weave magic beneath our lands, so this spell will weave our spirits together; and for every one of us that falls, the rest shall grow stronger."

The general begins to chant, words in a tongue I can't

identify; it sounds vaguely like Cherokee. He's signing along with the chant, though I can't really follow that, either—he's too far away and signing too fast, though I catch a couple of basic concepts like *share* and *brother.*

The chanting becomes louder, more strident, until it turns into a scream—and then a howl as the general shifts into were form. All the wolves join in, a single rising voice that echoes back and forth between the rocks, the most unearthly sound I've ever heard. Okay, maybe the wail that Elder God let out when I banished it was a little worse, but not by much.

The howl rises to a single, piercing note that sounds like it could shatter a universe. Some of it is coming from right beside me; Tair has transformed and is howling along with the rest of them. If I were on the other side of that wall, I think right about now I'd be seriously reconsidering my invasion plans.

But it's too late for that. The howl reaches its crescendo, holds it for a long yet timeless moment, and then just disappears. It doesn't stop, exactly; it just seems to climb up into a range human ears can't perceive.

In the ringing non-silence that follows, all the wolves lower their muzzles. Beside me, Tair does the same.

The gate in the wall swings slowly open.

Without another sound, or any apparent signal, the wolves surge forward.

I glance at Tair. He's crouched in half-were form, every muscle in his body tensed to leap. It's a good sixty feet to the valley floor—he'd survive, but he wouldn't be in any shape to chase after them. That's exactly what he wants to do, though; it's obvious in every trembling muscle in his body—

He jumps.

"Tair!" I blurt. I can't believe it; I keep thinking that something else is going to happen, that he's going to sprout wings or a parachute or just hang in midair like Wile E. Coyote. His plunge seems to last forever.

Nothing happens to stop his fall. Except the inevitable, of course.

He lies sprawled at the foot of the cliff, not moving. Unless he landed on a vein of silver he's not dead, but who knows how many bones he's broken. "We've got to get down there," I say—

We vanish and reappear, but not at the foot of the cliff. We're in another valley, not as narrow as the first one, with the remains of a shattered wall a little way down it. King Bloodsong the Second's monster house is just ahead of us, kicking the snot out of the soldiers milling around its huge, rooty legs. Arrows pepper the mobile fortress from archers stationed on ledges on either side, but they just bounce off; His Majesty wasn't kidding about his home being his armor.

"No! We have to get back!" I say.

"There's nothing I can do about it," Azura says. "We're being shown what the myth wants us to see—"

And then we're back, this time on the valley floor, on the other side of the gate. The Wolf Nation is attacking the Pharjee forces camped there, who despite their initial surprise are doing much better against an army of supernaturally pumped-up werewolves than their comrades are against an angry tourist attraction.

I turn around and sprint for the open gate. I don't know how long I have before I blink back, but I have to try.

I make it all the way to the gate before I get yanked to the other battle. The Pharjee are trying to get a round mirror the size of a wagon wheel into position, but the palace kicks it into a thousand shards.

Blink. I'm back at the gate. I sprint for the unmoving, furry form lying on the ground. I get all the way there before disappearing again.

The king, not satisfied with merely destroying the enemy army, is stalking farther down the pass. He comes to another mirror installation and destroys it.

Back to Tair. He looks up at me and whines, clearly in agony—and then he transforms, back into human.

That's what thropes do before they die.

NINE

But he's not dead, not yet.

Shifting shape while severely injured is not a good idea. Broken bones trying to re-form themselves can heal at the wrong angles, meaning they have to be broken all over again to heal correctly. Plus, it must hurt like a son-of-a-bitch.

But he manages. He looks up at me, breathing heavily, and says, "You called me Tair."

"What?"

"Thought for sure you'd call me Dr. Pete—" He winces as he tries to push himself into a sitting position.

"Don't move, for God's sake. Your spine probably looks like a candy cane that's been stepped on."

"Doesn't matter." He gives me a grin. "Thanks for coming back, though. Nice to have someone looking out for me."

"I'm not. I'm . . . why the hell did you jump, anyway?"

"Jumping was the easy part. The landing was tricky."

"Consider yourself lucky." I glance back through the gate, where the battle is still raging. "From what I saw, the wolves are taking heavy casualties. If you'd managed to join them, you'd probably have been slaughtered."

"I know. That's why I jumped instead of trying to climb down."

"You mean you did this to yourself on *purpose*?"

"Yeah. See, I know how this myth ends, Valchek: The Wolf Nation fights to the last survivor. The thing is, every time one of them dies the others get stronger; the last wolf standing gets all the mojo. And that's going to be *me*."

He hunches forward, straightening his spine with an audible *crack*. "Ah, that's better." He examines his left forearm critically where it's bent at an unnatural angle.

"But—you're just an observer, like us. You can't—"

"Can't I? Magic is about will, Valchek, and I've got plenty of that. A little knowledge doesn't hurt, either." He grabs his left arm with his right hand—and rebreaks the bone where it's started to set. Both bones, actually—radius and ulna. Well, he does have medical training.

"I don't believe you," I say. "You'd have to be part of the spell for that to happen. And if that were true, you'd be charging into the battle as soon as you could stand."

He chuckles, holding his arm in place while he waits for the bones to reset properly. "It's taking a lot of effort not to. But all I have to do is hold off long enough for the fight to finish."

"Except that every time a soldier bites the dust, the spell gets a little stronger. You're healing at an incredible rate—but the urge to rush in must be getting more and more powerful, too."

"That's why I changed into human form. Makes it easier to resist . . ."

And then I'm gone again, back to the northern pass, just in time to see another mirror get smashed into shiny pieces. A little too shiny; the sky to the east is rosy with a predawn light, and the bamboo castle has giant-spidered its way all the way to the end of the pass.

When the first rays of the sun hit it, it cracks and splinters under its own weight. The magic that lent it both strength and mobility evaporates in the morning sun, and the Palace Verdant crashes to the ground. I'm guessing that's the end of the reign of Bloodsong the Second.

Back to the southern pass, where the battle has reached its own inevitable conclusion. Dead bodies litter the ground, Pharjee soldiers who have been ripped apart by fangs or claws, wolf-weres that have been decapitated or impaled by silvered blades. A single huge wolf stands outlined against the dawn, its eyes glowing with a fierce golden light, the only apparent survivor. I look around for Azura and spot her on top of a boulder at the edge of the battlefield, watching the wolf intently.

And then I see Tair. He's in human form, striding across the battlefield toward the wolf. He has a battle-ax with a silver head in one hand.

The wolf leaps for him. Tair splits his skull with the ax, right between the eyes.

I guess I expect some sort of fireworks, but nothing else happens. Azura leaps down from the boulder, lands lightly, and walks up to me. "Your friend doesn't believe in staying on the sidelines, does he?"

"He's not my friend."

"Hey, I'm standing right here," Tair says. He tosses the ax away casually, his body language relaxed. There's a spray of blood across his face.

"So now what?" I ask. "You're some kind of über-wolf now? Going to sprout a cape and fly away?"

"It doesn't work like that," says Azura. "He injected himself into the myth, but he didn't really change anything. This is always how it ends."

"Yeah, except usually the guy who does the chopping isn't a thrope," says Tair. "The king's son is going to show up any minute, all sad and resolute because now that the wolves have helped save the kingdom, the last one is too dangerous to let live. He kills it for the good of everyone—well, everyone except the wolves, obviously. I think he's going to be a little confused this time."

"So that's how this ends? Everyone dies?"

"All the wolves do," says Azura. "That's the point of this myth: sacrifice. And in Nightshadow, it's more than a story—it's an explanation. No wolves have existed there for thousands of years; only the oldest Lyrastoi even remember seeing one in the flesh."

Tair looks around the battlefield. "Well, plenty of thrope flesh where I come from. Guess we're a hardier breed." He kicks the head of a soldier out of his way. "Or maybe we're just not stupid enough to die for somebody's else's survival."

"What are you doing here?" I demand.

"Came to see you," he says with a smile. "That, and skim off a little of the power floating around. I may not have absorbed the collective spiritual energy of an entire race—after all, this is just a myth, not the real thing—but I did grab some of it. Feels good, too."

"Thanks," I say. "I've always been curious about the parasite's point of view. Now I know."

"This myth is almost at its end," says Azura. "At which point it will begin again. Jace and I are prepared for that—are you?"

"No," he admits. "But I think it'd be smarter to take me with you than leave me here. After all, a few more run-throughs and I'll probably have enough power to break out on my own—and then I'll be even harder to deal with, won't I?"

"Maybe," I say. "Or maybe you'll just get stuck in a loop and I won't have to worry about you at all."

He shakes his head in amusement. "Come on, Valchek—you know I'm not that easy to get rid of. Anyway, I'm not asking for a free ride; I've got something to offer."

"Besides an attractive target for bullets?"

"You know who I'm working for. The deal you messed up ended with his property in someone else's hands, and he'd like it back. Considering the fact that it's being used to turn Vegas into a city-state for lems, I thought you and I might be able to work together to restore the status quo."

"This is all being caused by something Silver Blue sold Asher?" I ask.

"Not sold—it was stolen. The transaction was interrupted before payment could be made, and Asher took off with the artifact in question."

"And you're supposed to retrieve it. Just which artifact are we talking about?"

"You don't know? Guess your intelligence isn't as good as I'd thought . . . it's a little accessory I liberated from its previous owner when he came down with a sudden case of silveritis. You know, when that cowboy lem stuck a knife between his eyes."

"The Balancer gem, bonded to the Midnight Sword last I saw. That's a big-ticket item to trade for an errand-boy job; guess you aren't as ambitious as I thought—"

Azura interrupts. "The Balancer gem? Asher has the Balancer gem?" Her voice holds both disbelief and horror.

"For now," Tair says. "But I'm sure the three of us could get it back—"

"We accept," says Azura.

"What?" I say. "Hang on a minute—"

A man carrying a spear walks through the gate and pauses. He clearly belongs to the same race the king does, what Azura called a Lyrastoi. He looks around with a resolute expression on his face.

"Time to go," Azura says, and grabs Tair by one arm and me by the other. I never do get to see what happens when the prince can't find the wolf he's supposed to kill;

we exit the myth before it ends. Maybe he just decides to stab a corpse and call it a day.

All three of us reappear in the alley behind the Singing Fortune casino. I yank my arm out of Azura's grip. "Okay. A few ground rules if we're going to be partners: One, you refrain from killing anyone. Two, I'm in charge; I tell you what the plan is, and you follow it. Three, if you fail to follow rules one or two, I get to shoot you. All right?"

Tair gives me another of those easy grins he's so generous with. "Fine by me. What's the plan, boss?"

"We check in with *my* boss," I say. "And if he's not happy with this arrangement, you go straight into custody."

We make it back to the house we left Cassius at without any trouble. Cassius regards Tair with a cold, stony look when we bring him inside, but doesn't say anything to him until I've given him a quick rundown of what's happened.

"An alliance," he says to Tair when I'm done. "You'll help us get to Asher and take the gem, which then goes to an international arms dealer?"

"Better him than who has it now," says Tair. He's leaning against the wall, arms crossed, staring back at Cassius coolly. "But hey, Silver Blue won't be around forever—he's only human, right?"

And somebody's got to step into his shoes when he eventually dies. Guess Tair has more ambition than I gave him credit for—he's jockeying for a permanent kind of alliance, one where he can stab his current employer in the back and replace him when the time is right. If he's got Cassius in his corner, I have no doubt he'll succeed, too.

"The Balancer is too dangerous to wind up in the wrong hands," Cassius says. "When the time comes, you'll arrange to get it to me—or I'll tell Blue you're a mole in my employ and always have been. Clear?"

The grin fades from Tair's face. "Yeah," he says. "If that's how you want to play it."

"I don't play," says Cassius. "I don't make threats, either, they're usually a waste of time. Double-cross me and I'll eliminate you. Azura."

"Yes?" she says, practically snapping to attention.

"Are you familiar with the Balancer gem?"

"I . . . am, yes." She doesn't elaborate.

"You understand what it can do?"

"I do."

"Give me your assessment on this spell in light of the fact that Asher's using it."

She clears her throat before starting. "From what I understand, the Balancer works by moving energy around—shifting magical forces by increasing one thing while decreasing another or vice versa. You can use it to amplify or nullify the power of a spell, as long as you have someplace to draw energy from and someplace else to put energy into.

"The first site we visited embodied a creation myth. The site we just came from was about the sacrifice of an entire race. Creation and sacrifice are two of the keystones of the spell, but all that tells me is he's trying to create as opposed to destroy, and he's willing to kill a great many people to do so."

"He seems to be in the process of creating his own city."

"I don't think that's his ultimate goal. But I need the third keystone—and possibly the fourth—to fully unravel his intent. A two-legged stool will not stand on its own."

"And neither will we. We'll split into two teams, take one site apiece."

"Don't fight, ladies," says Tair. "Only one of you gets to have me at your side—"

"You're going with me," says Cassius. "I want you where I can keep an eye on you."

Tair shrugs. "If you insist."

"But first, you're going to tell me about Silver Blue and where he's holed up."

"Not just yet," Tair says. "I prefer to stay as indispensable as possible, don't you?"

Cassius doesn't bother to reply. He sits down on the living room couch and taps a finger on the map spread out on the coffee table. "Here are the other two sites. We'll take this one; Jace, you and Azura take the other. We'll regroup back here."

There isn't a lot more to be said. I take a minute to raid the kitchen before we leave; I stuff a few apples, some crackers, and a jar of peanut butter into a knapsack.

"Good idea," says Azura. She opens the fridge, rummages around, and hands me a stick of pepperoni. I hesitate—I'm a vegetarian, more or less—then take it and add it to the other supplies. "Thanks. No telling when we'll get to eat again."

"Or where," she says. "This Tair—you and he have history together?"

"Oh, yeah. History, psychology, and almost some biology. But it's a long story, and not the one we should be concentrating on."

"Fair enough. You ready?"

"Yeah. Let's hit the road."

And hope it doesn't hit back . . .

Site number three is apparently a theater, one housed in a gigantic, circular tent of bright yellow with blue stripes. It's on the Strip, situated appropriately enough where Circus Circus usually is.

"No convenient second-story windows," I note from the alley where we're lurking. "But I should be able to cut our way in through the fabric. We'll head around back—"

"I doubt if that'll work," says Azura. "There's a wind

blowing, but do you see even the faintest ripple of fabric? The cloth has been stiffened with underdead magics—an ordinary blade won't cut it, not with any ease. And once the sun's rays strike it, this entire structure will no doubt collapse."

"Stiff magic?" I say. "If I thought you had any idea what Viagra was, I could make about eleven different jokes right now."

"I know what Viagra is. It's what men take when they can't get tickets to see me."

"Tickets? Last I saw you were giving it away for onion rings and dollar tips."

"Don't forget the tequila." She grins.

I can't help but grin back. "Right. Guess I owe you a drink."

"You can buy me one inside. Come on, I've got an idea."

There's a vacant lot lined with trees right next door. We use them as cover to head around back, both of us careful not to be spotted by the lems guarding the front entrance.

The tent takes up as much space as the whole Circus Circus casino did, but the area that the hotel occupied now holds a thicket full of plants I've never seen before, pale blue mushrooms as tall as me with multiple stalks branching out from the main stem like a tree. There's a crow sitting on one, pecking chunks out of it and eating them. He seems to think they're pretty good, and eyes us suspiciously when we duck into the thicket for cover. It smells like apricots.

"Are these—you know, safe?" I ask nervously. They're spaced just close together enough that it's hard to crouch there without touching them.

"No, they're highly poisonous." Azura breaks a delicate-looking cap off and pops it in her mouth. "Fortunately, I'm hard to kill . . . they're fine, Jace. Delicious, in fact—they grow these out back for the casino crowd. Like peanuts, but less fatty."

"I'll take your word for it. How are we getting in?"

"See that laced-up flap over there? That's a knotlock. Same deal as the fabric, very difficult to cut. But if you know the right spell, you can just tell it to untie itself."

"And you know that spell?"

"No—but I have friends who will." She inspects the stalk of the mushroom next to us, finds a small hole in it, and leans in close. She whispers something I can't quite make out, other than the fact that it has a lot of clicks in it.

A few seconds later two long, feathery feelers poke out of the hole. They're followed by a bulbous pink head, and then a segmented pink body that flows sinuously out of the hole and wraps around the 'shroom's stalk. It's a centipede, made less creepy by the intricate markings on its back, electric-blue patterns that remind me of Celtic knotwork.

She's talking to it softly, in that same clickety language. It doesn't talk back—though that wouldn't have surprised me—but its feelers are bobbing up and down and side-to-side furiously. Azura puts her hand out, palm up, and moves it close enough so the feelers just brush her skin. She closes her eyes, brow slightly furrowed, clearly concentrating.

When she opens them, she nods once, then taps the centipede lightly on the head with her forefinger. It slithers back into its hole.

"What was that all about?"

"Sensipede. We use them as spies, plant a specimen in a grove like this, then place a simple enchantment on it to observe and remember one very specific thing—like the unlocking spell used on a door."

"Yeah? What happens if your creepy-crawly informant gets eaten or stepped on?"

"Oh, we don't use just one. The enchantment is passed on, generation to generation. There's essentially an entire species with just one job—as long as any of them survive, we can retrieve the information we need at any time."

I try to wrap my head around that one. A bug that lives only to discover one very basic piece of information, which is then passed on genetically for who-knows-how-many generations. Azura showing up and getting that data right now is like God dropping in and asking for the Ten Commandments back. I almost feel sorry for the poor little guy.

"So," I say, "you just happen to have a spy—sorry, a *race* of spies—living behind a place we need to break into?"

Azura grins. "I'm an Astonisher. I've got them behind every casino in town, and a few other places besides."

We slip out of the thicket and over to the flap. Azura touches the knot securing the door and mutters something under her breath. The knot writhes and undoes itself.

Azura pulls on the flap; the lacing sliding out of its holes with a dry, rasping noise. She steps inside and vanishes.

I can't see what's in there, but it probably doesn't matter—that's not where I'm going, anyway. I take a deep breath, and follow her.

I try to prepare myself for anything, but what I step into catches me completely by surprise. I could have handled a vampire version of Hell, a werewolf Paradise, even a golem bikini car wash—but what I get hits me far harder than anything alien.

It's my bedroom.

The very same one that Ahaseurus yanked me out of when he abducted me in the first place. That's my pile of laundry on that chair. That's my clock radio. That's my unmade bed.

No Azura—but I hear voices in the next room.

I draw my gun out of reflex. The bedroom door is open, and I peer cautiously out into the hall. The light's on in the living room.

"—yeah, her bed's been slept in but there's no sign of her." I recognize the voice; it's Rita Garcia, my supervisor at the St. Louis field office.

I holster my weapon and step into sight. "Rita," I say. "It's me, don't shoot—"

Rita ignores me, still talking into her cell phone. "—no, I *know* she was a little wasted when she went home last night, but the girl hasn't missed a day in four years—no *way* she'd just not show up." Rita's a tough little cookie, short wiry black hair cut with gray, no more than ninety pounds but mean as an alligator. Nothing wrong with her hearing as far as I know—

When I try to tap her on the shoulder, my hand goes right through her.

I freeze, then try again. Nothing. I'm a ghost, as insubstantial as a politician's promise. Then I notice that Rita's stopped moving, stopped talking; I'm a phantom and she's a statue.

"Disconcerting, isn't it?" a voice says from the kitchen. It's a voice I've only heard once before, on the night I was ripped from my own reality and into a world of monsters.

He walks out of the kitchen, dressed nattily in the same dark suit he wore then, but now sporting a crimson turban as well.

Ahaseurus.

I yank my gun back out, but he just raises his eyebrows. "Please. You're here because I want you here, Jace. That gun and its bullets are as ephemeral as you are at the moment."

I consider shooting him anyway. What if he just drops dead at my feet, I turn solid, and Rita jumps a foot in the air? Wouldn't that be great? And then I can call up Santa Claus and the Easter Bunny and we can go hunting unicorns together with our lollipop guns.

I lower the Ruger. "This isn't real, is it."

"Oh, it's real. When I noticed you had entered one of the other spell sites, I added a little detour to one of them. It brought you home, Jace."

"Did it? Then why can't I touch anything?"

He walks over to Rita, peers at her like an old man studying a piece of fruit. "Well, you're not *entirely* here—just your spirit, actually. I'm here in the flesh, though I'm just as undetectable as you are. The difference is, I can affect the world and you can't."

"What do you want?"

He smiles at me with that long undertaker's face. "I want to show you what you're missing, Jace. How worried your friends and family are. How much effort they're about to put into doing the impossible: finding you. Effort that really should be spent on more deserving cases, don't you think? Missing children, killers on the loose?"

"Absolutely. If I was here in body as well as spirit I'd give you a high-five. So why don't you arrange a little reunion between me and myself, and we'll pretend none of this ever happened?"

He turns his attention from Rita to me and chuckles. "I wish I could, Jace. I really do. But that just wouldn't fit into my plans right now. However, I might be persuaded to do so if you were willing to do something for me."

"What?"

"I know it wasn't you that tried to kill me. There's only one person it *could* be, and I'm growing tired of her. Her name is Azura; I want you to find her, and bring her to me. Do so and I'll bring you home for good."

I keep my face neutral. Azura told me that an Astonisher that didn't want to be found couldn't be, and the fact that she's inside one of Ahaseurus' spells right now without him realizing it seems to support that claim. "Let's say I do. What happens then? To her, to Vegas, to all the lems?"

"All just a dream, Jace. Your memories of that time will fade, and none of it will trouble you ever again."

Sure. I can just abandon Charlie and Cassius and everybody else, because hey, it was all just a crazy dream, right? They did just fine before I came along, and they'll do just fine afterward. This is what I've been working for, right here and right now, and all I have to do is give up an annoying spy-stripper that I just met and don't even like. Pfffft.

"No," I say. I'm a little surprised, myself.

"Don't be so hasty. Maybe you need a little reminder of what your life used to be like . . ."

He points a finger at me. Suddenly I'm in the FBI field office, listening to the other end of the phone conversation Rita's having with Zachary Tucker, my current partner. We'd only been working together a week when I was abducted, so I don't exactly have any strong feelings about him—he's a new agent, fresh from Quantico and so gung-ho he probably wears Eliot Ness Underoos. Nice kid—thin, nerdy, bulging eyes—but not exactly an anchor in my life.

The office is, though. And Ahaseurus, that bastard, has made sure that even though I can't touch anything, my other senses work just fine: burned-coffee smell that comes out of the break room because nobody ever cleans the burner; wood shavings and graphite from Crenshaw's desk because he uses that electric pencil sharpener whenever he's bored; sweet pastry aroma from an empty, icing-stained box on top of Yumio's workstation, from Angelo's down the street.

It's enough to bring tears to my eyes, blatantly manipulative though it is. Olfactory memories are some of the strongest ones we have, wired directly into our emotions; talk to any reasonably lucid ninety-year-old and I guarantee she'll still be able to remember smells from her childhood.

"You can have it all back," says Ahaseurus from behind me. "No more vampires. No more werewolves. No more monsters at all."

"Except the human ones," I say.

"That's what you do, isn't it? Of course, once you return there's nothing to stop you from going into another field. You need never face another monster again . . . not unless you find yourself dwelling on the past."

The office vanishes, replaced by darkness. There's a damp, earthy smell in my nose, undercut with something foul and rotting. I know exactly where I am; I had nightmares about this place for years afterward.

"No," I whisper. I'm in a root cellar, beneath an old farmhouse twenty miles outside Augusta, Georgia. I'm waiting for the forensics team to get here so they can start digging, but I already know what they're going to find.

I know Ahaseurus is in here with me, but it still makes me jump when I hear his voice. "Not a happy place, is it?"

"Okay, we've seen the Ghost of Valchek Present and the Ghost of Valchek Past. What's your point?"

"My point is that I can bring you back here anytime I want, Jace. You think the nightmares were bad? Imagine experiencing this in the middle of lunch with your colleagues."

Everything changes again, and—

I don't want to talk about what I see next. Not unless you're a licensed therapist.

When it's over, I try to get myself under control. I force my breathing back to normal, wipe my eyes, cross my arms to keep them from shaking. Funny how I can still feel my own body even though nothing else seems solid.

We're back in my apartment. Rita's still frozen, phone to her ear.

"That's what you can expect if you turn down my very generous offer," Ahaseurus says. I can't believe he's smiling. "Scenes from the very worst of your past, vivid as the first time you experienced them. They'll occur at random, without warning and without respite. Is that how you want to live the rest of your life?"

Turn the most mind-boggling experience of my life into a bad dream, or suffer horrible flashbacks with no rhyme or reason for the rest of it. Great, I'm either the lead in *The Wizard of Oz* or a character from an episode of *Family Guy*.

I stare at Ahaseurus, standing just behind Rita, take a deep breath—

And then Rita winks at me.

"Gonna have to go with option number three," I say. "Do my job, bring you down, and get takeout to celebrate afterward. It's kind of a ritual with me."

"I'm afraid the only ritual you'll be performing," he says, "is *urrk*—"

Pretty sure he meant to say something else, but *urrk* is what comes out. That's because Rita's slammed her elbow into his throat, and is now following through with a mule-kick to his midsection. He goes crashing backward into my bookshelf, knocking it over and strewing paperbacks all over the floor. I never liked that bookshelf.

He doesn't try to get up. He points at me with one hand and croaks out a few barely audible syllables—guess she didn't hit him hard enough to completely disable his windpipe, though she was obviously trying to. I feel a shimmer in the air around me—

"Jace!" Rita shouts in Azura's voice—no surprise

there—and dives toward me. I can't feel the impact when she hits, but her momentum pushes me backward and through a hole I didn't know was there; we're falling through a place that feels familiar and completely alien at the same time, and then I land on my butt on very hard, very solid ground with someone on top of me.

"Oof," I say. That's me, always witty in a crisis.

Rita rolls off and springs to her feet, shifting back to Azura in an instant. "We've got to go," she says.

I don't bother arguing.

We run. Again.

TEN

We've landed in the same spot we entered, just outside the tent flap, and now we sprint for the vacant lot next door and the cover of trees. I'm always surprised by just how green Vegas is—though if fields full of blue mushrooms keep popping into existence, that'll eventually be more like teal . . .

Shut up, brain.

I'm really getting sick of running, and have no desire to hide in another swimming pool. We round a corner and I stop, leaning in close against a wall and drawing my gun. Azura skids to a halt a few feet away.

"What are you *doing*?" she hisses.

"The unexpected," I hiss back. "He comes around this corner, he's going to find out just how solid these bullets are."

"That's—" She stops, and I can see her actually considering the idea. She darts over and flattens herself next to me. "Worth a shot," she whispers.

"Worth a clip," I say grimly.

We wait. I wonder if he's going to be floating a few feet up, all scary-wizard style, or riding some kind of demonic beast, or maybe just striding along with a really pissed-off expression on his face.

Nothing happens.

Well, my nerves fray to the approximate thickness of a supermodel's diet, but that's it. And I have a few centuries or so to think about whether or not I should have taken Ahaseurus up on his offer, and how shooting him is going to strand me here forever.

"I don't think he's coming after us," Azura says at last.

"Maybe you hurt him worse than I thought."

"I doubt it. I think the opposite may be true."

I glance at her. "I don't follow."

"He released a spell before we left. It seemed to be—well, just reinforcing something that was already there. Did he do anything to you while you were in there?"

I think about where he took me and what he made me relive. "No," I say. "Not directly, anyway. He threatened to, though."

She looks worried. "How do you feel?"

"Angry. Tense. Sweaty. How about you?"

"Let me know if you feel anything . . . odd, all right? Sudden urges, itchy body parts, cravings for—well, let's just say cravings. Okay?"

Great, just great. "Hey, that angry/tense thing? Totally gone. You've managed to replace it with a carefree feeling of dread and a lighthearted sensation of gibbering panic. *Good* job."

She doesn't reply, just pushes off the wall and walks away. After a second I join her.

"I need to make a stop before we rejoin Cassius," I say. "At my motel room."

"What for?"

"Something in my luggage. It's a mystic item, and I

think it might be charged with this myth-magic Asher's using. I don't know how to use it . . . but maybe you do."

"What is it?"

"A comic book." I tell her about the Kamic cult, and how they committed murders that were then vividly re-created as comic books—including adding the blood of their victims to the ink. The book I have is one the government created detailing the cult's defeat; it's one of the last copies in existence, and presumably quite powerful.

"I'll take a look at it," Azura says. "But don't get your hopes up. If it was created specifically to counter another enchantment, chances are we can't use it for anything else."

"That's just it—it was printed after the cult was already beaten. That's never made sense to me; I mean, what's the point in countering something when it's already gone down?"

Azura shakes her head. "Magic bends natural laws, Jace—that includes cause-and-effect. In this case, it sounds as if they were borrowing from the future—essentially, drawing on power that didn't exist yet, then creating that power after the fact."

I stare at her for a second. "I hate that."

"It's just the way magic works—"

"You call that working? It's . . . it's contradictory. And *unreliable*."

She shrugs. "I know. But magic is an expression of universal principles that are also contradictory—besides, if it *were* reliable, it'd be science. But it's not."

If I were the type to sputter, I'd be sputtering right about now. But I'm not, so I settle for muttering instead. "Stupid magic. Can't even follow a proper sequence of events . . . I'll bet this world's Einstein died in a mental hospital drooling in his soup . . ."

"Who?"

"Never mind."

We decide to retrieve the comic anyway—even if it isn't the battery of magic energy I thought it was, it could still be very useful as a focus. Besides, the motel isn't that far out of our way.

We approach cautiously, cutting through yards and keeping to alleys instead of streets. I don't know if Caleb Epsilon is still keeping an eye on the place, but the last thing I want to do is run into a javelin-chucking lem.

Azura does a careful reconnoiter first—I figure her Astonisher skills probably make her a pro at detecting anything hidden—and when she comes back to the Dumpster I'm crouching behind she reports that nobody's watching the motel.

I get in, find the comic, and get out fast. I don't go into my former ops center—Wilson's body is probably still in there, and I don't need a reminder of how badly I've screwed things up.

When I show Azura the comic, she asks me if she can touch it. I hesitate, then offer it to her. She doesn't take it, just reaches out a single finger that she holds about an inch away. After a second, she touches it lightly.

"Hmmm," she says.

"Well?"

"I'm not getting anything."

"Nothing at all?"

"A very slight residue of magic, like it had some kind of masking spell on it. Nothing major—definitely nothing as powerful as mythic magic."

"So it's what—empty? A dead battery no one bothered to throw away?"

"I don't think so. It's probably a fake."

That's a possibility I never considered. People will counterfeit just about anything that's worth money, including rare collectibles—why not magic comic books? Dr.

Pete never claimed it had any special abilities; that was my own conclusion.

"Thanks," I say, sticking the book in my bag. "Guess it's nothing but a keepsake now." If Azura's telling the truth . . .

I ask her if she learned anything from the site.

"A little. The myth was about the Lyrastoi, and how they were created. They're essentially were-bats, but they figured out something no one else ever had, a way to fuse two different kinds of mystic energy together: zombie magic and were magic. The result was a were that had many of the attributes of a bat, but lost the ability to change shape; in return, they gained the immortality of the underdead."

"An undead were-bat," I say. "In other words, a vampire."

"Yes. There are a few minor differences, but the Lyrastoi are basically pires. They need to drink blood, they can't stand sunlight, they're vulnerable to silver or wood."

"How much of the myth did you experience?"

"Only the beginning, but that was enough to recognize it. As soon as I realized you weren't with me I focused on analyzing the spell. It took some doing, but I was able to follow the same channel that diverted you. I took a chance and gambled that Asher would bring you back to where you first appeared; most spells are naturally circular in nature."

"Sure. Except when they aren't."

"I think you'll find that being angry at the nature of reality tends to be counterproductive."

"Everybody needs a hobby, Tinker Bell. Besides, my rage-aholic group would miss my brownies." I pause. "So how does the myth end?"

"With the Lyrastoi becoming the rulers of Nightshadow, as I remember. It was a long, gradual process, but that's the nice thing about immortality: You can take the long view."

"Creation, sacrifice, immortality—those are the mythic themes so far. What does that say to you?"

"That Asher has larger plans than just taking over Vegas . . ."

When we get back to the house, we find Tair waiting for us—but no Cassius.

"We got separated inside the story," Tair says, leaning back on the couch and putting his feet up on the coffee table. He pops open a can of beer with one thumb and takes a long drink. "When it ended, I got out. He didn't."

"Not good enough," I snap. "How do we know you didn't stab him in the back? You could have betrayed him to your boss, or Asher, or even Stoker."

"If I'd done that, would I have come back here?" He meets my eyes calmly. "Especially knowing how . . . *volatile* you are? Frankly, I'm surprised you're not aiming that ridiculous weapon at me yet. It's been, what, at least an hour since you pulled it out? I don't know why you even bother with a holster."

"Tell me what happened."

Azura doesn't say anything, but she's staring at him just as hard as I am.

"Sure," he says. "I mean, that was the point of this exercise, right?"

He sets down his beer, leans back, and puts both hands behind his head. "Okay. The story was about lems. When the very first one was made, who made it, how they spread all over the world."

"Golems?" Azura says. "That's not a myth from Nightshadow; there aren't any golems there."

"I'm just telling you what I saw. Do you want to hear it or not?"

"Go on," Azura says.

"A wizard was responsible. He used another supernatural being as a template, a kind of zombie called an underdead. Used fundamental animist principles to instill the spirit of an ape into a stone body, then locked it in place with the underdead template."

"Were magic fused with zombie magic," Azura says. "That's not been done since the birth of the Lyrastoi race . . . but lems aren't pires."

"No," I say. "But pires start as were bats, and lems start as statues—statues that are animated by the life force of animals like bulls or bears, not bats. Same principle, very different end result."

Azura frowns, rubbing her chin. "Not quite the same. The balance would have to be very different—more Chaos than I would have thought, less Order . . ."

"I wouldn't know about all the technicalities," Tair says. "Myths tend to paint a picture with big strokes, you know? Not so much on the finer points."

"Any details at all could be useful," Azura says. "Names, places, mystic items used—"

"The zombie's name was Brunt," Tair says. "The wizard's was Ahaseurus."

The second name doesn't come as a surprise to anyone—Ahaseurus is widely known as the creator of the golem race, and the spell that animates them is the stuff of basic biothaumaturgy. Not much is known about the man himself, however—and I suspect very few people are aware that he's still alive and going by the name Asher. Cassius probably does, though I've never confronted him about it.

But it's not the wizard's name that Azura reacts to—it's the zombie's.

"Brunt?" Her eyes do the impossible, getting even wider. "Are you sure?"

"Well, they only said it once, so maybe I got it wrong—could have been Grunt, I guess—"

She steps forward and knocks the beer out of his hand with a slap. *"Are you sure?"*

He glares at her. "Yeah, yeah, I'm sure. Why? Is he important?"

"Recount the myth. In detail. *Now.*"

I'm sure Tair could take her head off in one swipe if he bothered to transform, but he just looks up at her from where he's sprawled. Blinks. Then says, very carefully, "Okay, I'll do my best. All right?"

Azura takes a step backward, but keeps her eyes focused on him. Tair's body language tells me he's seriously considering bolting out the front door, though I doubt he'd get far. Tinker Bell, it seems, has a scary side.

"It went like this," he says. "A long time ago, there was a wizard. The wizard was from . . . a mystical realm." Tair's voice changes in mid-sentence, losing the snarky edge and becoming both dreamier and more formal. I knew what was happening; he was in the grip of the same kind of repetition that had been drilled into my head by the first myth I'd encountered.

He came to this Earth from there, and was troubled by what he saw. Where he was from—though they were called by different names—pires and thropes and humans lived together in harmony. Though they sometimes warred among themselves, they did not prey upon one another as wild beasts do; but in this new land those that drank blood or changed form seemed to consider human beings no more than sustenance.

And so he decided to change things.

Mankind was not as long-lived or as strong as the supernatural races, so the wizard judged that they needed an ally to fight alongside them, one both loyal and invincible.

They would be the protectors of men and women, and he would sow their seeds all over the world.

He chose to model his creation on man himself, to give it a form familiar but different. He chose to use earth itself for their substance, so that they would always be plentiful, strong, and difficult to destroy.

His last decision was the most difficult. He needed to instill them with life, but he did not want them to be merely offshoots of the human race, as both pires and thropes were. They needed to be something that did not rely on transforming humans to reproduce—as pires did—nor something that could prey on humans, as thropes sometimes did. A kind of life that would not compete for the same resources, but would still be dependant on the goodwill of human beings.

The problem perplexed him. He could have instilled this new form of life with energy stolen from pires or thropes, but that would put them at endless odds with two races, a war that would inevitably lead to the destruction or enslavement of one side. He considered using beasts of the field, but this would simply produce animals in another form, one with no more loyalty or intelligence than the most clever of creatures—a monkey or a dog, perhaps.

At long last, he realized there was only one person he could turn to for advice. It was a decision he would have preferred to avoid.

He made his way to the top of the very tallest mountain in the land, a journey of several weeks. There, on a barren, windswept peak, was a deep crevasse in the rock, filled with snow. He made a fire upon the snow, and used his magicks to keep it burning as the snow melted. When the fire had melted a shaft down into the bottom of the crevasse, he extinguished it and then lowered himself down on a rope; there, behind a glassy wall of ice, was a great door carved into the rock itself. The wizard kicked aside the ashes of the fire, settled into a cross-legged pose, and began the chant that would unseal the door.

For three days and nights he chanted, for the spell was a long and involved one that needed to be repeated several times; any mistake or error would cause the crevasse to slam closed like a giant clapping his hands, crushing him instantly.

But he made no mistakes. And after three days and nights, the stone door swung open, smashing the ice into shards at the wizard's feet.

The wizard whispered a few well-chosen words, and a ball of light appeared over his head. He entered the dark, bitterly cold doorway.

Inside, steps carved into the rock led down. He followed them for many hours, deep into the very heart of the mountain. They led him to a single room at their base, a simple cube with nothing in it save a slab of table-shaped rock in its center.

On that rock lay chained a monster.

He was of the race known as the underdead, an unliving creature that was once a man. He resembled a man, though a very large and ugly one.

His name was Brunt.

"Hello, wizard," the monster said. "Have you come to torment me further?"

"I have come to ask your advice," said the wizard.

"And why should I advise you of anything?" the monster replied. He did not turn his head to look at the wizard, instead keeping his gaze fixed on the roof of his stone prison cell. It was a view he was accustomed to.

"Because if you do I will free you," the wizard said.

The monster considered this. "Tell me what you seek advice upon."

*The wizard told him of his dilemma. "You exist to be
of service to the living," the wizard said. "Tell me, should
I base my new creation on you?"*

*"No," the monster said. "You should not, and you al-
ready know this. My kind needs a steady supply of fresh
corpses to thrive, and that's the sort of thing that can get
out of control. What you need is cold reason wedded to the
hot flame of life, mixed in a crucible composed of neither."*

*The wizard thought about this. He had not told the
monster about shaping bodies for his new creations from
clay, but now he saw what needed to be done; the clay
would be fired from within by the heat of life, and cooled
to a durable shell without by cold intellect.*

*"I thank you," said the wizard. "And I believe I know
where to obtain two of the three elements required. But the
cold reason you speak of—only the underdead possess this
in its purest form, and you are the last of your kind."*

*"Then use me to create this new race," the monster
said. "For I am tired of being alone."*

*The wizard weighed his words carefully. The monster
was imprisoned for a good reason, but perhaps his legacy could be one of good and not evil. "Very well. But be
warned; the experience will not be pleasant, nor will you
survive it."*

*"After an eternity chained here, any experience will
be welcome," the monster said.*

And so the wizard—

Tair pauses, his eyes refocusing. He starts to speak
again, then stops. "—the wizard worked his magic on the
zombie. He diced it up into a thousand pieces and put
each of those pieces into a different golem. When he in-
fused the golems with energy from sacrificed animals—
the first one he used was an ape—they came to life. They
had some of the characteristics of the animals that powered

them, but also the intelligence of the underdead that—ironically—had granted them life. Or at least some version of it."

Tair stops again. "That's about it. Everybody knows what happens next, anyway; he starts in China—guess that's where the mountain was—then travels around the globe, teaching other people the spell so they can make their own."

Azura's studying him coldly. "And what happened after the thousand pieces were used up?"

Tair shrugs. "The story didn't cover that part—"

"Perhaps he ordered out for more. But no, that wouldn't have been possible, since Brunt was the *very last of his race*." The edge in her voice could cut steel. "You're lying. That ending makes no sense. There are millions of golems alive today, and *none* of them has a piece of an underdead warrior at his heart."

And suddenly she's a lot closer to Tair. I don't see her move at all; she's just *there*, and she's holding her fist about six inches from his right eye. Something long and slim glints from between her knuckles.

"I can put this needle into your brain before you can twitch," she says. "Pure silver—your eyeball will smoke and explode in the instant before you die. *Now tell me what really happened to Brunt*."

Tair keeps himself very, very still. "Hey, Jace," he says. "Are you really gonna let this psycho stick a needle in my eye?"

"Not if you cross your heart and hope to die," I say. "She's right. Your story was terrific most of the way through, but you blew the dismount. See, you might be able to pull off the whole I'm-just-a-dumb-thug with everyone else, but I *know* you're a trained biothaumaturge—that's what got you into a life of crime, remember? You helped make illegal lems for the gray market. And someone with that kind of experience doesn't fudge the details of how the very first lem was made. Not unless he doesn't want anyone else to know them."

Tair smiles. "Worth a try, right? That's what I like about you, Jace—you don't let me get away with a thing. But I'm afraid the details of what really went down have to stay locked up in my head for now." He stares into Azura's eyes. "Unless you think you can extract the story from my skull with your pointy little stick."

"I'm less interested in what happened to a zombie in a fairy tale," I say, "than I am in what happened to my boss. What did you do to Cassius, Tair?"

"Nothing. That part was true."

"I'm not so sure. Convince me."

He sighs. "I went first."

"Excuse me?"

"When it came to swapping myths. I told you mine first—if I was planning on a double cross, wouldn't I get *you* to go first? That'd give me better options. I could tailor my lie to something you wanted to hear, or just hit the road—I don't think Miss Jabby here could keep up with me if I really poured it on. Instead, I told you what I know—mostly."

"You're going to have to do better," Azura says. "Or I'll put this through the center of your pupil. Mostly."

He shakes his head, ever so slightly. "I don't think so. See, you need what I know—"

He pauses. His nostrils flare, and his smile gets wider. "Oh, and you're going to need my help in a minute or so. You can't smell them, but we're about to have visitors . . ."

"Who?" Azura snaps.

He sniffs again, theatrically.

"Mercenaries," he says cheerfully. "Heavily armed, too."

ELEVEN

"Before you get the wrong idea," says Tair, "they're not with me. They're Stoker's men."

"You mean the guy you came to Vegas to broker an arms deal with?" I snap. My gun's already out.

"You know any *other* homicidal human terrorists with that last name?" he says. "Seven of them. A pire female and six male thropes—Dobermans, I think they call themselves."

"Mbunte," I say, with a glance at Azura. "Guess she recovered from the inoculation you gave her—if Tair isn't trying to con us. Again."

"Oh, they're out there," she says. "My nose may not be as keen as his, but it's not the only thing I rely on."

"If you're going to kill me, hurry up and get it over with," Tair says. "I'd really like to be in a position to defend myself when they attack, if you don't mind."

Azura stares hard at him for a second, then takes a step backward. The needle vanishes. "This conversation isn't over," she says.

"Oh, I know," he says, getting to his feet. "And I'm really, *really* looking forward to continuing it . . ."

I'm trying to cover every entry point in the place with

my gun simultaneously. Any second now, a thrope or a pire is going to come crashing through a window or kick down the door—unless they decide to soften us up with a barrage of crossbow bolts or nerve gas first . . .

I dive for my bag and fish out the comic. I toss it to Azura. "Okay," I say. "Do something impressive."

She gives me an incredulous look. "Like what?"

"Whatever that thing does!"

"I told you, it doesn't do *anything*—"

"I know, I know. But you were *lying,* right? You were going to swipe it later and use it yourself to take out Asher but that's not going to happen if we're both *dead* so quit blinking those oversize Bambi eyes at me and *do* something, damn it!"

"Hey," says Tair. "I used to have that issue."

Azura stares at me, then grabs the comic and rips it in half. "I. Wasn't. *Lying,*" she growls.

"The love and trust in here," says Tair, "is making me choke up a little. Really."

"Oh, crap," I say wearily.

"That was a collector's item, you know," Tair says helpfully. "Unless it was a fake, of course. I used to own one of those. Looked like the real thing, though."

"Oh, *crap,*" I say again, just in case the first time didn't take.

There's a knock on the front door.

I look at Azura. She looks at Tair. Tair looks at the door. I shrug.

"Who *is* it?" says Tair in a falsetto voice.

"We want to parley," says Mbunte's voice.

"Hey," says Tair, "great. I'm always up for a good parley. Did you bring snacks?"

Incoherent Teutonic muttering from the other side of the door. The only phrase I can make out is *was sind diese* snacks?

"Just come in, already," I say. If they were going to attack, they'd have done it already. "We won't shoot if you won't."

The door opens slowly. Mbunte looks a little worse for wear than the last time I saw her, her clothes torn, her hair and skin streaked with grime and dust. She glances around nervously, then walks in, signaling for the Dobermans to follow her. They all crowd in, the last one shutting the door behind him.

"Glad you could make it," says Tair, beaming and clasping his hands together. "Bathroom's down the hall, you can put coats on the bed in the master bedroom, and try to keep the door closed—we have a cat."

"Not to look a gift merc in the mouth," I say, "but why aren't you trying to kill us?"

"That was never our mission," says Mbunte. "We were tasked to bring you in alive."

"Not all of us," says Azura.

"No, not all of you," Mbunte admits. "Just Valchek. But that's ancient history now."

"Yeah, Asher's really kicked over the anthill," says Tair. "I don't know about your boss, but mine wasn't really expecting a full-fledged revolt. Would have brought more party favors if he had."

I was still mulling over the fact that Stoker wants me alive. "And I didn't expect my partner to go rogue—all of us got caught with our pants down. What's your point?"

"My point is that we should unite against a common enemy," Mbunte says. "We've been on the run since the lems took over; you're holed up here. I say to hell with Stoker, Asher, and Blue—let's pool our resources and get out of town in one piece."

"Ah, the loyalty of the mercenary," I say. "It's inspiring, it really is. Why, I'm prepared to trust you with my life already—I mean, I will as soon as I can scrape together some funds. Do you take debit?"

Mbunte glares at me. "I don't have to justify myself to you. This is about survival. We have a much better chance against the rockheads together than standing alone—"

"You mean *we* do," says Azura. "Because two of us are human, and none of you are. You've noticed the lems are treating human beings differently from pires or thropes."

"True. But we've got numbers and weapons. It's a fair trade."

"Really?" I say. "A six-pack of thropes, a few bows and blades, and a pire who specializes in poisons that *don't work* against lems? Why do I think our end of this proposed alliance is going to involve the phrase *human shield*?"

"It doesn't matter," says Azura. "Escaping from the city won't do you any good."

"What? Why not?" Mbunte demands.

"Because the fourth spell site was about the birth of the golem race. Creation, Sacrifice, Immortality, Birth—or if you prefer, Chaos, Death, Order, and Life. The four prime elements of the Universe. If Asher's initial myth had invoked the destructive side of Chaos, he would have been weaving an Apocalypse spell—but he didn't do that. He told a Creation myth."

"That's good, right?" I say. "The opposite of Apocalypse is good."

"Creation and Destruction are always entwined, Jace. Creating something inevitably involves destroying something else."

"What's he trying to create?" Mbunte asks.

"A new world," says Azura. "Vegas is just the launching point."

I have a sudden, horrible feeling. I stop watching Mbunte and her pet soldiers and start looking around frantically.

"Remote, remote, where's the remote," I mutter. I spot it lying at the base of the flatscreen TV, scoop it up, and hit the POWER button.

"—reports are now coming from other parts of the state," the newscaster says. She's more composed than the last one, but her eyes are a little glassy; I think she might be on the equivalent of thrope tranquilizers. "Fighting continues to rage in the streets of Reno, while Carson City is now reported to have fallen to the insurgents. The golem manufacturing facility in Sparks is under golem control, and management has been taken hostage. Nellis Air Force Base in Las Vegas has been occupied, and there are unconfirmed reports of experimental aircraft out of Area Fifty-one in the Nevada desert now being used by the golem revolutionary forces. The group claiming responsibility for this insurrection is the radical golem rights organization known as the Mantle, which is calling for golems across the globe to join them. We have this statement from their leader, Tom Omicron."

They cut away to a shot of a gray-skinned lem sitting behind a desk. He looks solemn, but that's sort of the default expression on most lem faces. He's not wearing a shirt, but he's got a jagged black circle painted on his chest—the logo of the Mantle. "I wish to assure the members of every supernatural race that we will make this transition as painless as possible. My people were created as guardians and helpmates to the human race, and we have failed terribly in our duty. Human beings are nearly extinct; current projections show they will not survive into the next century. We cannot let this happen.

"Not all of us have forgotten our heritage. We still remember who made us, and why. And if the hemovores and lycanthropes will not safeguard their lives, then we will. I urge all humans listening to this broadcast to contact the nearest lem authority; we will protect you from the tragic but unavoidable dangers of this war. And when it is over, we will return this planet to its rightful owners—you."

The camera cuts back to the anchor. "We're being joined now by Crispus Damian, senior analyst for the White House and deputy chairman of the Domestic Golem Affairs Bureau. Mr. Damian, what exactly is going on? Why this insurrection, why now, and why the sudden shift in policy from golem rights to human fealty?"

Crispus Damian is an imposing, dark-skinned pire with a shaved head and a square jaw. "We're still investigating, Kelly, but at this point we think it's one of two things: either a preemptive attempt to shift blame, because they know this terrorist action has no chance of succeeding; or an ill-fated partnership with a faction of human terrorists, who are demanding certain conditions in return for their cooperation. Either way, there's no chance of this revo— excuse me, of this insurrection surviving."

"Are human beings really that valuable as an ally?" Kelly asks. "I mean, there are less than a million alive, most of them widely scattered or in seclusion. The kind of language Tom Omicron was using was—well, almost subservient. Is this a political alliance, or is something else going on?"

"If you're trying to imply there may be some sort of sorcery at work, I can assure you we have our best government shamans working on that. If there is some kind of spell being cast, there's no danger of it getting past the confines of Nevada. We have wards already in place, and there's absolutely no risk to the people in the neighboring states—"

"We're screwed," says Azura.

"So this going to *spread*?" Mbunte asks. "No. No way. They'll use HPLC—"

"High Power Level Craft won't stop this," says Azura. "Not unless they want to tear the entire planet apart. It might come to that, but I doubt it; there are too many lems in important military positions, and they won't let that happen." There's a bleak certainty in her voice. *"This world will fall."*

In the end we accept the mercs' offer of an alliance. It seems like the prudent choice.

Mbunte doesn't try to take over, for which I'm grateful; I have enough on my plate without worrying about fighting a battle-hardened mercenary for dominance. I get the impression that she's a career soldier, one more comfortable with following orders than giving them—though I can't let myself forget that I was the one who killed Koltz, her last commanding officer. If she has a problem with that, she doesn't let it show.

The Dobermans take over two of the bedrooms to stash their gear and claim floor space; they seem to think we're going to be holed up here awhile. Azura goes to work setting up some perimeter spells, while Tair studies the news and ignores everyone. I grab some lunch in the kitchen—peanut butter on white bread—and try to figure out what our next move should be.

I can't stop thinking about what Omicron said on his telecast: that humans were the rightful owners of the planet, and the lems were planning on giving it back to them.

Was that such a bad idea?

Of course, being one of said human beings, I wasn't exactly a disinterested observer. I was a member of an endangered species that had just been handed a winning lottery ticket and told to get aboard the space shuttle for the next flight to Shangri-la. Okay, maybe my metaphors needed a little less time in the blender, but overall things looked a lot better for the human race in this reality than they had for a long, long time.

Sure. All that's needed is a bloody revolution that will cost countless lives. And in the end, what do we wind up with? An aristocracy of a million or so human beings, ruling over a police state? A big stone jackboot on the neck of every pire and thrope alive? Golems all magically brainwashed into our faithful servants, making us a culture of slavers?

That wasn't a better world. That was just a world where I was one of the oppressors instead of the oppressed.

I wish Cassius were here. He's got a lot more experience with this kind of big-picture political dilemma; I try to focus on the immediate and specific, like catching a killer before he puts another body in the ground. There are too many variables at work here, too many consequences to any given action. Just keeping an eye on Tair and Azura is using up most of my concentration.

I come to a decision, and call everyone to the living room for a war council. Azura seems to be done with whatever spell she was putting in place, and Tair switches off the TV.

"We need to find my boss, David Cassius," I say. "He's got the resources and the knowledge to turn this around, and he's already here in the city."

"If he's here," says Mbunte, "where is he?"

"Probably trapped in the repeating cycle of a myth." I give Mbunte a brief description of what Azura, Tair, and I have experienced at the spell sites.

"If Tair was able to break free, why wasn't he?" Mbunte asks. She gives Tair a flat, evaluating glance.

"Good question," says Azura. "After all, Tair claims to have done it with sheer willpower. Is Cassius the weak-willed sort?"

"Not hardly," I say. Now we're all giving Tair the hairy eyeball. "But if he is in there, we should go get him out.

And if he isn't—well, maybe we should have a little chat with the last person to see him. Right?"

Tair doesn't seem fazed by this at all. He smiles. "Hey, don't look at me like *that*. Even if he isn't in there, how do we know what happened? He could have escaped and then been captured or killed by lem forces. Asher could have zapped him into another dimension. Just because I made it out and he didn't doesn't automatically make me the bad guy."

"That's true," I say. "You're a bad guy all on your own."

"In any case," he says, "what good is it going to do to rescue him, anyway? He's trapped here, same as us."

"Don't underestimate him. Cassius always has a plan."

"Yeah, look how well things have gone for your mission so far."

"That's not *his* fault—"

A ringtone starts playing; it takes me a second to recognize it as the theme song from *Gilligan's Island*. Part of my brain notes that for future reference—I collect music that's the same here as in my original reality, regardless of genre—while the rest of me scans the room for the cell phone that's making it. I find it on a bookshelf and pick it up.

The incoming call is from a number I recognize. I thumb the answer button. "Hello, Charlie."

"Hi. This a bad time?"

"Depends on your point of view. Your side seems to be doing okay."

"It's not my side, Jace. It's *our* side."

Everyone in the room is staring at me. They're all probably wondering if I'm about to betray them.

"Right, right. Me as a member of the master race and you as one of my loyal subjects. That how you see this?"

"It's not like that. We're just trying to do right by the people that made us."

"Listen to yourself, Charlie. This isn't you, this is magic. Your judgment is being warped by a spell."

"No, it's not."

"Yeah? Who's better at pool, you or me?"

"What?"

"Answer the damn question."

". . . that would be me. You always scratch on the eight."

"Who's a better dresser?"

"Are you kidding? You buy your clothes in bulk."

"Who's a better dancer?"

"I am. You keep trying to lead, which I wouldn't mind if you knew *how*—"

"Who's your master?"

There's no answer. I let the silence drag out for a few seconds, then say, "Well, congratulations. You actually managed not to say it. You sure wanted to, though, right? How's *that* make you feel?"

"I'm sorry, Jace."

"Sorry? *Sorry?* I don't want you *sorry,* you walking bag of cement mix, I want you *angry*! What the hell good is a partner who won't even stand up for his own rights when he's being turned into a windup toy for a *lunatic*?"

"You want me angry?" His voice is cold. "Okay, Jace. You got it. Just try to remember I'm doing this for your own good."

The line goes dead.

"Uh-oh," I say.

"What?" Mbunte says. "What did he say?"

"I think I finally pissed him off. But not in a good way . . ."

"Get down!" Azura yells.

I have the bizarre urge to yell back, *Get funky!* but fortunately that part of my brain isn't in charge of my reflexes. I drop to the floor.

Glass shatters. Mbunte's head explodes.

This world doesn't have bullets, but it does have golems that can pitch iron-cored silver ball bearings around three times as fast as Nolan Ryan. Mbunte must have accumulated quite a time-debt as a pire, because her body hits the ground as mostly dust.

The Dobermans dive for their weapons—either compound bows, axes, or machetes—transforming into were form on the way. At least one is carrying a broadsword. Azura is scrambling on hands and knees for the kitchen, and Tair—Tair is just gone, nowhere in sight.

Me, I've got the Ruger out and ready, trained at the front door. Guess I should have asked Charlie where he was calling from.

"I thought you had alarm spells set up!" I hiss at Azura.

"I do! They went off! That's what the yelling was about!"

A grenade sails through the broken window, lands on the floor, and starts spouting white vapor. I recognize the smell: CNS agent laced with silver, designed to target thropes. The Dobermans are already slipping gas masks over their muzzles, though—they're professional soldiers, after all.

But they're not Charlie.

He comes in through the front door, just smashes right through it like it was made of cardboard. He's dressed in sand-colored desert fatigues and a combat helmet instead of his usual suit and fedora, which somehow I find more shocking than anything else. He's got a battle shield strapped to either arm, basically a razor-edged disk the size of a manhole cover with a steel viewing mesh near the rim. I've read about them, but never seen one in action before.

The Dobermans with bows let fly. Charlie blocks with the shields, holding one high and one low, a posture a human fighter could never maintain. The arrows bounce off.

Then it's Charlie's turn.

He cuts one of the thropes almost in half with a single swipe. He doesn't have a lot of reach, but he doesn't need it; he advances relentlessly, using a combination of brute force and nearly ten feet of cutting edge to make every battle up close and personal. He kicks one thrope through a wall, slams another into the TV with the flat of a shield, and opens a third from groin to gullet with an upward slash. The look on his face is one of intense, savage satisfaction.

For the first time, I really see the tyrannosaur buried in the black sand of Charlie's heart. It's terrifying.

The gas is getting thicker, turning the battle into vague blurs in fog. The thropes don't stand a chance, and all I can think of is that when he's done with them, I'm next.

I know that shield can turn away arrows, and maybe even one of the javelins that lems pitch—but I doubt if it can stop a silver-tipped .454 round.

Charlie won't kill me, I tell myself, trying to aim through the white fog. *Charlie won't kill me.*

Maybe not. But can I kill him?

TWELVE

He kills them all.

Six heavily armed mercenaries, veterans of wars and police actions from Africa to Afghanistan. Thropes the size of linebackers, each one a mass of muscle, claw, and fang capable of recovering from almost any wound short of decapitation.

It takes him under a minute.

When he's done he leans down and picks up the gas grenade, still hissing out white smoke, and tosses it casually out the window it came in. Then he turns to me. I can't see his face clearly through the fog.

I shoot him.

I remember the first time Charlie and I went out dancing.

It was in the middle of a case—my first case on this world—and I was basically being paraded around a small town as bait. That didn't stop me from getting in a little entertainment when I found out this town had a thing for swing bands—*especially* when I found out my new partner liked to dance. Yeah, I gave him a hard time about it, but not so hard he wouldn't hit the floor with me.

Did I find the idea of a dancing golem strange? Well, at

the time I was so overwhelmed by strangeness that it was just one more thing to add to the recipe. When I had some time to think about it later, though, it seemed perfectly natural, like just a little sugar in really strong coffee. Not so much that it becomes sweet; just enough to cut the bitterness.

He was a wonderful dancer.

The bullet takes him at the base of the throat. He gets the shield up in time, but not high enough; it smashes through the wire mesh that rings the circumference about six inches from the killing edge.

In a way, that makes it worse. The slug, tipped with silver but carved from teak, shatters, turning what could have been a through-and-through into a blizzard of shrapnel. It does about as much damage as a load of buckshot would if fired into a plastic jug filled with sand.

"Charlie isn't there to spy on you or keep you in line," Cassius told me the first time I met my new partner. "He's there to protect you, and inflict serious damage on anyone that gets in your way. He's your enforcer, not your babysitter."

That turned out to be only half true. Charlie was certainly capable of destroying just about anything that might pose a threat to me, from neo-Nazi thropes to ninja pires, but he did his fair share of babysitting, too. He was the one who hung out with me when I was feeling blue, the one who'd show up with a Bogey movie and a pizza on a lonely Friday night—even though he didn't eat. I didn't think of him as a friend, because on this planet he was the closest thing I had to family. I trusted him with my life.

Black sand sprays the air like fossilized blood. A golem's life force is embedded in the substance that composes them; you can patch or even replace the thick plastic skin that gives them their shape, but if they lose enough dirt, clay, or sand, the spell that animates them is broken. They die, just like any other living thing.

Charlie staggers backward a step. The mist clears just enough for me to see the look on his face, and nothing has ever made me hate myself more. I think I could have stood it if he looked angry, or surprised, or even if he looked sad—but he doesn't wear any of those expressions. He wears no expression at all; his face is a blank, a Halloween mask with no one wearing it. I've turned him into an object, a thing. My friend isn't *in* there any more.

He falls backward, hits the floor with a very solid *thump*. He doesn't move.

"Charlie?" I say. My voice doesn't sound like me. "Charlie?"

"Jace." My heart jumps—but it's not Charlie's voice, it's Azura's. She's standing in the door to the kitchen. Maybe she's hungry.

"Jace, we have to go. Other lems are on their way. Jace, *please*."

It's just noise. I stare at Charlie's body, waiting for him to get up and glare at me for putting holes in his new suit. No, he's not wearing a suit. What *is* that thing he's wearing? Boy, am I going to give him a hard time about *that*.

As soon as he gets up.

Azura's tugging at my arm. I'd shoot her, too—hey, I'm in Vegas and I'm on a roll—but I don't seem to have my gun anymore. Azura seems to have it. Tricky, that girl. Wonder why she's so agitated? Guess she's never seen someone shoot their partner before.

"Jace, we have to *go*." Yeah. Yeah, she's right. Charlie is not going to be happy when he wakes up, and he'll probably blame the whole thing on me. Best thing I can do right now is go find a whole lot of duct tape, then come back with a sheepish expression on my face and help patch him up. He'll forgive me, eventually.

That's what a good partner does.

The next little while is kind of a blur.

I remember thinking that I sure was running a lot lately. Ever since I got to Vegas, that's all I seem to do: run toward one thing, then run away from something else. Maybe I should get a bike. Or a skateboard.

I don't know how far we run, or for how long. Azura eventually picks another house with the door standing open and we go inside. "We should be safe here for the moment," she says. "I think he tracked us through the mercenaries."

"He?" I say. "Oh, yeah. Charlie."

Things get kind of dark right around there.

I wake up crying.

It's a weird sensation. I must have been dreaming, but when I try to remember my brain refuses to let me. Maybe that's a good thing.

I killed Charlie.

I can't process that for a minute. I mean, it just refuses to compute. The thought begins, it bounces around in my head for a while, but nothing comes out.

I try another approach. *Did* I kill Charlie?

Better results with this one, as a whole swarm of rationalizations surge into being. Maybe the damage didn't look as bad I thought. Maybe he was only unconscious. Maybe there was a lem team right behind him and they had a medic with them. Maybe that wasn't even Charlie.

I huddle around these possibilities like a woman freezing to death crouching over the ashes of a fire. For the first time since I was a child, there's no trace of sarcasm

or irony in any of my thoughts. I want one of them, *any* of
them, to be true so bad it hurts. It hurts a *lot*.

But deep inside, I know better.

Azura walks in from the other room, holding a mug of
something steaming. She looks concerned. I sit up on the
couch I'm lying on, and take it without a word. Tea. I take
a long swallow, not caring if I burn my mouth.

No, that's not true, either. I want it to burn.

She perches on the arm of an overstuffed chair across
from me, but doesn't say anything. I look around for the
first time, taking in my surroundings. Bigger, better house
than the last one, with more expensive furnishings and art
on the walls. Guess we've moved up in the fugitive world.

"Where are we?"

"Swenson Street. About seven blocks from the last
place."

"Think they'll find us again?"

"No. Not unless they start doing door-to-door searches,
and they don't have the manpower for that right now."

"But they will." Every lem in the world will be at Asher's
beck and call pretty soon, and that's 19 percent of the overall population. They can run the whole city through a sieve
and *sift* us out if they want.

I drink more tea. It has whiskey in it. Funny I didn't
notice that before. I wonder if it's drugged, too, and sort
of hope it is. Nice little chemical vacation to no-thought
island. But then she probably wouldn't have bothered
with the whiskey. Damn.

We just sit there for a while, not saying anything. She
doesn't ask about Charlie. She doesn't ask how I'm doing.
She just sits there, waiting, and when I'm done with my tea
she gets up and gets me some more. There's more whiskey
in it, this time.

"If you're going to get me drunk," I say at last, "at least
have the decency to join me."

"One of us should stay sober."

"Why? If they *do* find us again, they'll bring a squad. Sober or not won't make much difference, then."

She shrugs, gets up and gets the bottle. No glass. Guess she's a traditionalist at heart.

We sit and drink. When I've finished the second cup of tea, she passes me the bottle.

"How long have you been doing this?" I ask her at last. "The spy-slash-stripper-slash-magician thing?"

"A long time," she says. "Since I was eighteen or so. It's all I ever wanted to be."

I nod. "Yeah. I graduated the Academy at twenty-six, but I was in school before that. Always working toward the same thing, the whole time. Wanted to catch bad guys." I take a swig from the bottle, then correct myself. "No. Wanted to *stop* bad guys. Catching them was incidental."

"Bad guys. Doesn't matter which reality you're from, there's always too many of them. And not enough of the other kind."

"Yeah. Ain't that the truth." I study her for a second. "You ever have a partner?"

"Me? Astonishers have to be independent. You never know where you'll be sent, or what role you'll have to play. It doesn't leave a lot of room for . . . allies."

"You didn't answer the question."

"I—no, I guess I didn't. I suppose I did have a partner, once. Someone I trusted, someone that meant a great deal to me. His name was Brunt."

"The zombie from the myth?"

She nods. "The very same. He was . . . more than he appeared. Not the monster that Asher's made him out to be, not at all. And I don't understand how he could be the last of his kind, either—as you saw in the morgoleum, the underdead are not in short supply."

"Just because we saw it doesn't mean it was real. We're

talking about *myths,* right? By definition, they're not real."

She shakes her head. "All myths have some truth to them, or they wouldn't have the power they do. But it's possible—even likely—that Asher is bending those truths to suit his purposes."

"Like Tair did when he killed the last wolf. That was pretty smart, actually."

"I get the feeling Tair's not one to pass up an opportunity."

"He's a killer." I grab the bottle, take another drink. "But then, so am I."

She doesn't contradict me, for which I'm grateful. "How about you? Ever kill anyone?"

"Yes."

She doesn't elaborate, and I don't push.

"You know, I bet one part of that myth's true," I say. "The part about Brunt fathering the golem race. That sounds more like the Brunt you describe than a monster."

"It does," she says softly.

"Then I guess I have him to thank for the best partner I ever had," I say. I pour a little of the whiskey into my mug, then hand the bottle to her. "To Brunt."

She raises the bottle and I raise my mug. "To Charlie," she says.

We drink.

Things get a little blurry after that.

I wake up in the bathtub, fully clothed. Whiskey must have been magicked up to let it affect pires and thropes—I have a tendency to head for the tub when I drink it, though I have no idea why. Beats waking up with my head in the toilet, I guess.

I haul myself out, body stiff and complaining. "Azura?" I call. No answer.

I find her in the living room, passed out on the couch, cradling the empty whiskey bottle under her chin. The ungodly noise coming from her mouth tells me she's still alive, though I wouldn't call her healthy—people who tell me *I* snore should listen to her. If the real Tinker Bell had sounded like that, Peter Pan would have smothered her with a marshmallow.

I stumble to the kitchen and find that there's no coffee, only tea. Fine. I put the kettle on, then turn on the small TV on the counter. Nothing, just a blank blue screen. Lems must have disabled the cable system, or maybe they're disrupting broadcasts. I wonder how long the power will stay on.

I do my best not to think about Charlie. I focus on the hangover instead, concentrating on how bad my body feels as opposed to my heart. It works, kind of.

My turn to show up with a hot beverage and a kind word. "HEY!" I yell.

She sits bolt upright and says, "Whazza*fug*?"

"Morning, Tink. Time to rise and be shiny."

She favors me with a bleary, red-eyed expression. "I whuffa *nod*."

"Thanks for sharing," I say with a big, sunny smile. "No idea what that means, though. Here." I offer her the tea. She squints at it, more in befuddlement than suspicion. Poor girl, I forgot she masses at least twenty pounds less than I do. Guess all those Astonisher poison immunities don't extend to alcohol.

"Pardon me," she says carefully, then bolts off the couch and for the bathroom.

"Astonishing," I murmur, and take a sip of the tea myself.

She comes out a few minutes later, looking less like a plague victim and more like herself. "You," she says, "are a bad influence."

"So I've been told. We need to strategize."

"Can it wait until I reattach my head to my body? I might need it later."

"Nope. We need to find Cassius."

"Your superior."

"I wouldn't go that far. But yeah, him."

She totters into the kitchen, and I follow. She finds a glass and fills it with water from the tap.

"We're outgunned and outmanned," I say. "Or outlemmed, which is the same thing."

She takes a sip of water and makes a face. I don't blame her—I've tasted the water in Vegas. "That's what you were saying before we were attacked."

"And I'm still saying it. If we're going to go after Asher, we're going to need backup. Cassius can lay his hands on all kinds of NSA resources that could help."

"And you can't?"

"He's a general—I'm only a grunt. Well, maybe a sergeant. But I can't call down the lightning the way he can."

Azura finishes her water, pours herself another glass. "He may not be able to, either. Every military and police organization relies heavily on lems, which means they're all about to be plunged into chaos. What does he have that can counter that?"

Well, there's his membership in a secret society that pretty much runs the planet, and an ancient suit of gladiator armor powered by sunlight—but neither of those will help much at the moment, especially when I don't even know where he is.

"I'm not sure," I admit. "But Cassius is always prepared. He's someone we want onside, believe me."

Which means the first order of business is to locate him. The NSA likes to keep track of its agents, and that includes GPS emitters in their cell phones. Mine got trashed early on, but if Cassius still has his—

I stride out of the kitchen.

"Jace? What are you thinking?" Azura follows me.

I find what I'm looking for in one of the bedrooms. A laptop. I open it up and it comes to life, still online and apparently unencrypted. Excellent. I sit down and start tapping.

"Should have thought of this before," I mutter.

"What are you doing?" Azura asks.

"Contacting a friend. The lems have already killed the TV stations, and the phone system will no doubt be next. Fortunately, this is exactly the kind of situation the Internet was designed for in the first place, to enable communications during a military emergency . . . ah. Here we go."

Damon Eisfanger's wide, ruddy face fills the screen. "Jace!" he says. "Are you all right?"

"No. Where's Gretch?"

"She's a little busy—the lems have all just gone on strike. The office is at half strength and I'm here helping to fill in the gaps. Is Cassius there?"

"That's why I'm calling—I need you to find him for me. Use the GPS in his phone."

"I can do that." He starts tapping furiously at his keyboard. "Listen, Jace, things are getting really bad here. I don't know what kind of intel you have access to, but this general strike isn't the worst of it. There are protests happening in every major city in the world. Riots are starting to break out in some of the larger centers—Sao Paulo, Paris, Tokyo."

"It's going global," Azura murmurs behind me.

"Damon, listen. This is the result of a spell that's being generated here, by Asher." I hesitate, but what I know is too important to keep to myself anymore. "Damon, *Asher is Ahaseurus*. Understand?"

"We—we know, Jace." He looks deeply disturbed. "Listen, I'm not supposed to tell you this, but there's something *you* should probably—"

The screen freezes.

I try refreshing the page, and now I'm getting a message that I'm no longer online. Damn it. Looks like the lems are moving faster than I thought.

And what the hell was Damon about to tell me?

We decide that the best thing to do is have breakfast. Okay, maybe not the *best* thing—according to my stomach, not even really a *good* thing—but at least it's something we can actually accomplish. Thankfully, the people who live here are thropes and not pires, because the last thing I want to be faced with now is a fridge full of blood.

Azura opens a can of soup, and I find some oatmeal. But when I try to turn on the stove, nothing happens. At first I think the lems have finally gotten around to cutting the power, but then I notice the stove's gas, not electric. Gas is still flowing, too—it's the pilot light that's gone out. I dig through a drawer and find a pack of matches, but the damn things must be wet or something; I can't get one to do anything more than spark.

After the third one, Azura says, "Oh, no."

"These are useless. Maybe there's a lighter around here somewhere—help me look, will you?"

"Jace, do you know why I didn't take your gun with me when I posed as you?"

I've found a lighter, but I can't get it to work, either. "I wondered about that, actually."

"It's because I don't like using any weapon that relies on fire. Or even having one around, really. See, where I come from—"

"—Fyre is an actual, evil entity," I finish. "Yeah, I got that—had it drilled into my head, remember? So what?"

"So there's an enchantment in my land that prevents fire from existing there."

"Yeah, but we're not—"

I stop. I stare at her. Both of us walk over to the window and look out.

No matter where you are in Vegas, you usually have a pretty good view of the mountains. Same here.

Except these aren't the same mountains.

"I don't think we're in Vegas anymore," Azura says.

THIRTEEN

It's twilight, once more. The mountains are a lot closer and a lot taller, and the sun behind them turns them into a sharp-edged, red-tinged line of jagged black. Somewhere in those peaks is a mountain pass littered with the bones of an army of werewolves.

Or so the story goes.

"Asher's done it," Azura says. "He's pulled the entire city into Nightshadow. Which means Night's Shining Jewel is now in *your* world."

"But we're not trapped inside a myth. Are we?"

"This is no myth. This is my home."

I glance around the kitchen. "Oh? Nice microwave. That a Sears model?"

"Well, it's not *literally* my home. Clearly, physical structures have been transposed."

"But the microwave's still working. Why hasn't the electricity gone out?"

"Good question. Electricity wouldn't be bothered by the spell, but it's being generated on your world. The two must still be connected."

"No fire," I say. "That means no cars, no planes. And my gun's useless."

"We need to see exactly what's been switched over and what hasn't. Come on." She heads for the door, me right behind her.

We discover the neighborhood looks pretty much the same as it did when we first got here—streets and sidewalks lining deserted homes, with a few abandoned cars still in the driveways. It's getting darker, and the constellations overhead aren't the ones I know.

We don't see any lems or thropes, but there are plenty of were creatures wandering around, looking puzzled or nervous or just plain freaked out. A guy with the head of an elephant and a build like the Incredible Hulk is working out his frustration on a '99 Dodge, smashing his giant gray fists into the roof over and over. The car alarm screeching at him just seems to make him angrier, and we give him a wide berth; he's hammered the roof down to the level of the dashboard. A thing that looks like a cross between a rat and a ten-year-old kid darts from under a hedge and grabs handfuls of glittering safety-glass shards from the ground, stuffing them into a leather pouch around his neck.

No jets screaming by, but that doesn't mean the skies are empty; I see large, winged shapes outlined overhead, some of them clearly large birds, some of them—much higher, mostly—the triangular shape of hang gliders.

"Looks like a few tourists got sucked in here beside us," I say, pointing them out to Azura.

"Those aren't tourists, they're Lyrastoi," she says. "Nightgliders from the Royal Keep. No doubt trying to figure out what's going on, and what to tell the king."

We also see more than one underdead, blank-eyed zombies with grayish skin, usually just standing in one place and staring straight ahead. They look like robots that are waiting to be told what to do.

The one thing we don't see are human beings—or, as

Azura calls them, trues. Every were has shifted into half-
or full-animal form out of panic, and more than a few
seem to be stampeding for the city limits. We try to stay
out of their way—being trampled to death by a herd of
fleeing were boars is not how I want to be remembered.

We make it down to Las Vegas Boulevard, the Strip.
The skyline looks the same, but the streets are full of
empty vehicles, wild animals, and confused zombies. It
looks like some sort of apocalyptic movie being filmed
where the director suddenly had a nervous breakdown
and none of the actors knows what to do next.

Including us. "Why are we even here?" I ask Azura as
we watch a half girl, half gazelle clear an SUV in a single
leap. "We're not architecture."

"I don't know," she says. "But both of us jumped from
our respective worlds to the one we just left via magic.
We may have been ejected the same way."

Makes sense—as much as anything does, at the moment. Ahaseurus is the one who brought me across the dimensional divide in the first place, so I guess he might be
able to kick me out as well.

Azura doesn't seem bothered by the zombies at all,
brushing past them like they're not even there; me, I'm a
little more worried about being turned into cerebellum
sushi.

"Hey," I say. "These underdead—what exactly do they
eat?"

She looks at me like I've just asked her why chocolate
is a good thing. "They're not alive, Jace. They don't *eat*
anything." She pauses. "Well, that's not strictly true. They
do transfer entropy from themselves to organic sources—
plant matter, mostly. In essence, the organic matter de-
cays instead of their own body. It's sometimes called
feeding, though in truth the process is actually one of ex-
cretion."

"They make other things rot," I say. "That's not really an improvement over eating brains."

"Not as such, no. But don't worry—they don't attack people."

We discover the buildings that had been turned into spell sites have been returned to normal, which Azura seems to think is a bad thing. "The spell is complete," she mutters, watching a large hawk swoop through the shattered glass doors of the Paris casino.

"This is where we sent Tair and Cassius," I say. "If the myth is no longer running, then where is he?"

She doesn't answer, but the look on her face tells me more than enough. Spells, like any mechanism, require energy to power them—and that energy all too often comes from the souls of living beings.

"You think he was—what, *eaten* by the spell?"

"It's possible."

"But he's a *pire*! He's not even *alive*!"

"There were no doubt many pires caught in the spell, as well as thropes and the underdead. You don't need to draw breath to have a soul, Jace."

Cassius, dead? I don't believe it. He's too damn slippery to let himself be caught and killed that easily. If Tair could escape from the myth, so could he.

It's much more likely that Tair sold him out, which means he's probably in Silver Blue's hands. But if the whole city's been sucked into another dimension, where would the arms dealer have wound up?

We haven't seen any trues, which means they were probably all transported to Nevada along with the city of Night's Shining Jewel. Silver Blue's human, so he's probably in NSJ as well. In fact, I might be the only person in Vegas right now—besides Azura—who even knows what a slot machine is, unless Tair managed to somehow come along for the ride. I'm still unclear on how exactly thropes and pires fit into all this—I haven't seen either one on the street, which could mean that both inhabitants and buildings have been swapped. Presumably, there are a bunch of dazed tourists wandering around the mossy streets of NSJ and wondering where all the neon went.

"We've been sidelined," I say. "No offense to your place of birth, Azura, but I think all the action's happening in the place we just got kicked out of."

"Which means there's a good chance your boss is here, as well," she points out. "Asher will want to keep any potential trouble as far away as possible."

"We've got to get back."

"Agreed. But I can't do that on my own—which means paying a visit to *my* employers. The Lyrastoi."

I glance up at the nightgliders still circling far overhead; it's dark enough now that I can barely make out the tiny triangles. "Think we can get a lift?"

"No. I'll have to make my way overland, to the Royal Keep—if I can get a ride on a were stag or something similar, I should be back within a day."

"Wait a minute. You're not taking me?"

She shakes her head. "Sorry, but you'd just slow me down. Best if I find you a safe haven here and have you wait."

"But—"

"You'll be fine. Trues are treated well here, and if you have any trouble you can contact one of the were-hawks for assistance; they're members of the City Guard, charged with keeping the peace. Fellow lawmen, in other words."

Sure, if a renegade zombie decides he'd like to broaden his diet and turn me into a rotting corpse, I'll just wave to the friendly cops flying overhead and they'll swoop down and save me. I'm sure they'll take the side of a complete stranger who doesn't understand the language, the culture, or any of the rules.

"Here," Azura says, fishing what looks like a large seed from her pocket. "Swallow this. It'll let you speak the local language—each of the were tribes has its own dialect, but there's a common tongue that's used in the city."

I take it hesitantly. "It's not going to sprout roots in my lower intestine, is it?"

"No, that would cause it to be digested much too quickly." She doesn't elaborate, and I decide I'm better off not knowing. I stick it in my pocket and hope I won't need it.

Then we go looking for a safe hidey-hole for Jace Valchek, intrepid criminal profiler and special agent in charge of twiddling her thumbs, to sit around and do nothing.

Yeah, like that's going to happen.

We eventually decide on a casino for me to hole up in, because they're reasonably familiar territory to me and largely being avoided by the locals. That'll change, I'm sure.

I pick Wonderland, a casino and hotel based on Alice's adventures—I guess pires have a certain fascination with mirrors that don't behave like they're supposed to, and thropes do love their rabbit. According to a sign next to the blackjack tables, their buffet features over twenty bunny dishes—from hasenpfeffer to March Hare Macaroni.

I'm not interested in food at the moment, though. What I need to do is find a counting room or security office that I can get into and then lock behind me. That shouldn't be too difficult, right?

Wrong. Maybe on my world—the one with guns, nuclear bombs, and *Buffy the Vampire Slayer* reruns—but this particular version of Vegas was built by shamans as well as gangsters. Every door I might want to hide behind seems to be already locked, with magic as well as steel.

"I thought you were good at this," I say as Azura fiddles with another door.

"I am. But there's a big difference between a jailhouse lock and something protecting a big stack of cash. I can break this, but it'll take me an hour—and it won't be much good afterward."

I sigh. "Maybe I should just grab a cardkey from the front desk and use a room. At least then I'll have hot water."

"Until everything in the storage tanks cools off."

"I'm not planning on being here that long."

In the end, that's what we decide on doing. I'm tempted to go for one of the high-roller suites, but I don't want to be that high up in case the power dies. I choose a room on the third floor—high enough that random looters won't stumble across me right away, and close enough to the ground to be able to leave in a hurry.

We raid the kitchen for supplies—there's food in pots and ovens that's still hot, which is more than a little unnerving. Azura loads up on fried chicken, bread, and a jug of water, while I stick to fresh fruits and vegetables and a tray of sushi I find on a counter. It's only half made, so it must be fresh.

"Stay inside," Azura says. "Once the shock wears off, there'll be looters aplenty. They won't care about money, but something like this—" She holds up a long, gleaming butcher knife. "—is worth a king's ransom. We've no fire and thus no steel—every blade we have is either imported, obsidian, or hardened with underdead magic." I've noticed her speech seems more formal since we've gotten here; it's like her native accent is returning because she's home.

"I'll be careful."

"See that you do. Your gun won't work, and the criminal element here is just as dangerous as any large city."

"Yes, Mom."

"I'll be back as soon as I can."

And with that, she's gone. I grab my supplies and head upstairs.

Ah, Las Vegas. City of endless possibility, decadent hedonism, seductive abandon. What to do, what to do . . .

I eat crackers in bed.

They're good crackers, don't get me wrong. But I eat them alone, with only the TV remote for entertainment. Not the TV itself; it's showing nothing but blue movies, and by that I mean a screen of solid blue. The only channel I can find that still seems to be functioning is the one you use to check out of your room automatically. I watch that for a while, but the plot's kind of predictable. I wash down the translation seed with some water for desert— might as well be prepared.

I find myself thinking about Charlie.

And that's just not something I'm ready to deal with yet, so I think about raiding the minibar. But I'm far too vulnerable—in more ways than one—to get drunk by myself, so that's not an option. Besides, the little binge Azura and I indulged in has left me feeling less than eager for any more booze.

I peek out the window through a crack in the drapes at the street below. There's a pack of what look like spider monkeys wearing bandoliers exploring a Winnebago in the parking lot; it's a little unsettling when one of them morphs into a full-size naked man, apparently to better pry open the sunroof.

But there's more than just spider monkeys out there.

Thropes get bigger when they transform, so I've seen large and hairy plenty of times before. But I never thought about what that would mean for something like, say, a lion . . .

The pride strolls down the center of the boulevard in

half-were form like a street gang daring someone to stop them. There are seven in all, five females and two males, and I notice three things right away: first, that the females are clearly in charge; second, that any of these were-lions could bite a thrope's head off in one chomp; and third, that the males have obviously spent a *lot* of time fussing over their manes. Little braids dangling beneath the ears, streaks of red or blue dyed in, highly polished bones artfully woven into carefully brushed fur at jaunty angles; some cultural traits just seem universal.

The females are highly alert, their bodies in a semicrouch as they pad along on two feet. The males are more or less in the center, much more relaxed, their long pink tongues lolling out of their mouths like dogs on a hot day—

Suddenly I don't feel so good.

I lurch back from the window and sit down heavily on the bed. My head's spinning and my stomach's trying to copy it. Maybe that sushi was sitting out longer than I thought—

No. This feels familiar, and I know why.

When I first got here—here being the world Cassius and Ahaseurus yanked me into, not the one I'm currently trapped in—I came down with a syndrome called RDT: Reality Dislocation Trauma. Symptoms included nausea, headache, hallucinations, and fainting spells; basically, I was allergic to being in an unfamiliar universe and my body was trying to reject it.

Dr. Pete gave me an herbal remedy called Urthbone, and after a few months the symptoms disappeared and he pronounced me acclimated enough to stop taking it.

Now it seems my symptoms are back. I shouldn't really be surprised; this *is* a different reality, after all, and apparently I don't travel too well. If Azura were here she might be able to help—it seems like the type of problem she'd know something about—but I'm on my own.

Did I mention that the condition can be fatal?

No reason to panic, I tell myself. RDT takes a while to progress—when I went off my meds in a misguided attempt to eliminate certain side effects, I lasted at least a week before I started to hallucinate. I've only been here for a few hours.

I lie down and close my eyes. Slowly, the feeling subsides. When I'm sure it's gone, I open my eyes again. There. Perfectly normal, nothing to worry about.

For some reason, though, I can't get the image of that male were-lion out of my head. It bothers me, in a way that goes beyond simple fear of a large carnivore. It reminds me of—

Jace.

I hear the voice quite clearly. It's coming from between my ears, and it's not mine; I'm intimately familiar with how I sound inside my own head, and that's not *my* overly verbose brain that just spoke up.

It's Cassius.

"Uh . . . speaking?" I say. I have a sudden conviction he's going to ask me if I'm satisfied with my current long-distance provider.

Jace. Stop thinking about phone companies.

Sure, thanks a lot. Now that's *all* I can think about—

JACE.

Ow. Okay, okay. *That really you, Caligula?*

Yes, it's me. I'm using a telepathy charm. It won't last long, so pay attention.

I'm all ears. Brains. Whatever.

I'm sorry I didn't make it back to the meeting place. I wasn't able to escape the myth on the first go-round, though I sensed that Tair did. Did he come back?

Well, what do you know—tall, dark, and shaggy was telling the truth. *Yeah, he did. We didn't have long to chat, though—Stoker's mercenaries showed up with their tails between their legs, wanting to buddy up so they could make it out of Vegas in one piece. Good plan, bad execution—Charlie was right behind them. He made kind of a mess when he crashed the party.*

Anyone survive?

I wonder how much of my grief is leaking into my thoughts. *Azura, Tair, and me. Charlie . . . didn't.*

We need to meet, Jace. Right away.

I don't know what stuns me more, the coldness of his reply or the forcefulness that comes after. He sounds almost desperate.

Where? I ask.

High ground. I'm at the top of the Eiffel. Come NOW.

The last word isn't so much a shout as a command, as if he could somehow yank me there through sheer willpower. I've never heard Cassius sound like that before—but then again, I've never been in the man's head before. Or was he in mine?

Either way, the whole experience is over as suddenly as it started—I can't hear him, and I assume he can't hear me. I mean, I *hope* he can't hear me; a telepathic boss is one of my worst nightmares. He did say the effect wouldn't last long, but with Cassius you never know just how much of the truth he's telling.

Doesn't matter. I wanted to find him, and now he's found.

All I have to do now is figure out a way to get to the top of the Eiffel Tower . . .

The real Eiffel Tower in Paris, France, is just over eighty stories tall and made out of eleven thousand tons of steel. The one in Vegas is five-eighths scale, around 450 feet tall, and right next door to the Wonderland. The enormous steel girders of its base begin inside the casino itself, curving up and through the ceiling; to me it looks like the aftermath of an absinthe binge by a French architect with an industrial teleporter.

The real tower has a swimming pool between its giant legs. This one has a restaurant on the eleventh floor and an elevator that goes all the way up to a viewing platform on the top—except that the elevator is currently locked down and I don't have the security codes to bypass it.

Which means I take the stairs.

For a thrope or a pire, loping up forty-five or so floors is no big deal. For a merely human NSA agent—who keeps in shape, thank you very much—it's more of a deal. Not big, exactly, certainly not humongous, but edging from medium-size into the somewhat larger-than-normal variety.

I have plenty of time on the way up to think about why he chose this particular place to rendezvous. "High ground" was the way he put it, and that makes a certain amount of sense. It's probably fairly easy to defend from any attack but one from above, which limits potential hostiles to were birds and Lyrastoi—unless there's some other flying species I'm not aware of.

I slow down and take a breather when I'm five floors away, so I'm not out of breath when I show up. Vanity, I know, but Cassius always looks like he just spent an hour in front of a mirror with a team of personal stylists and I don't want to show up wheezing like an old car—

"Hello, Jace," a voice whispers from the stairs above me.

I freeze. It takes me a second to realize that the voice belongs to Cassius, because I don't think I've ever heard him whisper before. Or if he has, it didn't sound like *that*.

"Came down to meet me, huh?" I say. "Thanks, but I don't think the last few flights would have killed me—"

"Wanted to make sure you were alone," he says. I can't

see him clearly; he's standing above me and behind a beam. "I'll see you up there."

I don't hear him leave—no footsteps echoing through the stairwell, no sound at all but the wind blowing through the open beams of the structure—but when I round the corner, he's not there. I keep going.

I don't see him when I get to the top, not at first. I look around the deserted platform, see nothing but a closed tourist kiosk and the central column the elevator rides up in. The platform's glassed to shut out the wind, but I can still hear it battering against the structure, trying to get in.

"Cassius?" I say. "Where are you?"

"Over here." His voice comes from beside the elevator column. I start walking toward it.

"Stop," he snaps. Uh-oh.

"What's wrong? You don't trust me?"

"That's not it."

"Oh, I get it. You think maybe I'm Azura, playing one of her shapeshifter games. Well, let me clear that up right now . . . the very first time we met, I shot you. Okay?"

"Could just be an educated guess. You pretty much do that to most people."

His voice still doesn't sound right. Maybe I'm the one who should be checking IDs. "Yeah? Where did I shoot you, exactly?"

"In my office. Or the face, take your pick."

Yeah, it's him. "Are you all right?" I take a few more quick steps forward, rounding the corner so I can actually see him.

What I see is something of a shock. He's crouched on one of the steel girders overhead, and he's bare-chested. I've never seen Cassius without a tie, let alone topless;

he's not nearly as pale as I would have imagined a centuries-old pire to be.

What's even more disturbing is the look on his face. Cassius usually swings between radiating absolute authority or boyish, disarming charm; what I see now is a lot more primitive, something just below the surface barely being restrained. Anger?

"Hey," I say. "You Cassius, me Jace. I've heard of people losing their shirt in Vegas before, but I never thought I'd actually *see* it—"

"I ran into one of the locals."

"Guess they don't like Armani."

"Brooks Brothers."

"Ah. And you're up in the rafters because?"

"Tactically sound."

"Of course. Are you coming down, or is there a pigeon you suspect—"

"Shut *up*!"

Now, *that* shocks me. Cassius may be older than paper, he may be a supernatural blood-drinking creature of the night, he may run one of the most ruthless and efficient intelligence agencies in the world—but he's not rude. That would imply a lack of both control and judgment that he outgrew a few centuries ago—and a Cassius that's out of control scares me to the basement of my soul.

"I don't have the *time* for this," he spits out.

"Sure, I hear that from a lot of immortals." I regret saying it as soon as it escapes my mouth, but some reflexes are hard to suppress.

"This place. This *place*," he hisses. "I can't—I can't *think*. It's getting into my blood, Jace—into my *blood*."

You don't ever, ever want to hear a hemovore say *blood* the way Cassius just said it. It makes my heart stutter and my stomach clench and my breathing stop dead for a moment. It's kind of like hearing Hannibal Lector say, "A nice Chianti."

He leaps down, landing in a crouch and staying there. That must have been one hell of a scrap he got into, because he's missing his socks and shoes, too.

"When you say, 'this place,' I'm guessing you're not talking about the half-size Eiffel, right?" I keep my tone light, because I'm really not sure exactly what will happen if things get serious. Cassius is acting like a junkie who took the wrong drug and doesn't know how to handle it.

"It's the aging spell, Jace. It has to be." He keeps his head down, not looking at me. "It's interacting with whatever kind of magic permeates this place."

I get it. Cassius has been in a state of arrested development for hundreds if not thousands of years—but since he agreed to share the time-debt for Gretchen's child, that clock has been restarted. It's kicked his hormones back into gear, but other than a slight case of acne he was fine—until he came to Azura's homeland.

"I think I know what's happening to you," I say. "This place has some kind of root system beneath it that channels energy. It's got enough mojo to turn a walking stick into a walking Palace of Versailles, so I'm guessing it could definitely supercharge a pire's metabolism."

"Root system. That makes sense. The farther away I got from the ground, the more in control I felt."

If this is what he's like now, I'm glad I didn't run into him downstairs. "Look, you've got to stay up here, at least for now. The sun never makes it above the mountains in this place, so you don't have to worry about being flash-fried. But you can't walk the streets in your condition."

"I know. But I . . ."

"I'll get you whatever you need, okay?"

"I need . . ."

Oh, boy. Here it comes.

He straightens up, looks me in the eye. His eyes are blood red, and his incisors way too prominent.

"I need a hug," he says.

FOURTEEN

I stare at him. I blink. "I don't think that's such a good idea," I say, resisting the urge to turn around and run. "Not really office-appropriate."

He doesn't argue, just closes his eyes. Concentrates so hard I can see his body shaking. His fangs recede, and when he opens his eyes again they look normal. "I understand," he says. His voice sounds more exhausted than feral. "I'm sorry, I just—"

"No, I'm sorry," I say. I feel ashamed of myself for what I was thinking. This is David Cassius, not some newly turned Lugosi with a dollar-store cape and a head full of B-movies. If he seriously wanted to chow down on me, I never would have made it to the top of the stairs. "I trust you, okay?"

And then I just step forward and wrap my arms around him.

It's like hugging a statue, at first. His skin is cold, his muscles rigid. But I'm just as stubborn at hugging as I am at everything else, and I refuse to let go.

Slowly, gradually, his body relaxes. His hands touch my back, ever so lightly. If he were human, I'd be able to feel his breath on my neck—but he's not. He's an ancient being in a dangerous profession who's kept himself intact by evaluating every situation for its strategic value. Despite all that, he keeps on falling for humans—not because they're the practical choice, but because he can't help himself. We embody everything he's given up, and a man like Cassius hates surrendering anything.

He's not addicted to blood, he's addicted to life. And he hates admitting that he needs anything, let alone anyone.

"You can hold me tighter," I whisper. "I'm not going to break."

"I could snap your spine without even trying," he whispers back. He sounds more sad than threatening.

Everybody needs to be held sometime. By a friend, by a lover, by a parent—it doesn't really matter. It reconnects us, reminds us that we're not alone in this world. Someone like Cassius needs it worse than most, because it's not something he knows how to ask for; it took a spell, another dimension, and a sub-basement full of enchanted roots to get him this far, and I'll be damned if I'm going to let him down.

Basement. Roots. Down . . .

A wave of dizziness hits me, and for a second I think the whole tower's developed a serious case of tilt. My knees go a little wobbly, and I kind of sag. Cassius notices and keeps me upright, but he pulls back and looks me in the face. "Are you all right?"

I shake my head, trying to throw it off. "I'm fine. Just a little—woozy, I guess. It's not you, it hit me before."

"Of course." The formality is back in his tone, and I can sense him shifting back into Official Government Agent mode. I can almost hear the steel shutters slamming down inside his head—

"Thank you," he says softly. He looks me in the eye when he says it, and there are no shutters behind his eyes; they're wide open.

"Anytime, Caligula." I hate the joky tone in my voice, but I guess he's braver than I am. "Hey, we're standing on top of the Eiffel Tower and you're not wearing a shirt. Where's that damn photographer I bribed?"

"Probably been eaten by the were-grizzly I ran into earlier." He drops his arms, steps back. "Seemed disappointed I wasn't edible."

"So he ate your shoes? And socks?"

"No, I got rid of those myself. It was . . . an impulse."

"Well, sometimes you have to listen to those."

He smiles. "Yes. I suppose you do."

"I'm probably going to regret asking this, but are you . . . hungry?"

"I'm fine, Jace. I can go for days without blood."

"As a normal pire, yeah. But you're aging now, remember? Your engine's going to need more fuel." And I'm a little worried about what happens when the gauge hits EMPTY, too.

"I'll order takeout."

"Right. Stay here—I'll go find you something."

"Don't you mean someone? I don't think there are a lot of corner stores around here, Jace."

True. But there are pires, kind of—what do the Lyrastoi do at suppertime? If Azura were here I could ask her, but she isn't. She's not here, and neither is—neither is—

"I killed Charlie," I say. My voice sounds strange.

Cassius stares at me. I stare back.

And just like that I'm the one that needs to be held, because all I can see is that spray of sand as the bullet hits, I remember exactly how that felt against my skin, the impact of every tiny grain of Charlie's life . . . and then Cassius has his arms wrapped around me again as I bawl my eyes out and try to explain between sobs.

Everybody needs to be held, sometimes.

* * *

"You did what you had to do," Cassius tells me, over and over. "This isn't just another case, Jace. We're at war."

He's right, but I still hate it. And myself. And even Charlie, for putting me in that position in the first place.

But not a fraction as much as I hate Ahaseurus.

When I'm coherent again, I tell Cassius everything that's happened since he and Tair left. He pays close attention, but his body language's kind of jittery; he's obviously still having a hard time holding himself together.

"All right," he says. "Azura's gone, and we can't count on her coming back."

"I think she will. This is her home turf—she's got the resources and connections—"

"Jace," he snaps. "We can't trust her. She's got her own agenda, and she's the agent of a foreign power. We don't know what these people want, or what their allegiances are; they could be hammering out a treaty with Asher himself right now. Time is *not* on our side."

"Then what do you suggest? You have some NSA gadget in your pocket that'll yank us back home? No, you don't, because as you've told me many times before, interdimensional travel is major sorcery."

"You have to go," he mutters. "You can't stay here, Jace. It's not safe."

He's not just talking about the location; his eyes are looking redder all the time. "I'll go, but I'm coming back. I'll bring you a nice juicy rabbit or something."

"No. Just—wait for Azura to come back, then come get me. If I need . . . *sustenance* badly enough, I'll go find something."

"That's not much of a plan. In fact, it's probably the worst plan I've ever heard; it edges out the top spot previously held by 'Let's wait around and do nothing,' by the clever addition of 'Let's *split up,* wait around, and do nothing.' "

"You have a better idea?"

I sigh. "We jump off this tower in a doomed but futile attempt at a double suicide?"

"Take the stairs."

I'm halfway down when I realize I've forgotten to ask Cassius about what he experienced inside the myth he and Tair visited. I'm debating whether or not to go back up when the dizziness hits again, and this time there's a smell that goes with it. A rich, earthy smell, with something rotten underneath.

The dizziness gets worse, and I change my mind about talking to Cassius; going down doesn't have much appeal, but going up seems impossible. By the time I get to the bottom of the stairs, the world seems like it's gone sideways and I'm going to fall off.

I make it back inside the Wonderland and halfway across the gaming floor when my vision grays out and the floor smacks me across the face. The last thing I hear is the chime and ping of all the slot machines, lulling me into unconsciousness with promises of instant wealth, burbling sweet electronic nothings into my ear . . .

I look at the pictures spread out in front of me on the conference table. Agent Krisfell waits for my reaction; he's trying to see if I'll throw up or blurt out My God! *or maybe try to stonewall, pretend they don't affect me. I haven't been with the Bureau that long and this is my first really big case, so I'm an unknown quantity that he needs to evaluate, and fast.*

"I heard he was a trophy taker," I say after studying them for a moment. "Unusual choice, but it tells us quite a bit. He's been around strong women a lot, most likely his mother. Emotional abuse is more likely than physical. He lives in a house with a yard."

"Why do you say that?" Agent Krisfell is short, black, and completely bald. His voice is soft and smooth, like a DJ's. He's the first FBI agent I've met who has a manicure.

"Look at those cuts. Crisp, clean, with a slight curve to them. They were made by pruning shears. That means he's most likely a gardener, which means a yard. Childhood abuse is common in cases like this—and his choices indicate a desire to control certain aspects of his victims."

"Aspects embodied by his mother."

I shrug. "That's what I would say. If it were his father, he'd be killing men."

Krisfell nods. I suspect I haven't told him anything he doesn't already know, but hopefully I haven't missed anything obvious, either.

I hold myself together for the rest of the interview. That night I drink most of a bottle of scotch to get to sleep, and I wake up screaming at 3:00 AM.

Which is exactly how I wake up now.

It's not a proud moment, but those pictures . . . they got to me on a level I didn't want to admit, not to Krisfell, not to anyone. Not even to myself.

I get to my feet, still kind of shaky. When I had RDT before, it came with hallucinations of my ex, Roger, who seemed to be standing in for my subconscious and warning me not to trust anyone. This was different, more like actually reliving a memory than just recalling it.

This isn't RDT. It's the curse Ahaseurus threatened to lay on me, the one that's going to make me go through the worst moments of my life over and over again. The good news is, it probably won't kill me—it'll just make me wish I were dead.

And here I thought I was going to be bored.

Back to the third floor. If I'm going to lose my mind, I'm going to do it in private, preferably with a drink in

one hand and my feet up. I can stare out the window at
the wildlife and see how many subspecies I can identify—
bonus points for spotting anything truly bizarre. I'm hoping for a were-flamingo, myself.

But when I get to my room, my plans change. I can
hear a voice inside, and it's one I instantly recognize.

Aristotle Stoker.

The first time I met Aristotle Stoker, I didn't know who
he was.

I mean, I knew who he was by reputation: descendant of
the infamous Whitechapel Vampire Killer, an Irish novel-
ist named Bram Stoker. In a world infested by actual
bloodsuckers as opposed to the fictional kind, he went a
little batty himself and wound up slashing a few undead
prostitutes to pieces with a silver-edged knife. They caught
him and hanged him, but it did drive his novel *Dracula* up
the Victorian best-seller charts—and unlike the Bram
from my world, this one had decided to procreate.

Which, a few generations later, produced Aristotle. I
guess he figured he had a legacy to live up to, because he
wound up being the most wanted pire killer in the world.

He was one of the driving forces behind the human
rights group called the Free Human Resistance, until he
faked his own death and resurfaced as an assassin known
only as the Impaler; as the name implies, he was less
focused on activism than terrorism. He was almost a
complete mystery to intelligence agencies, with no photo
or even accurate description of him existing. Some professionals even believed he had to be a composite identity,
a fiction invented by the FHR to instill fear in the supernatural population.

There's no doubt he did exactly that. But he turned out
to be very real, very dangerous . . . and more than a little
crazy.

I take out my *eskrima* sticks and ease the scythe blades out quietly. Stoker stands about six foot ten, all of it muscle, and he's made a career out of killing beings stronger, faster, and more durable than he is. I don't know how he found me, but I need to take down both him *and* Ahaseurus in order to go home.

The last time I had the chance to kill him I didn't take it. This time I won't make that mistake—but who is he talking to?

I listen carefully for a minute, then shake my head and reholster my scythes. I open the door.

Stoker isn't in my room. He's on my TV.

Pretty sure I didn't leave the set on, but I doubt someone broke in, turned on my TV, then left again. More than likely it's some kind of spell, turning on sets all over the city in hopes of getting my attention. If I hadn't been so spaced out from my little abduction to Memory Lane, I probably would have noticed noise coming from other rooms on my floor.

The message ends, then starts over again.

"Hello, Jace," Stoker says. He's sitting, arms in front of him on a table. Some kind of white sheet in the background, probably hung over a window. He's wearing a buttondown white shirt, open at the collar. Simple, nonthreatening. His hair is a little shorter than the last time I saw him, but other than that he looks the same: broad, handsome face, eyes alert and intelligent under a heavy brow. "If you're watching this and you're not alone, you should know that only human eyes and ears can perceive this. Everybody else will be getting a recorded news update that's six hours old. Pay attention, okay?

"I'd rather talk to you face-to-face, but I don't know where in the city you're hiding. That's probably a good thing—but you need to think about your next move really hard."

He leans forward and clasps his hands together. There's no sense of scale in the image, nothing to compare those hands with, but I know he could pick up a bald midget by the skull while eating a sandwich. Him, not the midget.

"You're a smart woman, but even a smart woman can make bad choices if she has bad information. I'm sure you already have a pretty good idea what's happening, but there are a few things you need to be clear on.

"Asher's making a global power play. First Vegas, then Nevada, then the rest of the country, and finally the world. Basic strategy for any coup d'état: Control the army and you control the government. Asher controls the golems—because, believe it or not, he's the one who *wrote* the spell that created them in the first place.

"And he's one of us, Jace. Human. He doesn't want to slaughter pires or wipe out thropes—he just wants a world that human beings can live in without fear. A world that belongs to *us* again, instead of them."

He leans back, smiling ever so slightly. "You know, even though you're not here, I can still hear your response. *Oh, yeah? So now the human race is what, the landlords of the planet? Hey, sorry, I know Australia has a leaky basement but I can't send a plumber until Tuesday.* Or something like that, but more sarcastic.

"Look, I know you have no reason to trust me. The last time we talked—well, I wasn't exactly sane. I admit that, all right? The kind of magic I was exposing myself to, it affects your mind. I see now just how crazy my plan was, even though it made perfect sense at the time."

He shakes his head. "I'm not crazy anymore, Jace. I don't want to destroy the world or kill all the supernaturals. You and I should be working together—or you're going to wind up in the same position I used to be in. Leading a resistance against an occupying force, hunted by every law enforcement agency on the planet, forced to commit horrifying acts just to get your point across. That's . . . that's a terrible way to live, Jace. I know."

I'm sure he does. But the alternative seems even worse—taking the side of a world-conquering dictator who's just turned the remnants of the human population into the world's ultimate aristocracy. No way I could sign up to enforce that kind of status quo.

Yeah, you're a real rebel, my brain whispers. *Look how long it took you to accept a paycheck to hunt your own kind on a world where they're almost extinct.*

"Asher has both his and my people hunting you," Stoker continues. "You're probably wondering why he seems so obsessed with you. It's because of your counterpart—the Jace Valchek of my world. It's why you were targeted in the first place, why Asher brought you over. That's all I can tell you for now, but believe me—you want me on your side in this. I can protect you; Asher needs me, needs my connections in the human community."

He holds up a piece of paper with a number on it. "Call me as soon as you get this. I can only broadcast for a limited time—Asher's occupied at the moment, but I can't risk him seeing this. I'm taking a huge risk as it is."

He stares at me from the screen. "Please, Jace. I'm trying to save your life."

The message stutters for a second, then starts all over again. I pick up the remote and shut the TV off. "Help me, Obi-Wan Kenobi—you're my only hope," I mutter.

When I first arrived in thrope-pire-lem world—let's just call it Thropirelem for brevity's sake—I quickly came to detest magic. Magic is a detective's worst enemy; it breaks all the rules you need to rely on, it's contradictory and unreliable and frequently makes no damn sense whatsoever. However, over time, I've come to a grudging acceptance of the situation.

My new favorite concept to hate is the multiverse.

Parallel worlds, alternate realities, whatever you call them, it all boils down to the idea that there are other universes that exist right alongside our own. Each of these places is similar to the ones beside it, but the farther away from the original universe you get, the more differences there are. I started in my own, got yanked to Thropirelem, then wound up in Nightshadow.

And how many of these worlds are there, you ask? Three, four, a dozen, a hundred? Well, according to what my übergeek friend Eisfanger tells me, they're infinite. An all-you-can-eat cosmic buffet and salad bar, come back as often as you like. That is, if you've got the megapowered cross-universe mojo needed to hop from one to the other.

Which, apparently, my good buddy and interdimensional stalker Ahaseurus aka Asher does. And what's he using this power for, aside from overthrowing a planet here and there?

To grab me. Not even because of who I am, but because of who I could have been. Or was. Or might be. Or am, but not exactly.

You see why I hate this? Not only is it confusing, it makes me feel like a cheap bootleg of a more successful product. "I'm sorry, we couldn't get the real Jane Velsheck Action Figure in, but this Jace Valchek doll is almost as good. Look, you can twist her head right off."

What I don't know is what Asher wants with me, or what his relationship with my alternate is. Or was. They could be lovers, enemies, partners . . . I just don't know. She could be alive or dead—maybe he's got a whole dungeon full of them and just wants me to complete his set. It's always hard to track down that last variant edition.

I flop down on the bed and throw an arm over my eyes. I'm trapped in an alien dimension—a *different* one, hooray!—my gun's a paperweight, my boss is doing an impromptu version of the Phantom of the Eiffel Tower, my one ally can't decide if she's James Bond, Harry Houdini, or Stripperella, I put a bullet in my own partner . . . and I could be overwhelmed by the waking equivalent of night terrors at any point. Oh, and the psycho killer I'm supposed to put away would really, really like to friend me. Sorry, I mean the *two* psycho killers; I'm such a popular girl.

I just lie there until I fall asleep. Maybe if I'm lucky something will break down the door in the middle of the night and eat me.

No such luck. What I get is a knock at my door at Too Early o'clock.

"Jace Valchek?" a deep voice calls out.

"No housekeeping," I mutter. "Sleeping."

Then reality seeps in and I sit bolt upright. Geez, I didn't even get my shoes off before I passed out; I know waking up in Vegas is supposed to be a little disorienting, but this is ridiculous.

"Who's there?" I call out.

"My name is Dariek Nightstorm. I come at the behest of Azura of the Hidden Clan."

Well, that certainly sounds official. I stick my eye up to the peephole and hope I don't get an icepick through it. The man on the other side must be a Lyrastoi—he's tall, thin, and pale, with jet-black hair and pointed ears; I know Lugosis who would kill for his bone structure. He has a pale gray cloak draped over his shoulders, and it looks like it's the only thing he's wearing that's not made of leather—black boots and pants, a jacket of deep purple with white bone buttons.

I open the door. He enters cautiously, eyeing me like a

cat edging around a dog. "Gather your things. We must leave this place, and quickly."

"But checkout time isn't until noon," I say. This gets a blank stare, which is about what I was expecting. "Where's Azura?"

"She is waiting at our destination. Can you ride?"

I don't think he's asking about a bike. "As long as it's something resembling a horse, I think I can manage." I grab the few things not already in my knapsack and stuff them inside. "Where are we going?"

"Somewhere you'll be safe."

"Really? That'll be new. Listen, there's a stop we have to make first."

"I was not told about any stop." His tone lets me know he doesn't like the idea. I don't much care.

"I'm telling you now. My superior, David Cassius, needs to come with us. He's on top of that giant metal tower you passed on the way in."

"I cannot guarantee your safety should we do this—"

"Do I look like I want a guarantee?" I snap. "You can wait at the bottom if you can't hack the climb. Or did you bring the kind of ride that does stairs, too?"

He gives me a cold glare. "I brought steeds for two. Your superior will have to find his own transportation."

"Come on, let's take this argument on the road," I say, heading for the door. He's forced to follow me.

"You are being hunted," Nightstorm says. "Even now, there are groups conducting an organized search of the new buildings. We cannot tarry—"

"No tarrying, check," I say. "Try to keep up, I'm in kind of a hurry."

That last comment either confuses him or pisses him off enough to make him shut up, which is good. I desperately want some coffee and know I'm not going to get any—how the hell would I heat the water? There's probably bottles of iced coffee lurking somewhere in the bowels of this place, but I don't have time to look.

Outside the casino, two hostile-looking guys are waiting in the twilight. I can tell at a glance exactly what kind of were creature they are, because every inch of their skin— bare except for a little strategically placed pouch—is covered in alternating black-and-white stripes. Also, they have these six-inch-high mohawks that go all the way down the backs of their necks.

"No saddles, of course," I say. "Terrific. Bareback it is."

"I am Windrunner," says the first one. "This is Trailbreaker. He will carry you."

"Not just yet, he won't." The entrance to the tower is just steps away; I head straight for it. "Wait here—I'll be right back."

They don't, though—all three trot along after me. "We were instructed to keep you safe," Trailbreaker says. "We shall accompany you."

"Fine," I say. "Uh—try to hang back once we get near the top, will you? My boss might think I'm bringing him lunch."

But when we get to the top, Cassius isn't there.

"Damn it," I say. No note, no sign of a struggle— though it might be hard to tell if one *had* happened. Pires don't bleed as a rule, and there isn't any furniture to be knocked over. The tourist kiosk is still in one piece, but that doesn't mean much, either.

"He may have been taken by the same forces searching for you," Nightstorm says. "Which means—"

"I know, I know. Time to go." As much as I hate doing it, I'll have to leave Cassius on his own; I can't even risk a note, because there's no telling who might find it.

When we reach the base of the tower, the two zebra

weres transform. I've seen plenty of thropes do that, but there's a difference when the end result is three hundred pounds of hoofed stripes. It takes longer, for one thing, and there's a lot of snorting that goes on at the same time. The little pouch, in case you're wondering, winds up around the neck.

Trailbreaker looks at me with big black eyes and twitches his head in a gesture that clearly means *Jump on!* Well, okay . . .

Nightstorm does the same with Windrunner, and it's happy trails for us.

The trails might be happy, but after the first half hour my tail definitely isn't.

Ahaseurus clearly doesn't have NSJ under his control the way he does Vegas; there aren't any lem patrols, just the occasional underdead wandering around. The other weres seem to have all cleared out—though we still see were hawks circling overhead, and at one point a band of what look like giant weasels with hands scurry across the road in front of us.

It's obvious when we get to the edge of the trans-planted area: On one side there's a run-down motel with a car on blocks in the parking lot, and on the other, jungle.

Not like any jungle I've ever seen, though. The under-growth is thick and tall and lush, but it isn't made of plants; in a land with no direct sunlight, the only thing that flour-ishes is fungus. Not tiny little toadstools, either: There are mushrooms as tall as palm trees, with brilliant red under-sides and blue streaks down their stalks; there are 'shrooms shaped like reefs of bright orange coral, like bells, like fuzzy brown brains; there are delicate, feathery molds that sway like grass in the breeze, bright white puffballs the size of dinosaur eggs, spiky-looking mounds tufted with crimson strands.

"Wow," I say. "My butt hurts."

The zebra-man I'm riding on lets out a long, complicated whinny, the meaning of which is probably along the lines of, *You think your butt's sore? My back's killing me.*

There's a path cut through the jungle, wide enough for two riders side by side. "This is Edenheart," Nightstorm says. "We're going into it, but not far." He gallops off down the trail without waiting for my reply, and I follow. Well, Trailbreaker follows—I just hang on to his mane and try not to embarrass myself.

After ten minutes or so, we turn off the main trail onto a mostly overgrown and much smaller track. It leads us deeper into the jungle, ending at last in a small cluster of huts, most of them falling apart. The place appears to be deserted.

Nightstorm stops and dismounts, Windrunner shifting back into human form. I manage to get off my ride's back without falling on my face, but it's still not exactly graceful.

"Where are we?" I ask.

"This is Sporedrift," Nightstorm answers. "Once a way station for travelers, but long abandoned." He strides directly toward the one hut that still seems relatively intact, with a door made of spindly white twigs lashed together—dried mushroom stalks, I guess. He stops in front of the door, mutters a few words under his breath, and taps it lightly, twice. It swings open and he enters.

Both Trailbreaker and Windrunner motion for me to follow, so I do. Inside the hut, Nightstorm is clearing aside a pile of the same kind of twigs in the middle of the floor. I pitch in and give him a hand.

At the bottom of the pile is a trapdoor, with a heavy wooden ring set into a square of carved wood. The wood

has a strange, swirly grain to it; I suspect it didn't start
life as a tree.

Nightstorm produces a small, transparent globe on a
thin leather strap from his cloak. He taps it a few times
and whispers something to it, and suddenly the globe is
alive with fireflies, shining with a flickering but bright
light. He hands it to me. "Put this around your neck."

As I put it on, he grabs the ring and pulls it open. A
rich, earthy smell drifts out—

*"Wait for the forensics team," Krisfell tells me. I nod, too
shaken to speak. He pulls away, Crown Vic spraying
gravel from the tires. I wonder if he'll get to the hospital
in time, or if our suspect will bleed out in the backseat. I
can't say I care much either way.*

*I walk around the side of the house and look at the
cellar doors for a long, long time. They're the kind that
are set into the ground at a steep angle, with either steps
or a ladder on the other side. They're old, cracked white
paint over splintery boards, held together with rusty
nails.*

*It's not locked. I have the search warrant in my pocket.
No one else is in there—no one alive, anyway. I should
wait for the forensics team.*

*I pull the doors open, one at a time, and let them bang
all the way to either side. I take out my flashlight and
climb down the short ladder.*

*The walls and floor are made of dirt. There's a water
heater in the corner on a concrete pad, next to a furnace.
Black metal pipes crisscross the ceiling, suspended from
dusty rafters by strips of tin.*

*A mound of fresh dirt is piled up in one corner, with a
gardening trowel stuck in it.*

I approach it slowly. There's an ancient set of wooden

shelves against the wall on the other side, stacked with dusty mason jars that look like they've been there since the Civil War. Preserves: jam, pickles, fruit. Now they're just something for spiders to string webs between.

The air is rich and moist, that kind of heavy dampness that makes you feel like every inch of skin you own is sticky. And now I smell the odor of decay underneath it, the smell of something rotting just below the surface. Bodies give off all sorts of gases as they decompose, and they're a lot harder to cover up than you might think; they'll even seep through solid concrete.

There's a galvanized steel bucket standing beside the mound, half full of dirt. Nothing like a little compost spread around the garden.

Out of the eight women in the area who've gone missing, we've only found two bodies. I think I know where the others are—or most of them, anyway . . .

I come back to myself just as suddenly as I left, except now I'm lying flat on my back with Nightstorm hovering over me. At least I didn't scream this time. I hope.

"You have been cursed?" Nightstorm asks. His voice is matter-of-fact, as if he'd just asked how long I'd had that head cold.

"So it seems," I say, pushing myself to my feet. "Sorry. Smell kicked it off."

"Memory inducement," Nightstorm says. "Scent is the usual trigger. I would advise plugging your nostrils, but that's only a temporary solution; it will find another way to activate."

"Thanks for the advice. Any idea how I get rid of it?"

"Several. Do you have access to the Book of Aether, the left lung of an Eldritch Bogg, or a jar of distilled Lethe water?"

"Not so much."

"Then your prognosis is grim. Shall we go?" He motions to the dark opening in the floor.

"Sure. But if I pass out again, you may wind up carrying me."

"The curse will not manifest again so soon. And if it does, then carry you I shall."

Even though I'm the one with the light, he goes first. I have a hunch that Lyrastoi do pretty well in the dark.

We climb down a ladder about twenty or so feet, through a dirt tunnel shored up with boards. It widens out a little at the bottom, with three different tunnels branching out from that point.

We take the tunnel to the right. "These are smugglers' tunnels," he says as we walk along. "Many of the denizens of Nightshadow are weres with a predisposition for living underground: were-badgers, were-voles, were-ferrets. Not all of them are criminals, but a large number seem to have a fascination with shiny trinkets they don't necessarily own. There is an intricate system of passages that runs beneath both Night's Shining Jewel and, to a lesser extent, the Edenheart Jungle. They are constantly being modified to frustrate the efforts of the authorities, with new tunnels being added and old ones collapsed. Traps are always a hazard."

"Thanks for taking the lead."

"The route we're taking has recently been cleared. Stay close and stay alert, all the same."

Walking along behind him, I notice something for the first time: What I thought was a little batwing-shaped collar is in fact two tiny, vestigial batwings growing from the base of his neck. I wonder if his genetic heritage includes sonar, too.

"So you're a Lyrastoi, huh?" I say. "I learned a little about you when I was trapped in a myth-spell. Your species basically runs this place, right?"

"We are the noble class, yes. It is our responsibility to keep the denizens of Nightshadow safe from harm and govern benevolently."

"Which includes keeping the place fire-free?"

"Among other things. There are many tribes that live here, both herbivores and carnivores; before the Lyrastoi imposed order, tribal warfare was constant. It still occurs, but now there are treaties in place that prevent a great deal of bloodshed."

"Yeah, I can just imagine what happens when a tribe of werecoyotes moves in next door to a bunch of were-rabbits."

"It is not as one-sided as you might think. A hunter will only kill as much as he needs to survive, but tribes of plant-eaters are more likely to wipe out packs of carnivores from fear—and when both sides are armed, that's more than possible. We have a saying here: A poisoned arrow has no stomach."

"Poison. You supernatural types seem to have a real fondness for it."

"Poison means something different to weres; perhaps *impurity* would be a better word to use. They do not tip their darts or arrows with the sap of noxious plants—they use their own blood."

I thought about that for a second. Lycanthropy can be transmitted through a bite, a scratch, or genetics—but a blood transfusion works, too. "So what happens when a were-lion gets a dose of were-gazelle, or vice versa?"

"The same thing that happens when a true of one blood type is given the blood of one with another. The essential natures of the two beings are incompatible, and a war is waged within the body. The battlefield rarely survives—and when it does, the infected host is usually deformed, insane, or both."

So a wolf could be assassinated by sheep's blood. I

think about making a Silencer of the Lambs joke, but de-cide to keep it to myself. It's kind of strained, and not a cultural reference Nightstorm is likely to get anyway.

Also, note to self: Don't get scratched, bitten, or cut here, by *anything*.

FIFTEEN

It's hard to tell how far underground we are, but judging from the slant of the floor and the richness of the dirt around us, I don't think we've gone that deep. There are bugs of various sizes and degrees of creepiness scuttling on the walls and the occasional puddle of water on the floor, all of which suggests the surface is not far away.

We've been traveling for ten minutes or so when there's a flicker of light from around a bend in the tunnel. When we round the corner, I see that the tunnel empties out into a small room, with a dirt floor and what look like wicker chairs around a crude table. The table holds a larger version of the globe around my neck, and seated on the other side of it is Azura.

"Well, well," I say. "If it isn't the Mistress of Disguise and Sudden Exits. How was your vacation?"

"Nice to see you, too," she says with a grin. "My trip was most productive, though I've not slept since I saw you last. Sit, please."

I take a seat across from her, Nightstorm grabbing the chair to the left. She's got some kind of papyrus scrolls laid out in front of her, covered with symbols I don't understand; guess the translator seed I swallowed doesn't do print. Oh, well, it's a dying medium anyway.

"How are you, Jace?" she asks gently.

"Peachy. What did your bosses say?"

"She has a memory inducement curse upon her," Nightstorm says. "She underwent an attack while I was with her."

"Hey," I say, vaguely offended. "That's none of her damn business—"

"How long did it last?" she asks the Lyrastoi.

"Two, three minutes."

"Ah." Azura looks thoughtful. "Serious, then. I thought as much."

"Never mind that," I say. "What are we going to do about Asher?"

"I've consulted with the king," Azura says. "We agree that the only way to deal with Asher is to confront him here. On your adopted world, he has an army and all of its resources; here, we do."

"So we lure him here. How?"

"By disrupting the source of his power." She rolls up the topmost scroll and puts it aside. Beneath it is another, with a large, roughly circular diagram on it.

"This is a map of the stormstalk roots that run beneath Night's Shining Jewel. The stormstalks were planted by the Lyrastoi centuries ago; they are as much rock as plant, rooted in the granite cliffs of the Clawrock Mountains. They take their sustenance from lightning, drawing it from the storms that hover around the peaks.

"The stormstalks use a process called sorcerosynthesis to transform the lightning into living energy, pure life force; it is this force that flows down the roots like water from a melting ice cap."

I study the map, tracing the lines that snake down from

the mountains. "Tributaries of energy, flowing together like the headwaters of a river."

"Yes. They come together at these points," she says, tapping the map. "Forming seven main lines that run fairly close to the surface. All of them angle sharply downward here, near the center of the city; they converge in a central root bundle deep below the earth, one anchored to the very bedrock of Nightshadow itself. It is this root bundle that generates the enchantment that prevents Fyre from existing here, powered by the living energy delivered by the stormstalks."

"That's why the city is where it is, right?" I say. "Just like most cities spring up on a river. Only your river carries mystic energy instead of water."

"Yes. We use the energy of the stormstalk system for many things; any enchantment cast in the city has a natural, abundant source to draw on."

"A source," says Nightstorm, "that has now been stolen."

"That's not quite accurate," Azura says. "While it's true that the root bundle has been physically transported to Jace's world, its power continues to flow across the dimensional divide, in both directions."

"For how long?" Nightstorm snaps. "He needs the power from the stormstalks, but for his own ends. Already our shamans say the anti-Fyre enchantment weakens. Soon enough it will break altogether."

"But therein lies his weakness," Azura says. "We can disrupt the flow of energy across the divide. Ahaseurus cannot risk his own enchantment being interfered with; the myth-spell he wove allowed him to transpose the cities, but it is the power of the root bundle that allows him to control the golems."

"You suggest we cut our own throats?" Nightstorm says. "The better to drown our enemy in our very blood?"

"It's not that bad a strategy," I say. "He's going to cut

you off sooner or later, anyway. Do it yourself now, and you deprive him of options while increasing your own. How feasible is it to block the flow of energy? Can't you just sever the roots?"

"It's not that simple," Azura says. "Severing the roots would be like cutting open a pipeline. Life force would continue to flow, in much the same direction—it would simply diffuse more into the surrounding environment."

"Flooding Vegas with magic," I murmur. I wonder how Penn and Teller would feel about that. Probably thrilled, if they weren't stuck in a prehistoric city overrun by rogue golems. "But a flood is still better than nothing. The more magic draining into the landscape, the less there is for him to tap into, right?"

"True," Nightstorm admits. "But the price—Fyre will surely notice—"

"Let's deal with the problems we have right now," I snap. "I don't know how big and bad this Fyre thing is, but he's not currently trying to take over an entire civilization, is he? No? Then stop whining about maybe getting your fingers burned and *focus*."

Nightstorm glares at me—I get the feeling he isn't used to anyone speaking to him like that. I glare back.

"She's right," Azura says. "It's our only chance. The king and I have already come up with a plan." She taps the map with a finger. "We're going to dig tunnels between each of the seven points, or modify ones that already exist. A Lyrastoi sorcerer will be stationed next to each root. All the roots will be severed simultaneously, and the sorcerers will each attempt to direct the flow of magic down the tunnels to the right. If it works, the flow will form a circle; it will still inevitably swirl toward the center, but we will attempt to force it *up* instead of down."

"Creating a gigantic magic hurricane," I say. "Yeah, no way that can end badly."

"The danger is enormous," she says quietly. "But it is our only hope. The sorcerers will try to keep it contained, but should it break free—"

"We'll all end up wearing ruby slippers and talking to Munchkins," I say. I see the looks on their faces and sigh. "Never mind. It'll be bad, I get it. Can things be put back together afterward?"

"The sorcerers will try to sever the roots at the dimensional border itself. If we can return the cities to their proper worlds, the flow should resume its normal course with minimal effort."

"Great. A little interdimensional plumbing and problem solved. Now all we have to do is figure out how to take down Ahaseurus himself when he shows up in a towel bellowing about how his shower isn't working. With an army of killer golems behind him."

"There goes my weekend," Azura says.

So it's back to the original mission: take down the big A. Except this time, instead of an elite NSA strike team, I've got an Astonisher, a were-bat, and a bad case of flashback-itis. Oh, and supposedly a whole Magic Kingdom as backup, but I'll believe that when I see it. Most of them will probably be busy digging, anyway.

One other important thing has changed, too. The best weapon to go into any fight with is information—about your weapons, about the battlefield, and most of all, about your opponent. When I first got to Vegas I didn't know that much about Ahaseurus—but as it turns out, Azura knows a lot more.

"Ahaseurus is the name he used when he first traveled to your world," she tells me. We're sitting alone in the underground room, the zebra-men and Nightstorm on their way back to report to the king. "The world in which you live now, I mean. He did so because the Hidden Clan had banished him forever."

"The Hidden Clan—that's your organization of Astonishers, right?"

"Yes. Ahaseurus wanted to create an empire, with Nightshadow as its capital. He was conducting experiments on underdead subjects to transform them into unstoppable soldiers; the experiments used surgery to bond inorganic materials to the subjects in order to make them resistant to injury from weapons or sunlight. Underdead turn to stone when exposed to the rays of the Poisoned Star."

"I remember. Nightshadow Mythology 101."

"Ahaseurus had been regarded as one of the most powerful of the Hidden Clan. He was said to be charismatic, brilliant, persuasive, and filled with unlimited ambition. He was also said to be cold, impulsive, cruel, prone to sudden rages and many lovers. In his youth he courted notoriety with his study of Fyre, even going so far as to create a room within Nightshadow itself where Fyre could exist—in a tiny, much-weakened form, of course, but it was still the cause of much controversy. He claimed we could learn more by talking to evil than merely studying it from afar."

"Classic rationalization," I murmured. "What was he like when he was a kid?"

"He began life as a true, as we all do. His village—"

"Wait—everybody here starts out human?"

"Yes. Even the Lyrastoi. Most children born to a particular tribe of weres will choose to join that tribe when they become adults—but not all do. Some join other tribes, or remain trues."

"Why?" I ask. "No offense—I'm a true myself, after all—but it seems like this world offers a lot of inducements to go furry or fangy, and not a lot to stay as you are."

"There are several reasons, actually. One is the chance to become a sourceling; they are the trues the Lyrastoi use to feed themselves. To be a sourceling is many a young woman's most treasured dream; they live as the Lyrastoi do, wealthy and pampered and given only the very best food, drink, and clothes. Their lives are a swirl of elaborate parties, entertaining games, and even intellectual stimulation; study hard enough and one day your reward will be immortality, for that's also how the Lyrastoi replenish their own numbers. I wanted to be one myself, as a child."

"What happened?"

"I grew up." She sighs. "Only trues can be sourcelings—but the same holds for Astonishers. I chose the second path—and while it may hold more thorns, it allows me to do more than be an aristocrat's spoiled cow while waiting to give up daylight."

"I thought you didn't have that here."

"Not in Nightshadow itself, no. But there are lands beyond the Clawrocks, and I have been to many of them. The life of an Astonisher holds many opportunities."

I see the look in her eyes, that combination of weary acceptance and fierce pride, and for the first time I really see who she is; that cheerful I-believe-in-fairies persona is no more real than my sarcastic armor, though it serves the same purpose. She's not a striptease bimbo playing at being a secret agent, she's an intelligence operative who's willing to do whatever it takes to get the job done.

"You were telling me about Ahaseurus's childhood," I say.

"Yes. He was born to a small tribe of were-rats, on the northern edge of the Cemetery Sea. When he first applied to the Astonishers' Guild—that's the precursor to the Hidden Clan—he claimed to be from a long-lost tribe of were-panthers. That was eventually disproved, but it didn't disqualify him from membership; deception is our stock-in-trade, after all."

"Self-aggrandizing claims," I murmur. "These were-rats—you said they lived near an ocean? Were they fishers?"

"Primarily, yes. But they hunted other game, as well."

"Was Ahaseurus a hunter?"

"Yes. He bragged about his prowess often. His tribe usually hunted in groups—"

"But he liked to hunt alone, right?"

Azura gives me a puzzled look. "How did you know?"

"He wasn't hunting for the meat or fur. He was doing it because he enjoyed killing—and probably torturing—small animals. When he got older, he developed a taste for pyromania—even in a place where starting fires is almost impossible. I'm guessing he used to wet his burrow or whatever he slept in, too."

"I don't understand."

I shake my head. "You've got your skills, I've got mine. You may be an Astonisher, but I'm a profiler. And a damn good one."

"What does a profiler do? Portraiture?"

"In a way. I analyze how criminals think in order to predict their actions."

She frowns. "That would be obvious, would it not? A criminal will commit a crime—hardly a relevation."

"Yeah, but I try to figure out which crime he'll commit next. As well as important details like where he's living or working or drinking, what he drives, what his habits are."

Azura shakes her head. "Forgive me for saying so—but that seems like a great deal of trouble to catch a common thief."

"I don't catch thieves, Azura. I catch serial killers."

"Serial killer—I've come across the term while I was

in your reality, but never bothered finding out what it meant. I certainly understand what a killer is, but what does *cereal* have to do with it?"

It takes me a second to realize she's not just yanking my chain. What's happened to Azura is the same thing that happened to me all the time when I first got to Thropirelem: I'd trip over some little detail that was obvious to the natives, but not to me. "A serial killer is someone who kills over and over, often raping or torturing the victim first, often with a great deal of rage. Usually targets strangers, frequently takes trophies, derives a great deal of pleasure or satisfaction in the act. The word *serial* in this context means 'pertaining to a series.'"

I let her digest that for a moment. It doesn't shock her, but it does bother her. "And this is a profession that you've chosen, hunting down these killers. Meaning there are others who work in the same field."

"Yes. Hundreds of them, if not thousands."

"I am no stranger to murder, Jace. I have seen people killed for food, for sex, for revenge, or for personal gain. Now and then someone kills because they have lost the ability to reason. But what you describe—to visit such intimate horrors on a complete stranger, and then *repeat* that act, on *another* complete stranger—" She shakes her head. "And there are enough of these monsters in your world that an entire field of study is dedicated to catching them?"

"Not just catching them. Treating them, studying them, imprisoning or executing them. Writing books, TV series, movies about them. As much as we hate and fear them, they're a big part of our culture."

"With all that attention, surely such a creature would give himself away before very long."

"Not always. Some of them do it for years, even decades, before they're caught. They hide in plain sight, pretending to be normal—but they're not. Their minds are broken, usually in a very specific way, and I'm trained to figure out which way that is. And then use that information to track them down and stop them."

She nods. "I understand. Most people think that being an Astonisher is all about skill—that one must have finely developed coordination, reflexes, and speed in order to do what we do. But that is only part of it. An Astonisher must learn to *think* differently; to redirect our audience's attention to where we wish it to be. *That* is why we are advisers to royalty, not because of childish tricks we can play with scarves or cards."

Yeah. We're an odd partnership—Azura's job is to fool the public, while mine is to reveal the truth. And the truth is, I'm starting to see a pretty familiar pattern. "There are three traits that often turn up in the childhood of a serial killer, known as the Macdonald triad: setting fires, abusing animals, and bed-wetting. Ahaseurus has demonstrated the first one and most likely practiced the second. Understand, it's not these behaviors that *cause* the disease; they're just symptoms of something much worse, usually abuse. A child in pain looks for an outlet—fouling his bed, setting a fire, or tormenting a living creature with even less power than himself are what usually manifest."

"But that's in *your* world, Jace. Here, things are very different."

"Granted—his lone hunting and obsession with fire might be more about his culture than damage to his psyche. But I'm seeing other aspects that fit, too: his empire-building plans, the inhuman experiments, the promiscuity, the compelling but mercurial personality. To me he sounds like a textbook case of malignant narcissism: no conscience, pathological need to accumulate power, inflated sense of his own worth. His impulse control is no doubt poor, but he's obviously smart enough to have constructed an elaborate facade that he shows the rest of the world, one that lets him hide his real persona."

"He's a sorcerer intent on conquering an entire world, Jace. Are you saying that underneath that, he's even *worse*?"

"*Much* worse. Malignant narcissism has been called 'the quintessence of evil'; those who have it essentially build up their own low self-esteem by destroying others, and experience pleasure by doing so. They become addicted to the experience, and just like any addict, they need a bigger and bigger dose to get off. Many psychopaths wind up self-destructing; the malignant narcissist can function well enough to perfect his disguise even while his crimes escalate."

I've taken off the globe-light that Nightstorm gave me, and Azura's playing with it as we speak. She rolls it from knuckle to knuckle on the back of her hand, the fireflies inside swirling around like living bits of light. She's not really paying attention to what she's doing; even though it requires superb muscle control, to her it's obviously as mindless as tapping a pencil on a desk.

The room suddenly feels dark and cramped, the air thick and close. I don't usually suffer from claustrophobia, but I have the overwhelming urge to feel fresh air on my face. I stand up abruptly, fighting a surge of panic.

"Jace?"

No dizziness this time. One second I'm here, and then I'm *there*.

I squat beside the mound of dirt in the basement, but don't touch anything. A distant part of my mind is pleading with me: Don't look up, *it begs.* Just don't look up.

But no matter how real this all seems, it's just a memory. A piece of the past, projecting frame after inevitable frame on the screen inside my head. Knowing what comes next won't stop it.

I look up. The second-from-the-bottom shelf is level with my eyes. The jar right in front of me isn't nearly as dusty as the others, and I can see what's floating in there quite distinctly. I don't recognize them, though, not immediately; taken out of context, they're just lumpy, vaguely familiar objects.

But then something inside my head shifts, changing my perspective. Changing it forever.

In the jar is a human tongue. And two lips.

This time I regain awareness in the middle of a panic attack: heart pounding, hyperventilating, impending feeling of doom squeezing my chest and throat and brain. I'm lying on my back on the dirt, which makes it worse; the feel of the damp earth on my skin is almost unbearable. I shriek and sit bolt upright, but Azura grabs me by the shoulders before I can get to my feet.

"Jace!" she shouts. And I mean, really *shouts*—it's enough to make my ears ring. I jerk in surprise, and shoot her an angry look.

"What?" I snap. It works, though—kind of like an auditory slap. My heart's still going a mile a minute and I'm gasping like a fish on a dock, but I know where and when I am.

"Sorry," Azura says. "Memory attack?"

"Yeah." I focus on getting my breathing under control. "Old case. Bad one. I'm—I'm okay."

She lets go of my shoulders, then helps me get to my feet. She's surprisingly strong for such a small woman. I'm only upright for a few seconds when the dizziness hits, but there's no way I'm going to lean on the dirt wall for support.

"I've got to do something about this," I say. "I can't have this happening out in the field. I'll get someone killed."

"Probably you," Azura says. "Well, we can't have that. We'll have to fix you."

"You can do that? I asked Nightstorm, but he was less than optimistic."

She rolls her eyes. "All Lyrastoi fancy themselves wizards, but only a few really have the knack. Trues make the best mages—it's one of the reasons all Astonishers are human. Nightstorm himself probably couldn't pull it off—well, not unless he had a lung from an Eldritch Bogg or the Book of Aether handy, and those aren't exactly items you can pick up in the marketplace—but he's not the one that's going to cure you. You are."

"I am?"

"With a little assistance from me. Trues may not be able to change shape or resist injury on their own, but we do have an affinity for mystical forces—and that includes a built-in resistance to magic attacks, a natural immune system. Most people simply don't know how to access it."

"And you do, of course."

"It's the very first thing they teach us. Still dizzy?"

"No, I think I'm all right now."

"Good. Follow me."

She leads me out of the room, down one tunnel and up another. We end up facing a bare earthen wall in the middle of a tunnel, one that turns out to have a cleverly concealed entrance to another room in it. Azura pushes aside a piece of cloth that a moment ago I would have sworn was made of dirt and leads me inside.

It's larger than the room we were in, one wall lined with wooden barrels. There's a long, deep tub set into in the center of the floor.

"Where are we?"

"This is a ritual center. See those barrels? Filled with water from the Lethe River. Powerful stuff—which is good, because we're going to need it."

"Lethe? Nightstorm said something about using that to treat my condition. It didn't sound like he had any, though—"

She sighs. "Nightstorm doesn't know nearly as much as he thinks he does." She walks over to the farthest barrel and opens a stopcock. Warm, steamy water gushes from a pipe, then flows down a narrow channel in the floor and into the tub.

"Hot water?" I say. "I thought you didn't have fire."

"We don't. But we do have hot springs—geothermal heat is what keeps Nightshadow a tropical environment."

"So, a hot bath is going to cure me?"

"No, it's going to provide the proper support for you to cure yourself." She pauses. "It's not going to be pleasant, Jace. There's only one way to beat nightmares, and that's with a stick."

"I've got one of those. Two, actually."

"Good. You'll need them."

"You know, the last time I let you talk me into an aquatic environment, you tried to drown me."

"It was for your own good."

"So's this."

"I won't try to drown you."

"Can you remove the qualifier, please?"

She sighs. "I *won't* drown you, okay? Neither will the water. Or the lack of air in your lungs. Are those promises sufficient, or shall I find some paper and compose a contract?"

I give her a hard look. She waits patiently.

"Okay, okay," I mutter. "So what exactly are we doing here?"

"You're going to soak in the water, which will help you attain a meditative state. I'll be maintaining physical contact, my hands on your head. I'll guide you through some imagery."

"Is this an exorcism or a spa treatment?"

She smiles. "The memory curse will try to take you to a place where you feel lost, afraid, alone. We're going to subvert that—just like Ahaseurus detoured you at the myth site, we're going to send you to a different place."

"Please don't say 'a happy place.' I'll wind up drunk and half naked in Amarillo."

"Oh, you'll be completely naked. Take your clothes off." She kneels at the head of the tub and tests the water, seems satisfied. "But this isn't about relaxation or euphoria. It's about *fighting back*."

I kick off my shoes, skin out of my clothes. Azura seats herself cross-legged at the head of the tub.

"You're still going to recall an unpleasant memory, Jace, and it'll be connected to the other flashbacks you've been having. But you won't be helpless in this one; you'll be in a place of power. And most important, it won't have the same inevitability that a memory holds, because you'll have a powerful mystic resource counteracting that: the Lethe water. It'll make your memories malleable—you'll be able to act, to change things."

I step into the steaming water carefully. Nice and hot, just how I like it. "Change things how?"

"That's up to you. Just let your feelings guide you."

"Great. Throw in a few scented candles and some chanting and we can write the whole thing off as a religious retreat."

I sink into the water, which feels really, really good. Azura links her fingers together and cradles my skull as I lie back.

Despite the wisecracks, I'm actually scared. No cure is 100 percent, and I'm messing around with my mind here. What if Azura keels over from a heart attack halfway through? Am I going to be trapped inside my own memories forever, wandering through my history like a ghost in a maze? Add a trail of anti-psychotic medication for me to gobble along the way and I can rebrand myself as Ms. Pac-Man.

I close my eyes, trying to relax. "Breathe through your mouth. Keep your breathing deep and even," Azura says. "Focus on who you are, what you are. There's a stubborn little knot at the center of your being; feel it, know that it's you. Wrap your fist around it, hold it as tightly as you hold your weapon. Feel its power."

And I do. It's exactly like she's describing, a little knot. I clench my own fists as I try to grab it with my mind, hold it as tightly as I can.

"Now close your mouth. Inhale deeply through your nose. Smell, the dark, rich earth of the soil all around you . . ."

That's all it takes. The world spins away beneath me, swirling like water down a drain. But this time I have something to hold on to: myself.

I open my eyes. Seated across from me is a man in an orange prison jumpsuit, with long, greasy brown hair spilling down the sides of his head. He's bald on top, with a pinkish scar that starts at the top of his forehead and disappears into his hairline. It's where I shot him.

"Agent Valchek," he says. He's got one of those soft, butter-wouldn't-melt-in-my-mouth southern accents. "How nice to see you."

His name is Gibby Reddinger. He killed at least eight women and used them to fertilize his roses. He also cut off their lips and tongues and pickled them.

"Mr. Reddinger," I say. I open the file folder lying in front of me on the table. "I'd like to ask you a few questions about an open case."

Gibby smiles at me with prison-dentist teeth. "I'll do my best to help."

This is the man who gave me nightmares for years. I'm

not here because of a case—the case is bullshit, it's just fishing for information on a missing woman that Gibby probably had nothing to do with. But I volunteered to conduct the interview, because I was tired of drinking myself to sleep and needed to do *something*.

Something else, I mean. My first attempt to deal with Gibby hadn't gone that well.

"I'm investigating the disappearance of this woman," I say, pushing a photo toward him. He picks it up, studies it. He's not in restraints; despite his crimes, he's not classified as being high-risk to commit violence. He's been nothing but cooperative since we caught him.

Since *I* caught him.

"She does look familiar," he admits. Which is prison lingo for *I'm wasting your time because I have so much of it myself.* He raises his hand to his scar and winces, ever so slightly. "I'm sorry, Agent Valchek—ever since I was shot, my memory's been a little spotty."

Ever since I shot you, you mean. Ever since that bullet creased your skull and put you in a coma for three weeks, ever since you woke up handcuffed to a hospital bed and asked for a lawyer. Ever since you used that as an excuse to plead diminished capacity and claim you didn't remember all the horrifying things you'd done.

"Her name is Kendall Corliss," I say. My voice is worse than emotionless; it's actually polite. Personalities like Gibby's respond better to courtesy than they do threats. "Please try to remember."

"Mmm." He leans back in his chair, frowning in what I'm supposed to believe is concentration. Maybe it is, but if so, then what he's trying to think of is how long he can draw this out and whether or not he can get something out of it.

He winces again, running his middle finger lightly over the scar in a way that's almost obscene. "Yes, yes, Kendall.

Kendall Corliss. I'm sure I know that name, I most certainly do. My injury is acting up a little, though; it does that, makes it hard to think."

This is the point where I'm supposed to offer him something. Something to soothe his pain, so his poor, muddled brain can come up with the answers I'm looking for. I remember the little dance we went through well, how I dangled the possibility of conjugal visits with his celebrity-stalker girlfriend or maybe even early parole, while he tried to sound sincere and figure out how far he could con me.

I remember it all too well—even though it hasn't happened yet. Because here I am, with Gibby sitting right in front of me; it's happening right *now*. And even though I know every lying word that's about to come out of his mouth, I also know something else.

I know I'm sick of it.

"—I think a nice cup of tea would help me think," I say, at exactly the same moment he does. He stops and stares at me, puzzled.

"You know what would help *me* think?" I ask him. "Getting you out of my head."

"Have you been thinking about me, Agent Valchek?" he asks with a little smile.

"I have. I don't like to admit that, not to anyone—and especially not to you. But it's the truth."

His smile gets wider. "Do tell."

"I switched weapons because of you. Maybe I went a little overboard, but I didn't want to risk bouncing another slug off some deviant's skull. If I'd been carrying the Ruger instead of the Glock, you'd be the one underground right now."

"You'll catch more flies with honey than vinegar, Agent—"

"I can't believe I held back with you."

"I wouldn't call shooting someone in the head holding back—"

"Not then. Now. This interview, right here. I was actually *polite*. Me. I told myself I was working you, playing on your ego, but that was more lies. Truth is, I'm *afraid* of you, Gibby."

He stares at me, smiling but not saying anything. What I've just told him is every psychopath's dream come true: The cop who caught him has just admitted he has power over her.

"Everybody has their buttons," I say. "You hit mine. What you did to those women—cutting off their lips, their tongues—you were taking away their ability to criticize you, mock you, reject you. You took away their power."

"That's right," he says softly. "Took yours away, too, didn't I?"

"Yeah. You did. You shut me up. *And I let you.*"

"Well, that's—"

"Shut the fuck up. I'm talking."

I knock the files onto the floor with a sweep of my hand. "You sad, broken little man. You're more scared than I am—that's why you killed those women in the first place. They were strong, smart, and mouthy. Just like me."

"I'm not afraid of you." He gets to his feet. There's not a lot to do in prison but work out, and he's got the build. "I can kill you just as easy as any of those whores—"

I stand up. "No. You can't."

Tables in prison interview rooms are bolted down. He doesn't let that stop him; he grabs the edge and flips it to the right, tearing it right out of the floor.

Good. It was in my way.

SIXTEEN

I put the heel of my foot in his belly with a side-kick. He doubles up, all the air going out of him with a *whoosh*. I straighten him back out with an uppercut, using my elbow instead of my fist. He staggers backward, blood pouring from his nose.

Then I really go to work.

This isn't a fight, not really. This is me letting go of all the frustration and anger I've felt toward this piece of garbage for years. Even though it's technically not real, it feels like it is; every punch, every kick hits with as much force and fury as any scrap I've ever been in.

It's not completely one-sided, either. I guess I'm also fighting a manifestation of the curse Ahaseurus laid on me, one that's trying to drag me back into the pit of horror and fear it represents. Gibby gets in a few good punches; I'm bleeding myself before too long.

Doesn't mean he stands a chance.

How many people get a chance to do what I'm doing? Beat the crap out of a bogeyman straight from their sub-conscious? Gibby isn't just someone I tracked and caught, he's every person I ever wanted to tell off and didn't, every person who's ever scared me just by existing.

I don't know how long it goes on, but I know when it's over; Gibby lies at my feet, unmoving. I'm breathing hard, but not tired; in fact, I feel *great*.

"You know what?" I say, wiping blood off my mouth with the back of my sleeve. "You were a lousy gardener, too."

I come back to reality a little slower than I left it, all my senses fading into a gray nothing then gradually returning; I feel the warmth of the water, Azura's hands cradling my head. I open my eyes.

"Wooo," I say softly. "How long was I out?"

"About an hour," she says. Her voice sounds a little funny, kind of stuffed up. "How do you feel?"

"Exhausted. Sore. And really, really good." I sit up, taking my weight off her hands. I realize I can taste blood in my mouth. "I think I bit my lip or something, though—"

I turn around. Azura's got a crust of dried blood around her nose, lips, and chin.

"Hey, what happened to you?" I ask. "Was there a psychic backlash or something?"

"Backlash, yes. Pyschic, no." She dips her hand in the water, uses it to wipe away some of the mess on her face. "I thought I was out of range, but you've got one hell of a reach. Don't think it's broken, though."

"Sorry. Will the water help heal it?"

She looks puzzled, but it's replaced a second later by a look of comprehension. "Ah. Not really. Healing is not among its properties."

"I'm not so sure." I climb out, realize there's no towel, and decide it's warm enough to air-dry, anyway. "I feel a helluva lot better than when I got in there. A little wrinkly, maybe, but about fifty pounds lighter. That Lethe water worked just the way you said it would: I was living the memory, but I was able to change it."

She gets lithely to her feet. "I take it the outcome was more satisfactory this time?"

"Are you kidding? It was fantastic. Can we do it again? There's a pudgy little monster in the fifth grade I want to visit."

She smiles. "I'm afraid not."

It's amazing how many people give away a lie by not being able to hide that little trace of smugness that comes with getting away with something. "There's no such thing as Lethe water, is there?" I ask.

"Oh, there is. Just not here."

"This isn't a ritual center."

"It's a bathroom. In the sense of having a bath in it."

"If I didn't feel so good, I'd slug you."

"You already did."

I shake my head. "I should have known."

"You did it on your own, Jace—and yes, I lied to you, because that's what you needed to hear. Surprised?"

I stare at her, and then smile back. "No. Astonished . . ."

My initial high wears off pretty quickly, and Azura finds me a room to sleep in. I sink down onto a mattress that's probably stuffed with dried fungus, and fall asleep almost immediately.

If I have any dreams, I don't remember them.

I wake up feeling refreshed, though I'd gladly assassinate someone for a coffee. Azura showed me where the food and toilet facilities are—both about as crude as you'd expect—so I take care of my morning business first. When I'm done, I find Azura in the pantry, sitting at a round table and drinking something that smells like tea out of a carved wooden mug. The room has a high enough ceiling that it doesn't feel cramped and tapestries hung on the walls to cover the bare earth. It's almost like we're not underground.

"Sleep well?" she asks.

"Yeah, thanks. Is that—"

"Earl Grey. Not as good when you can't boil water, but passable. I picked up the habit in your world—care to join me?"

"God, would I." She pours some steaming water from a gourd into another mug, then adds a tea bag she fishes out of a leather pouch.

I rummage through a crude cupboard for food. There's no fruits or vegetables, but lots of mushrooms in various sizes and colors. Inside a wooden box with a leather-hinged lid, I find something surprising: meat, big chunks of it. It doesn't seem to be dried, salted, or smoked, but when I pick up a piece to examine it I discover it's as hard as a rock. Not cold, though.

"What's this, shank of boulder?" I ask, holding up a T-bone.

"Venison, I believe. Want some? You'd have to eat it raw, of course."

I make a face. "No thanks. You people must have teeth like diamond drills."

She laughs. "You don't eat it like that. It's got an underdead enchantment on it to prevent it from spoiling—similar to the process of refrigeration, but without the risk of freezer burn."

It makes sense. They use magic to keep themselves from decomposing, so why not do the same for food? "I'll pass, anyway. I don't eat meat, as a rule."

"Fair enough. I had you pegged as an herbivore, actually."

"Oh?" I know I shouldn't be irritated by that, but I am. "Why's that?"

"Any species can be aggressive, but it's the animals with hooves that really have the market cornered on stubbornness."

And that *should* tick me off, but doesn't. "Huh."

"Try the sporenuts in the basket—they're quite good."

I do, and she's right—they're crunchy, sweet, and just a little malty, like beer nuts if they were actually made from beer.

"So what's the plan?" I ask while I'm crunching away.

"We wait. Hopefully not for long; Nightstorm should be back before day's end. I thought I'd do a little scouting."

"I'm coming along."

She doesn't argue. "I was going to suggest it, actually. You should familiarize yourself with these tunnels, just in case."

After breakfast we head out—or deeper in, I guess. The glowing bugs in my little globe are still going strong, and I wonder what sort of magic they're charged with; maybe they're zombie fireflies. In any case, they give off enough light to let me see about ten feet ahead while we're traveling.

"We're headed back toward the edge of the city," Azura says. "I want to take a closer look at the border zone, specifically where the stormstalk roots cross it."

It takes us over an hour to get there; traveling on zebraback in a straight line is a lot quicker than making your way through tunnels that double back on themselves and are filled with hidden traps and blind alleys. Azura seems to know where all of them are, though every now and then she stops and frowns as if trying to remember something. I stick pretty close.

And then we come to the root.

It protrudes from the ceiling, about as thick as a telephone pole and a pale, creamy white that glows ever so faintly. It runs in a straight line along the roof of the tunnel like some kind of giant organic fluorescent, and gives off a hum as well; but where the noise from a bank of fluorescent lights can get on your nerves, this soothes them. I feel a strong urge to touch it, but resist.

"Is it dangerous?" I ask.

"Like electricity, you mean? Not usually. It's a power source, but the energy that flows through it is the stuff of life itself. It can power many kinds of enchantments, but direct contact is not generally harmful—though it can amplify any spells or mystic tools in your possession."

I wonder what it would do to someone who'd swallowed a magic translation seed, and decide I'd rather not find out. I could find myself speaking were-boar every time I got drunk.

We follow the tunnel right up to its end, where it dead-ends abruptly at a flat, gray wall. I tap the surface with one finger. "Concrete. This must be the foundation of a Vegas building."

Azura studies the root overhead. It melds with the concrete seamlessly, as if it had always been there. "This is the dimensional boundary. Energy is still flowing down the root—if there were any disruption, we would be able to see it."

"So this is where we dig?"

"To either side, yes. They'll lay down some sort of conductor between the roots, and when the new connection system is in place we'll sever them here, at the boundary. Cut the power and kill the spell."

It sounds like a workable plan. And of course, I'm sure that disrupting a massive magical power system is completely and totally safe.

Sure.

We go back to our little hidey-hole and do some strategizing; by the time we're done my respect for Azura has gone up a few notches. The girl's mind is *devious,* and she believes in planning ahead. I feel sorry for whoever marries her; the poor schmuck doesn't stand a chance.

And then we wait.

The work crew shows up the next morning—morning being defined under the current buried circumstances as the bleary period immediately following my waking up—and prove to be not exactly what I expect.

I grew up with a certain kind of mythology around the walking dead: mobs of rotting corpses with their guts hanging out, staggering around like frat boys on summer break and moaning, "braaaiiins!" while trying to chow down on those who still have a pulse. Big on appetite, not so much on the social graces.

So when I hear a polite knock on the door frame and pull aside the cloth that serves as a door, I don't expect to see a zombie standing there.

He's a big guy, six-four or so, muscular, with grayish skin. His hair is short, very black, and not combed. His eyes are—well, dead. His lips are black. Unlike the Hollywood undead I'm familiar with, he isn't dressed in torn funeral rags or clothes stained with the blood of his victims; he's wearing a black, toga-like thing and sandals. I know immediately what he is, because he radiates this sense of stillness that makes the most serene Buddhist monk I've ever met seem like a sugar-crazed toddler with ADD. If I was the fashion-conscious type, I'd label his look as Goth Greek.

"Hello," it says. He, I mean.

"Uh," I reply. "Hi."

He stares at me blankly. I stare back. *So that's what I look like when I first wake up,* goes through my head.

I realize after a few moments he's not going to say anything else unless prompted. "What do you want?" I ask.

"Nothing."

Well, duh. I'm going to have to be more careful about how I talk to these guys. "Why did you come to see me?"

"I'm to tell you that we have arrived. Azura is above. Follow me and I will take you to her."

"Wait here until I'm ready. All right?"

"I shall." He doesn't blink, not once. I pull the curtain shut in his face and get myself together.

"Okay," I say, emerging a few minutes later. "Let's go."

He turns and trudges down the tunnel without a word.

"You have a name?" I ask.

"Yes."

"Right. What is your name?"

"Zoran." Zoran gives off a very faint reek of decomp, but only when I get too close.

"My name's Jace. Did you come alone, or bring friends?"

"I did not come alone."

He reaches a ladder and begins climbing; I let him get a few rungs ahead before I follow. Turns out we're not that deep underground, maybe only seven or eight feet. When Zoran gets to the ladder's top, he pushes open a hatch and climbs out.

When I emerge behind him, I see what he means.

"Wow," I say. "That's a whole lot of dead folks."

We're still in the Edenheart Jungle, but it's not nearly as empty as the last time I saw daylight—filtered, dim, dusky daylight, but still brighter than fireflies in a snow globe—because apparently a morticians' convention is in town and they've unloaded all their samples right here.

Row after row of the underdead stand, unmoving, in front of me. Hard to tell how many at a glance, but at least a hundred; men, women, all of them dressed in the same simple black tunics and sandals, all of them with the same gray skin and black lips. Unlike Zoran, each of these has some sort of digging implement: usually a gourd cut in half to form a scoop, sometimes with a longer handle lashed to it. They look like the kind of work crew you might hire in the parking lot of a Home Depot in Transylvania.

Azura is over to one side, talking to a short, wide man with a bushy orange beard, a guy who's clearly not dead. He's got the biggest hands I've ever seen, with long, extremely dirty fingernails. Azura is showing him the stormstalk map she showed me, and he's nodding as she talks.

I walk over. "I see the contractors have arrived. I just hate remodeling, don't you?"

"Jace, this is Gorrick Diggur—he's going to be overseeing the operation at this site."

"Jace Valchek," I say. He doesn't offer to shake hands, for which I'm grateful. He does give me a skeptical glance, then turns his attention back to Azura.

"Aye, we can start right away. We'll be digging westward, while the team to the east approaches here. They'll finish before we do, no doubt; we've farther to go to the next one. We'll drive a few sounding posts into the ground to let them know when they're getting close."

"Good. And the new roots?"

Gorrick scratches one bushy orange eyebrow with his index finger; if he miscalculates, I'm sure he could gouge out his eye. "On their way. The king's got men stripping every piece of tapestry or fixture in the castle with a shred of dried stormstalk in it; the royal seamstresses are going to weave it all together into a braid of true hair, were fur, and any leather they figure will conduct a charge. It'll be patchy and leaky as a wineskin made from a dead porcupine, but it should get the flow going the way we want."

"And once we've established a circular pattern it should hold," Azura says. "It's the timing that'll be tricky."

Gorrick shrugs. "That's your lookout. We'll lay the pipe, but you'll have to decide when to open the valves."

"I'll let you know," Azura says. She gives him a curt

nod that signals the discussion is over, and Gorrick stomps over to the tunnel entrance. "First twenty, single file and follow me!" he bellows, then climbs inside. The underdead do so without a word, moving with nary a stagger. There's something unnerving about how compliant they are; it feels like they're just waiting for my guard to drop, and then they'll go all Romero on me.

"Here we go," Azura mutters.

There's not a lot to do after that but watch them work. Gorrick, I gather, is a were-badger, which makes him something of an expert in the field of digging. Once he gets them started, he organizes some of the others into groups, cutting down tall fungus-trees and hacking the stalks into support posts with obsidian axes.

"How long do you think it'll take?" I ask Azura.

"We hope to be finished within two days," she says. "The earth is soft, and we can work nonstop."

"Why even bother with tunneling? Couldn't you just run this makeshift cable out the tunnel and through the jungle?"

She shakes her head. "Sadly, no. We're trying to redirect powerful forces with improvised materials, and the earth will help provide a directional channel. Should we attempt this aboveground, most likely the cable would break—it probably will anyway—but without a tunnel to enclose it, it would release the energy into the open air. No one knows what that would cause, but it makes all the mages very, very nervous."

"Magically charged life force spewing into the atmosphere? Why do I get the feeling that statement should have started with, *A wizard, a zombie, and a were-goat walk into a bar?*"

"Oh, I know that one. It has that funny punch line where

a mad sorcerer takes over the world and kills both of us for fun."

"Look on the bright side, Tink—if this doesn't work, the giant mystic hurricane we're trying to create will probably kill us."

"Thanks for putting it all in perspective."

"Hey, it's what I do."

The underdead deposit the dirt they haul out of the tunnel in a pile a little way into the jungle. I wonder at first why they aren't just dumping it right beside the tunnel mouth, but after a while I understand. The pile becomes a mound, then a hill, then a foothill. Before too long the edges of it are creeping close to the tunnel mouth itself. According to Azura, Gorrick hopes to hit a tunneling speed of around 220 feet an hour, an amazing 4 feet per minute. If he can do that—barring obstacles like boulders that will have to be removed or detoured around—he can tunnel the mile or so to the next site within twenty-four hours.

Too bad he doesn't get the chance.

The attack happens in the middle of the night, when Gorrick's forces are around the three-quarters mark. Azura and I have pitched tents aboveground so we won't be in the way, and both of us are fast asleep when it happens.

I wasn't conscious when it began, so I can't accurately describe the entire event—but it's part of my job to reconstruct crime scenes in my imagination, and it must have gone something like this:

The underdead dig silently, intently. There's no swearing, no laughing, no talking; no grunts or pants or sighs. Four thousand feet of tunnel already exist, with a steady stream of workers flowing one way with empty pails and the other with full ones. At the digging face, workers put support struts in place and reinforce the walls and roof with underdead enchantments that harden the dirt into something like concrete.

Gorrick is at the digging face, supervising. He gives orders only when necessary, when the diggers encounter a large rock or unexpected water; then he instructs accordingly. He is not immediately aware when the attack occurs, because it happens at the other end of the tunnel.

A pulsing ring of energy expands from the point that the stormstalk root melds into the blank gray concrete, painting a shimmery circle on the wall. When it's as wide as the tunnel itself, at least thirty stainless-steel javelins six feet long erupt from it, turning the short passage into the barrel of a gun. The tunnel being dug is at a right angle to the wall, so only a small number of workers are disabled, but this is only the initial assault.

Golems charge out of the widened dimensional rift. They don't carry flamethrowers or nerve gas, because they know neither will be effective—but they are armed with heavy-duty bows, axes, swords, and javelins. They break into two columns, one moving down the tunnel to the right, the other advancing over the bodies between them and the exit.

By this time, the underdead that were aboveground when the javelins hit have raised the alarm. Underdead may be literal but they're not stupid—mostly—and they know what an attack means. Unfortunately, they're not prepared for war; crude digging implements don't mean a lot against stainless-steel blades and arrowheads. The golems rip them apart in a matter of minutes.

I'm reconstructing all of this in my head, because that's really all I can do. I'm blindfolded and gagged, my hands and legs are bound, and I'm locked in the back of what I think is an armored truck. We fought as hard as we could, but they took us anyway. We were slung over the backs of two soldiers and hauled through the dimensional gate, then locked up. The truck roared away immediately, no doubt on its way to deliver us to Ahaseurus. Azura's right next to me, unconscious but alive.

I think.

SEVENTEEN

Being carried over the shoulder of a golem like you were a bag of laundry is extremely uncomfortable. These golems are also wearing some kind of body armor that's all ridges and edges—well, mine is, anyway—so by the time we're hauled from the truck to the inside of a building, I'm sore in all sorts of places.

I'm placed on a chair and strapped securely to it. Before they do that, though, they remove every single stitch of clothing I'm wearing, and they don't bother untying me first; they just cut it off, like doctors in an ER prepping a patient. The very last thing they remove is my blindfold, though the gag stays in place.

I blink in the suddenly bright light and look around. I'm in some sort of office, and Azura's in the chair right next to me. She's also bound, but they've let her keep her clothes on. Figures.

I realize whose office I'm in the second before he walks around from behind me. The plaques on the wall are too far away to read, but the picture of him and the president shaking hands is kind of a giveaway.

Tom Omicron stands in front of us and crosses his arms. He's not as big as some golems, maybe a few inches shorter than Charlie, and he's wearing only a wide leather belt with multiple pouches on it over his slick plastic skin. He's filled with some sort of gray dirt, which I understand is a political statement; it's a color not normally used for lems, a mineral-based dye that has to be added after the fact. I guess he wears the belt because he couldn't find a flattering purse.

"You two," he says with a frown, "have caused us some serious problems."

I really wish I could respond to that, but the gag is making that impossible. Fortunately, Azura's willing to take up the slack.

"Good," she says. "Wouldn't have been much point in causing non-serious ones."

"You think we enjoy destroying the underdead? They're more like us than the pires or the thropes."

"Then why do it?" Azura asks.

"It's for the greater good."

"It's what your master commands."

"Not true." If she's trying to get under his skin, it's not working; Omicron sounds like a patient parent trying to explain something to an unruly child. "This is a strategic alliance between equals—one that will ultimately benefit both golems and humans. I think you're letting personal feelings cloud your judgment."

"Well, that's just how us human beings are. We get all caught up in emotions like loyalty and trust and what's that other one? The one about not letting a psychotic sorcerer overthrow the world?"

Omicron shakes his head. "I would think that of all people, you would have a different point of view. But in the end, it really doesn't matter what you think; it's up to Ahaseurus to decide what to do with you. I've asked him to be compassionate."

Gee, what does that mean? We get milk and cookies

before he chops off our heads? I glare at Omicron, but apparently he's not telepathic; he just gives me a bemused look and walks away. I hear the door shut a moment later.

I look at Azura, and she looks at me. "Well," she says. "I think we both know who the next person to walk through that door will be, and he won't be nearly as polite as Mr. Omicron. What*ever* shall we do."

I roll my eyes.

"If only they hadn't gagged you," she continues, "thereby taking away your ability to utter a spell. If only they hadn't removed any and all devices you might have secreted on your person that you might use to escape your bonds. Oh, these golems are too clever for us by half." She puts the back of her hand to her forehead dramatically. "If only—"

She looks at her freed hand in mock amazement. "If only," she says, getting to her feet, "they had mistaken one of us for the other."

She grins at me with a perfect replica of my own teeth, then undoes my gag.

"Pfah!" I spit. "I don't know what's more disturbing—the fact that I've wound up naked—*again*—or that anyone looking at me sees *your* body. I feel disguised and exposed at the same time."

"Enjoy it while you can," she says, working on my ropes. "Damn, they've got these magicked up. Going to have to cut them . . ."

She produces a knife from nowhere and starts sawing away. In another moment I'm free. "Here's your gun," she says, doing that same out-of-nowhere trick. "They took your scythes, but didn't bother with this."

"One of the advantages of having a weapon no one takes seriously. I'm surprised they didn't confiscate the knife, though."

"They would have had to find it, first. One of the advantages of looking like an NSA agent while being an Astonisher—they simply didn't look hard enough."

I stand up with a wince, rubbing my sore belly. "Well, they sure *feel* hard. And speaking of hard, being around you is *extremely* hard on my wardrobe. Do Astonishers all have some kind of clothing-repellent field they naturally generate, or is that just you?"

She takes off the black top she's wearing and hands it to me. "Here. Unless you'd prefer the pants?"

"This is fine."

"I don't know why you even care. In a moment, anyone who looks at us will see two golems—you'll be more concealed than if you were bundled head-to-toe in burlap."

"Yeah, but burlap's scratchy. I got this top at the Gap."

She shrugs, tells me to stand still, and murmurs the same illusion-casting enchantment she used to swap our appearances. A few seconds later we look like two rocky gray army grunts, complete with desert camo outfits and lace-up combat boots. Azura even alters our voices so they've got that deep, rumbly sound to them.

"Ready to do this?" she asks.

"No," I say. "Let's do it anyway."

Discussing strategy the night before, we realized our best option was assassination.

It wasn't my first choice. I've been told killing Ahaseurus kills my chances of ever getting home—but Azura managed to convince me that it's still possible with help from Nightshadow's mages. I want to believe she's telling me the truth, but even if she isn't she has a pretty strong argument: If we don't stop him, Ahaseurus is going to own at least one planet, and he really doesn't seem like the kind of landlord who responds well to complaints. I can be selfish at times, but how can I compare being stranded with that? At least the planet I'm stranded on has coffee, cineplexes, and the internal combustion engine—if I get trapped here, I'll have to get used to mushroom tea, puppet shows, and grumpy zebras.

But I'm going to have to be the one to kill him.

I hate that. I'm a cop, not a hit man. I've never killed except in self-defense, and I've never enjoyed it. Killing someone should always be an officer's last resort, because using it means you've failed to do your job.

But Azura's a born strategist, and she knows what she's talking about. Ahaseurus will have all sorts of magic wards set up, meaning Azura won't be able to get anywhere near him; she points out what happened the last time she tried. It'll have to be done quickly, from a distance, and with the kind of force that won't permit any chance of survival.

That means my gun. A regular .454-caliber bullet fired from an Alaskan Super Redhawk hits with more than thirteen hundred foot-pounds of energy; I'm not sure how silver-and-teak loads compare, but the former was expressly designed to take down an angry grizzly or charging moose, and my version can blow a hole the size of a pineapple in an enraged thrope. Ahaseurus, for all his sorcery, is still only human.

If we have to do this, I'd much prefer a thrope or pire sniper with a compound or crossbow—silent, just as deadly, and more accurate at long range. But if that's not available, then me and my boomstick will have to step up.

Neither Azura nor myself expected a mass attack. We thought Ahaseurus would send some kind of strike team to nab me, but we didn't think he had the power for an all-out assault; we were still operating under the assumption that popping from one universe to the other was difficult to do. We didn't understand that once the sorcerer had his foot firmly wedged in the dimensional door, shov-

ing it open a little farther didn't take much more effort.
Not when he had a powerful mystical conduit right at his
fingertips, anyway.

But that still didn't change the basic plan. We were inside his defenses, we were free, and we were armed.

"Good luck," Azura whispers as I open the door that
leads from Omicron's office to the hall.

"You, too," I say. And then I'm striding down the hall,
not looking back, doing my best to seem like a golem on an
important mission. Both of us have roles to play, and we're
going to have to split up for our performance to succeed. If
it doesn't work we'll both die, as well as a whole bunch of
other people.

If it *does* work, it'll probably just be us.

I have no idea where I am. Don't you love it when a plan
comes together?

I march down the hall, studying my surroundings furiously while trying to look like I'm not. I've already figured out that I must be in the headquarters of the Mantle,
but I don't know exactly where that is—somewhere in
Vegas, in some kind of office building? Is this where
Ahaseurus is based, or has he set himself up in some kind
of opulent pleasure palace?

No, all the fancy hotels are in Nightshadow now, which
means this building must be outside city limits. Makes
sense—he has to keep track of what's going on in the rest
of the world, which means access to modern technology.
Right now there are a bunch of dazed thrope and pire tourists wandering around a whole lot of bamboo structures
and tents, wondering where all the blackjack tables went
and why they can't get a cell phone signal.

I feel about as lost. I get to the end of the corridor and
a bank of elevators; there are two other lems standing
there, both in desert fatigues. One of them is talking in

that deep, subsonic bass language I heard over the radio—
but this time, thanks to the translator seed I swallowed, I
understand it.

"—not going to take very long," the lem says. His stripes
mark him as a sergeant.

"Not once Europe falls," the other replies. "I understand Africa is now ours?"

"Reports are still coming in, but there's very little resistance."

The elevator doors open.

Charlie steps out.

I freeze up completely. The other two lems step in, still
talking, and the doors close behind them. Charlie's got a
big brown patch over his throat where I shot him, and his
color seems different—they've replaced some of the black
volcanic sand with gray, giving his skin a lighter tone.

He walks right up to me—but then keeps going, striding past me down the hall the way I just came. I finally
notice what he's holding in his hands and realize where
he's headed in such a hurry.

I turn around and chase after him. Here's where I see
just how well Azura's managed to disguise my voice.

"Sir!" I call out. He doesn't stop.

I catch up, but don't try to grab him—I don't know how
extensive this illusion is. I get in front of him and block his
way instead. "Sir, please!"

He stops. "Get out of my way, Private."

Great—couldn't Azura have given me a higher rank?
"Sir, I have a message from—uh, General Omicron."

"Yeah?"

"He needs those, sir." I point to the scythes he's holding in his hand—*my* scythes. "I was instructed to take
them to him immediately. Sir."

Charlie, it appears, has been made a captain. He could
just order me to get out of the way and continue along—

but I'm hoping that invoking his superior's name will at least slow him down.

"Why?" he snaps.

"I don't know, sir. But he was very clear that it be right away, and that I was to deliver them personally."

He glares at me. I feel light-headed; all I want at this moment is to throw my arms around him and tell him how sorry I am. Instead, I stare straight ahead and keep my face as impassive as possible. *I'm made of stone,* I say to myself. *I'm made of stone.*

Yeah. Sure I am.

His glare lasts a long time. I wonder if I've made a horrible mistake. Maybe he's on his way to give my scythes back because he's overcome the spell and wants to help me escape. Maybe I should just tell him who I am before he decides to take my head off with my own weapons—wouldn't that be a great way to die, decapitated by my partner with my own—

He shoves them at me. "Go ahead, take them. I don't know why I grabbed the damn things anyway."

I take them from him. "Thank you. Sorry to bother you, sir."

"I was bothered before you got here, Private." He turns and stalks away, presumably still headed for the room he thinks I'm being held in. Once he gets there, it won't take him long to figure things out. I have to assume that when he does, he'll raise the alarm.

I don't have much time. I don't know how to find my target. I may have just intercepted my former partner on his way to murder me.

So why am I suddenly so damn happy?

If I were a world-conquering wizard, where would I be?

At the hub of things, the place where I could guarantee the maximum amount of protection plus the most up-to-date information. The command center. This world doesn't have explosives, but they have screamer missiles and silver-nitrate-laced napalm, so I'm guessing the command center will be as heavily fortified as possible.

I head for the basement.

The elevator takes me all the way down to the bottom level without any problem—I just crowd into a car with a bunch of other lems. We're let out into a parking garage that's been converted into a staging area; it's full of military vehicles, tables stacked high with arrow-filled quivers and bundles of javelins—and many, many lems. In all the hustle, it's easy for me to pause and decide which way to go.

There's a large whiteboard propped against one wall, with arrows pointing in various directions. MILSUP ARM is on Level 3, stalls J17 to J23. MILSUP TAC EQ is on Level 1, stalls A3 to A14.

COMMAND is on Level 4, the level I'm on. I don't need the arrows to tell me where, either; it's obviously behind that large double door being guarded by four extremely large, midnight-black lems. There's no way I can just stroll in there without being challenged—and even if I do get past the guards, getting too close to the Big A will no doubt cause my disguise spell to trip one of his mystic safeguards. I need a certain amount of empty space between me and him for this to work, and this environment just isn't providing that.

I consider the brave but stupid option: bluff my way as far as I can get, then start shooting as soon as I meet resistance. Yeah, that'll get me another twenty feet or so before I get turned into Jace Valchek, the human pincushion. Suicide won't solve anything.

My best bet is to camp out here and wait for him to put in an appearance—except, of course, that any moment now some master sergeant is going to notice the dumb private twiddling his thumbs and start shouting orders at me. Which means that what Azura is working on probably isn't going to help that much—

The lights go out.

As far as diversions go, it's a pretty good one. I'd feel better about it if I hadn't noticed a table stacked high with night-vision goggles against one wall, but it's about the best I'm going to get.

I pull my gun from its shoulder holster, hidden inside the illusion that surrounds my body. I can't see a damn thing, but I remember where that door is; I'm going to have to go for it, because this is the only shot I'm going to get—

A shot I can't take. The emergency lights flare to life, and my window of opportunity—small as it was—has passed.

I pretend to study the whiteboard as I frantically try to come up with an alternative plan. *Come on, Jace, there has to be something you can do.*

And then one of the headings on the board registers for the first time: TUNNEL.

Of course. There are tunnels leading inward where I just came from, so there must be something similar here going the other way. All those lems must have come through the dimensional interface from somewhere.

Not only that, but there seems to be a steady stream of lems moving in that direction. I join them; if nothing else, it gives me a purpose and makes me look less suspicious. If I can't assassinate Ahaseurus, maybe I can find a way to disrupt the flow of energy between the two realities, shut down the spell that's controlling the lems.

The lems head for Level 2, where I see that a large hole has been punched through the concrete wall at the end of the car park. This tunnel is a lot more high-tech, with power cables, electric lights, wooden planks along the floor, and the throb of pumps getting rid of groundwater.

The tunnel's wide enough for two golems side by side, but fortunately the one next to me doesn't seem talkative.

I start having second thoughts. What if I just get marched right back into Nightshadow? I might be able to escape, but I'm no closer to my target than when I started.

That doesn't happen, though. The tunnel widens out into another staging area, where they have a couple of big javelin batteries set up—basically oversize crossbows stacked on top of one another, capable of throwing six-foot-long steel shafts half a mile or so. They're aimed at a wall of bare earth that looks different from the tunnel walls I just marched through: darker, richer, wetter. This is the edge of the city of Night's Shining Jewel, its damp, fertile base. And at the top of the wall is the stormstalk root itself, looking as if it were cleanly bisected—hard to believe that the other end of it is located in another reality. The interior of the root is glowing with a soft white light, with an almost hypnotic pulse to it; energy, flowing from there to here.

"So, great minds think alike," a voice whispers behind me.

I look around. All I see is another golem—it takes me a second to recognize Azura.

"What are you doing here?" I hiss. "We were supposed to rendezvous behind the Circus Circus afterward."

"Afterward? You mean you managed to—"

"No, I couldn't get near him."

"Even with the lights out?"

"You mean in the ten or so seconds before the emergency lights kicked in? No, amazingly enough, that wasn't enough time to sneak past four heavily armed guards, penetrate the nerve center of a global military-industrial conspiracy, and assassinate its über-powerful wizard-dictator. Guess I shouldn't have paused to stick my bubble-gum on the wall."

"Well, tactics clearly aren't your strong suit. Why'd you come down here?"

"I saw an opportunity to cause trouble and screw things up. You?"

"I came up with a slightly more constructive plan. You see the earth-face the stormstalk root protrudes from? That's where the original tunnel appears to dead-end. In fact, there's another tunnel just behind it, running parallel. A short distance to the right there's even a hidden entrance connecting the two. Unfortunately, the tunnel that leads to it is not currently in this dimension."

"How short a distance?"

"Five feet, give or take."

"Let's say we dig through five feet of Las Vegas soil—what then?"

"Then we're in the network of tunnels that underlie Night's Shining Jewel. They'll let us move about undetected, and reach the root bundle buried at the heart of the city."

"And do what? Destroy it?"

She shrugs with massive golem shoulders. "I don't have the kind of power to do that—and I wouldn't destroy the bundle even if I could. But I might be able to disrupt or redirect the golem spell."

"Then all we have to do is get through five feet of soil. Any ideas?"

"I have one," a voice says behind us.

We both turn. Tair, in fully human form, smiles at us. "Hello, ladies," he says. "Nice glamour spell. A shame my nose is a lot sharper than a lem's . . ."

EIGHTEEN

"Oh, crap," I say wearily.

"Nice to see you, too, Jace. Well, smell you, anyway." He's dressed a little sharper than the last time I saw him, in a two-piece suit of dark gray with a thin purple silk tie and a white linen shirt. He must have raided a clothing store while they were all deserted.

We're standing a little way off from the main body of lems milling around, and no one else seems to have noticed us yet. I wonder if simply shooting him and yelling *Spy!* is the best option.

"Take it easy, both of you," he says. "I'm not going to blow your cover. Not as long as you behave."

"What do you want?" Azura asks tersely.

"That is the question, isn't it . . . well, for now let's just focus on what my employer wants. Actually, let's start with what he *doesn't* want."

I take a stab at it. "Silver polish that gives him hives?"

"Have you been looking at my Christmas list? No, what Silver Blue really, really doesn't want is a planet run by rogue golems."

I frown. "But—he's human."

"He's a human *arms dealer,* Jace. International conflict is his stock-in-trade, and he does extremely well at it. One of the by-products of this takeover will be a unified world government—okay, a world *dictatorship,* but the quaint notion of separate nations is about to get dumped in the junkyard of history. Mr. Blue would prefer to stay an independent entrepeneur in an unstable world, rather than a pet aristocrat in a police state."

"Understandable," Azura says. "I take it that he hasn't made his objections known to Asher yet?"

"Mr. Asher is convinced that Mr. Blue is onboard and heartily approves of all the changes being made. This is why I have free run of the place—though my failure to capture you two has, sadly, reduced my stature in certain eyes. You can't have everything."

"Yeah, where would you put it? Oh, wait, I guess you could always store it on the planet you just conquered. But if the guy whose side you're *not* on has everything, what does our side have to offer?"

I'm sorry I said it as soon as it leaves my mouth. Tair gives me a long, thoughtful look before answering. "If only you didn't look like a big plastic bag full of sand at the moment . . . I guess I could close my eyes, but it just wouldn't be the same."

I glower at him, but it's hard to tell how much gets through the illusion. Lems tend to be pretty good at glowering—Charlie sure as hell is—but I've only experienced it from the other end.

"Anyway, here it is," Tair says. "Zombie magic."

"Zombie magic?"

"Zombie magic."

"I see," Azura says. "And in return?"

"I won't turn you in. In fact, I'll help you get to that hidden tunnel entrance you were whispering about, and do my best to prevent anyone from following you."

"Wait," I say. "I *don't* see. This is about the underdead?

About turning corpses into cheap labor? How does an international arms dealer profit from that on a planet where thropes live for three hundred years and pires don't die, period?"

"It's not about the underdead themselves, Jace," Azura says. "It's about the enchantment they channel."

"What, you mean the way they can make other things decay instead of themselves?"

"Or stop that decay entirely," says Tair. "I understand it has something to do with strengthening the atomic bonds that hold matter together. I'm sure you've seen examples of it over the last few days: cloth made rigid, or bamboo given the tensile strength of steel. And all without increasing the weight of the object at all."

And suddenly it makes perfect sense. In a Stone Age culture like Nightshadow's, it let you make more durable structures, gave you stronger and sharper tools, provides an alternative to refrigeration. But in a technologically advanced civilization, the effect would be staggering: super-strong, super-lightweight materials—available at practically no cost at all—would revolutionize every industry from transportation to housing, as long as you protected the outer surface from direct exposure to sunlight.

But the very first business to feel its effects would be the military. Body armor, planes, tanks, blades with an edge a molecule thick that never broke or wore down. No wonder Silver Blue wanted the secrets of the underdead; they could make him the wealthiest, most powerful man in the world.

As long as that world wasn't being overrun by golems in the service of a mad sorcerer.

"Okay, I get it," I say. "But why are you asking me and Azura? The underdead I've seen aren't exactly hard to catch—why not just grab a few of the ones you plowed through to get to us?"

"It's not that easy," Azura says. "The underdead channel the enchantment, but they do not understand it. If they were removed to another world, they would not be able to replicate it, nor could the enchantment be duplicated by another shaman through studying the underdead. It is a secret held by the Lyrastoi alone, for within it is the secret of their own immortality."

"Oh, don't be so modest." Tair turns his smile on her. "I'd think that if anyone had access to Lyrastoi spells, it would be their most trusted advisers—right?"

Azura doesn't answer, which is answer enough.

"So here's the deal. I get you to the root bundle, you get me the underdead recipe. You save the world and I get a big fat bonus from my boss. Cool with you?"

And after a moment, Azura nods.

Tair's plan turns out to be amazingly simple. He tells us to follow him, then approaches a couple of other lems and tells them to go get a couple of shovels. When they come back, he hands them to us and tells us to get to work. The lems he talks to don't question anything he says; apparently he has more clout down here than I thought.

And then we dig. Tair instructs a couple more lems to shore up our new tunnel as we go, then decides we aren't digging fast enough and gets us and them to swap jobs. The digging goes a little faster.

And when we've gone far enough in, Azura gives Tair a nod and he pulls the other two lems out. He tells them to get a tarp and cover the mouth of the tunnel with us inside, then guard it. Neither of them asks a single question as to why; sometimes, you just gotta love the military.

Tair sticks his head around the edge of the bright blue tarp from the other side. "Sooner or later somebody's going to check up on this," he says. "I'll do my best to stall them—but I'd hurry, if I were you."

"If you were me," I snap, "you'd already have stabbed Azura in the back."

"Maybe," he says cheerfully. "Luckily for you, I happen to think *your* back is worth guarding." And then he's gone.

"Interesting," Azura murmurs.

"What?"

"Nothing, nothing. The entrance should be right around . . . here." She probes with her hand into the earthen wall, then pulls. A hinged trapdoor that looks like it's made out of dirt swings out. Azura goes through, then me. I close the hatch behind me.

The new tunnel isn't completely dark; there's a faint white glow ahead, probably being given off by the storm-stalk root. Azura heads that way and I follow her.

Sure enough, there's the root, running along the roof of the tunnel. The tunnel only follows it for a few yards before angling off to the right.

"We're about to enter the part of Night's Shining Jewel known as the Burrows," Azura tells me. "It's far more complex and chaotic than the tunnels we've been in thus far. The Burrows is home to the city's thieves and black marketeers; they tap into the stormstalk system wherever they can and bleed off power. The City Guard tries to discourage this, but those who live here are both crafty and stubborn; they're always finding new ways to conduct their business."

I'm reminded of the elaborate drug tunnels the DEA keeps finding beneath the US–Mexican border. "Yeah, I'll bet. So this isn't going to be a straight run down to the root bundle, huh?"

"Hardly. Fortunately, these tunnels should be deserted at the moment; that'll make getting through easier. But before we go any farther—"

She stops and makes a few passes through the air in my direction, muttering under her breath. Both our disguises fade away, leaving me in a black blouse and Azura in black pants and a sports bra. "Better we don't look like soldiers of an occupying force," she says.

"Yeah, much better to look like refugees from a burning building. Or whatever the equivalent is—"

Azura takes her pants off with what I assume is years of stripper-experience efficiency. "Here," she says, handing them to me. "I'm fine with undergarments alone. Besides, you look absurd."

"No argument there," I say, putting them on before she changes her mind. "I can pull off the shirt-as-a-skirt look, but the shoulder holster kind of ruins the effect."

We set off down the tunnel.

While we travel, I have time to think.

The more I consider it, the more I realize how far reaching the effects of zombie magic could be; so much of what's possible is limited by the strength and weight of materials. Take those limitations away, and the sky's literally the limit; even wild science-fiction ideas like an Earth-to-orbit elevator become doable.

But while the idea of thropes establishing a full-time colony on the moon is interesting—party time, dudes!— it's not what I find scary. It's what could be done with golems.

Right now, golems occupy an interesting social niche, somewhere between second-class citizens and walking guns. And while the human-size lems working in law enforcement are comparable to Glocks, the bigger military ones are more like tanks.

But even tanks have to pay attention to physics, especially ones that stand on two legs. Weight goes up faster than height, which means that if you make a golem ten times bigger, you're also making it a thousand times heavier. For already heavy beings, this means they can't get above a certain size before collapsing under their own weight.

But zombie magic changes all that. You could build an armada of golems the size of Godzilla and have them stomp all over any city that got in your way. Some of those military lems already have internal flamethrowers built in, too. If I were Tokyo, I'd be awfully nervous right about now . . .

It takes us the better part of a day to reach the nexus of the stormstalk system, largely because we have to go slow and careful. Azura manages to locate and avoid every single trap—which range from pits full of sharpened stakes to confusion charms that swap left with right—and the only real trouble we have is with an angry snake that was left in a concealed recess at head height. It ignores Azura for some reason, but decides I'd be perfect to chomp on. Fortunately, I have my scythes out and ready; all I see is a flicker of movement before my reflexes cut in. I'm not even aware of what it is until it's in two still-twitching, neatly severed pieces on the floor.

"I'm impressed," Azura says, nudging the corpse with her foot. "Deep vipers are notorious for their speed and stealth. Even so, I'm embarrassed it got past me."

"Nice to know I'm not just deadweight."

"Not yet," she says cheerfully.

The tunnels don't take us directly to the bundle; that's protected by all kinds of major mystical mojo, enough that Ahaseurus figured it was easier to just steal the whole city. The root we've been zigzagging around takes a sudden turn downward, diving toward the spot where it connects with the other six major stormstalk roots deep below.

We descend by means of a ladder that parallels it around fifteen feet away, light provided by one of Azura's handy globes. The ladder goes down at least another hundred feet before ending at a small alcove and a much smaller tunnel, no more than three feet or so high.

"This leads close to the central chamber," Azura says. "We'll have to dig to break through."

"How far?"

"I'm not sure. Ten feet, maybe more. We must be quick; this far underground, a tunnel collapse will be fatal."

"Terrific."

I'm not usually given to claustrophobia, but crawling into a narrow, dark tunnel on my hands and knees doesn't qualify so much as a phobia as simple common sense: *Don't go in there—you'll be buried alive and die.*

Shut up, brain. You may be right, but I'm still in charge. Stupid, but in charge.

The tunnel doesn't go far, maybe five feet or so. When Azura gets to the end, she starts to dig with her hands. I wish I could help, but there isn't enough room for both of us side by side. I take the dirt she's pushing backward and try to move as much of it as possible behind me. The soil is wet and muddy, and before too long I know how an earthworm feels after a downpour.

Strangely enough, I feel *great.* I find myself humming the *hi-ho, hi-ho* dwarf song at one point, which is cheerful but a little crazy. Azura's warned me about this—the stormstalk roots radiate pure life energy, which makes everybody around them just a little perkier than normal. Magic Prozac radiation, provided free of charge; if I do die by being buried alive, at least I'll have a smile on my face.

I never thought it would take so long to travel ten feet in my life. When Azura finally breaks through, my happiness level zips up into the red. I actually burst into tears of joy.

I scramble out of the hole behind her. We're in a large cave, with the world's biggest, weirdest chandelier hanging from the ceiling: seven glowing stormstalk roots, each of them as big around as a subway train, extend from the far edges of the cave roof to the center, where they're woven together into one massive, braided trunk. The trunk dangles down toward the floor of the cave, but never reaches it; instead, it somehow gets farther and farther away as it gets lower, shrinking until it vanishes into the distance.

"Neat trick," I manage eventually. I've been staring at it for a while, but I'm not sure how long.

"Yes," Azura says. "I know it's difficult, but try not to stare at it. It's quite hypnotic."

I tear my eyes away reluctantly. "Okay, so we're here. What happens now?"

"I'm going to make physical contact with the bundle."

"How? It's like a gazillion miles away."

"That's largely an optical illusion. All you have to do is stand directly beneath it and reach up—as long as you have the proper training, of course."

"What'll happen then?"

"I'll commune with the energy coursing through the bundle. More than likely, I'll encounter another myth, the central one that Ahaseurus is using to tie all the others together. I'll see if it can be altered or disrupted."

Like Tair did with the thrope myth. "I'm going with you."

"You'd only be in the way."

"Not buying it, Tink. At the very least, you're going to need someone to watch your back while you try to undo things. I'm going."

She sighs. "Very well." She holds out her hand, and I grab it.

Together, we step under the bundle.

I don't know what I expected, but I'm pretty sure a gigantic, 3-D sign announcing that the following trailer was rated General for All Audiences wasn't on the list.

"What the hell?" I say. At least I have a body this time; I'm standing in the middle of Las Vegas Boulevard, just one of a crowd of tourists who are looking up into the sky.

"Cultural bleed," Azura says from beside me. I glance over and notice that we're both dressed like clichéd tourists; loud Hawaiian shirts, baggy Bermuda shorts, tacky straw hats. I've still got my gun in its holster, though, and both my scythes. "This is a Nightshadow myth seen through the eyes of people from your world—your adopted world, I mean."

The sign in the sky disappears. I'm almost expecting a big, *Star Wars* type of prologue to start scrolling into the clouds, but what I get instead is the Voice—specifically, that deep, slightly vibrato Voice that every movie trailer in the universe uses.

"In a world of magic and monsters," the Voice intones, *"in a time of upheaval and change, a great evil will rise, threatening not only those who live . . . but the dead as well."*

Scary music swells. Either this is the trailer for a horror movie, or it's about to go off the rails into parody. I know which one I'm hoping for.

"When there's no more room in Nightshadow . . . no more Mr. Nice Zombie."

I glance around nervously, but most people are still looking up, staring at what looks like a green-tinted comet, streaking across the sky. I seem to remember something about a comet from the original *Night of the Living Dead,* and it didn't have anything to do with household cleansers or one of Santa's reindeer.

To the cinemyth's credit, it doesn't go with the standard zombies-clawing-their-way-out-of-the-grave bit— but then, it's hard to claw your way through asphalt and concrete.

The zombies appear from the casinos and hotels,

dressed as blackjack dealers and cocktail waitresses, croupiers and bartenders. Their skin is gray, their eyes dead; a few have eyeballs dangling down their cheeks or similar gory nastiness exposed. They're not so much staggering as shambling; maybe that's a petty detail, but I'm a detail-oriented person. Especially with corpses.

And then they change.

A light flares in their eyes, a sickly green light that matches the light in the sky. Apparently this is a signal from outer space that informs them that they are no longer the brain-eating, mostly brain-dead zombies that like to shuffle from place to place; no, now they're the new, modern zombies, the kind that like to move at an all-out gallop and are really, really pissed off. Hey, I'd be mad, too, if I came back from the grave and discovered I was stuck in a permanent marathon.

They lunge at the crowd, clearly bent on mayhem. And then the people around us start to transform—not into zombies, but weres: were-lions, were-bears, were-bulls. Everything but wolves, which tells me that despite the Vegas trappings, this is still a Nightshadow myth.

The two groups slam into each other. The Voice declares, *"A war will be fought, a war for the very soul of a land. Fought on the streets, in the jungle, in the mountains. A war with only one possible outcome."*

"Not liking where this is going," I shout at Azura. Shouting seems to be the only way to communicate in the middle of the snarling, howling, bellowing battle that's going on all around us.

And then it all changes, jumping to another scene. We're in the middle of the New York, New York casino's reproduction of the Brooklyn Bridge, which doesn't go anywhere but has a great Irish bar in the middle. That's where we are now, crouching behind locked doors with furniture piled up against them as a crude barricade.

Through the cut-glass windows of the door I can see them coming, stalking toward us from one end of the bridge: a crowd of weres, maybe even the same one we just saw fighting for their lives.

Apparently they lost.

"Uh, 'Zura? Is zombieism contagious in your world?"

"What? No, of course not. The underdead are an expression of Order and Death—contagion is a mixture of Life and Chaos."

"Guess these guys failed Elemental Metaphysics 101, then." The same eerie green light shines from the weres' eyes, and there are underdead scattered throughout the crowd as well. "Pretty sure they're all playing on the Boneyard Team now."

"When every new victim adds to the horror," the Voice intones, *"there can be no escape."*

Claws rip at the doors. Rotting hands press against windows, which melt away like they were made of ice. Most people don't realize that glass is actually a liquid; it just flows at such a slow rate that it looks solid, and now underdead magic is speeding up that process, aging it centuries in seconds. I can only imagine what will happen if they get their hands on us—we'll either dissolve into puddles of goo or become underdead ourselves. Azura and I back away, but there's nowhere to go.

A hulking, gray-skinned form smashes through the doors and furniture like they're not even there. The were-rhino stops and glares at us with piggish, glowing green eyes beneath the curving horn that juts from his forehead.

Another jump and now we're running, no longer in the bar but some hotel hallway. I can hear something big and heavy thundering along behind us, though I can't see what's making the ruckus until the were-rhino fails to make the corner and smashes into the end of the corridor. Lots of dust and plaster fly around on impact, very cinematic.

"Those who survive," the Voice says, *"know only one thing."*

Another jump-cut. When I see where we've reappeared this time, I shriek out of pure reflex and flail about for something to grab on to.

Azura and I are on the very top of the Luxor, the giant black glass pyramid on the Strip. Both of us have managed to grab an edge and the angle isn't that steep, but it becomes immediately clear that falling off isn't what we should be worrying about.

It's what's coming up the sides toward us.

"Sooner or later," the Voice says, *"they'll run out of places to run."*

Zombie weres of every description are scrambling up all four sides of the pyramid: were-cheetahs, were-gorillas, were-crocodiles, a stampede of undead wildlife heading right at us with bared fangs and hellishly glowing green eyes.

"This is impossible!" Azura snaps.

I don't bother arguing. I don't know how much good my gun will do—or if it'll even work—but there's only one way to find out.

The first shot catches an underdead square in the chest, making a large and extremely messy crater. It also throws him backward, knocking over some of the zombies behind him and sending them tumbling down the glass incline. I try the same strategy a few more times, which produces only semi-satisfactory results; it slows them down, but only on one front and only temporarily. Seems like a head shot is necessary to take any of them out permanently, just like in the movies.

I always carry extra ammunition with me, but I don't have enough to take on this kind of assault—hell, the USS *Nimitz* probably doesn't have enough. I spare a glance at Azura, and discover she's holding both my scythes out and open.

"You know how to use those?"

"Aim the sharp part at whoever you don't like?"

"Sure, get all technical on me."

And then the horde is upon us.

I don't get a chance to witness just how quick a learner Azura is, because the scene jumps again. Somewhere, an otherworldly film editor is cackling and rubbing his hands together.

We're back at the stormstalk bundle, but no longer standing directly beneath it; we're off to one side, in the shadows. Standing in the center of the cavern with arms raised toward the bundle is a Lyrastoi, his back toward us, his collarwings pierced with rows of gold rings. He's holding a spear in his hands.

"But all may not be lost," the Voice says.

"Hooray," I whisper.

"For there are other worlds, other realities. And for the last two members of their respective races, one of those worlds is their last hope."

"Last two?" I whisper. "I count three people here. But we seem to have been relegated back to the audience, which means there's only one—"

"The spear," Azura whispers back.

And now I notice that the head of the spear is kind of unusual. It's similar to the obsidian head of the spear Baron Greystar planted in the middle of the road, the one that became the Palace Verdant—but this one is longer, more even, and iridescent instead of black. In fact, it looks oddly familiar—

It's the Balancer.

The gem flares. A swirling miasma of light and shadow rises from it like smoke from a magic cigar. The swirl shapes itself into a gigantic wolf's head.

The next words aren't spoken by Mr. Moviephone, but by the Lyrastoi. "Soul of the Wolf Nation," he says in a voice nearly as deep and resonant. "I call upon you for one final task."

"Have you not asked enough of me?" the wolf's head growls. "Have I not given my all for the sake of my homeland?"

"You have. But that land's time grows to a close. Death rules unopposed. I am the last of my kind, as you are the last of yours. I offer you a chance for both of us to survive— and for new life for your race."

"I am but a spirit."

"And I will join you shortly. But I can use the power of the gem and the power of the stormstalks to send both our spirits to another world. We will be reborn there."

"Reborn to die again. Alone."

"No. We will be the fathers of a new race, each of us. Our blood will spread our essence in the same fashion that the underdead now spread theirs—but this new land will have no underdead. And one day, both our races will be as numerous as they once were."

"So all will be as it once was?"

"No. The voyage will change both of us, how I cannot say. All I can promise is that your tribe will run free again."

"What would you have me do?"

"Help me to rend the dimensional veil. Between us, we will tear it asunder . . ."

The wolf's answer is to surge upward, toward the root bundle, and seize it in his jaws. The Lyrastoi rears back and launches the spear into the bundle as well.

The roots crackle and spark with energy. The wolf savages the bundles with his jaws until it begins to bleed lightning. The outline of the Balancer gem, now buried deep inside the bundle by the spear, is still visible as it throws off a brilliant, pulsing light.

Then everything blows up. It is using the language of a big-budget movie, after all.

Fade to black. No Voice, no studio logo, no announcement that it's coming soon to a theater near us. Azura and I are standing beneath the root bundle once more, which is looking pretty intact after that explosion. Well, they are roots—I guess they grew back.

"Are you suddenly craving popcorn and a large Coke, or is that just me?" I ask. "That had everything but Nicholas Cage in a starring role—"

"No," Azura says. Her voice is shaky.

"Are you all right?"

"No, no, it *can't* be," she says. Her voice breaks on "can't."

"Take it easy, it was only a story. Even if it's partly accurate, it all happened a long time ago—"

"No, Jace, you don't understand. That wasn't a myth, not like the others." Tears course down her cheeks. "That was a *prophecy*. That's how my world is going to die . . ."

NINETEEN

We hunker down and talk. It seems Azura's plan of disrupting Ahaseurus's spell has hit a major snag: It isn't being focused through the root bundle after all.

"It *is* powering the spell," Azura says. "But that doesn't help us. I can't do anything to stop it—it would be like trying to halt a river with my bare hands. I need to get to the equivalent of a dam, where the power is being collected and channeled—*that,* I can manipulate."

"And that's not here. Okay, let's table that for a second and go back to the whole apocalypse thing. Explain."

"The myth we just observed. It's more than a story from my world, it's a story from yours, as well. Your home away from home, I mean—the one full of pires and thropes. It's the story that links both places together."

"So the Lyrastoi and the wolf—the place they came was here?"

"They were the progenitors of the lycanthrope and vampire races. Changed by the transition to another world, but still essentially the same."

"But—there have been pires and thropes here for centuries."

"Yes." Her voice is sad. "Surely you've noticed that the

flow of time is different in different realities? The story we experienced is a myth to you and a prophecy to me, Jace. To you, it is something that happened a very long time ago, in another reality entirely. To me, it is something that hasn't happened yet—I'm not only from another dimension but another time. And I've just seen how my world will end."

I hate time travel almost as much as magic; it confuses everything. "Look, I refuse to believe in all that predestination crap. Past, present, future, whatever—we're still in charge of making our own choices, and I choose to kick the snot out of Ahaseurus and put the brakes on his DIY empire. How about you?"

"I don't know . . . while I was aware of the power of the Balancer gem, I had no idea it housed the spirit of the Wolf Nation." She shakes her head. "And the gem must be what Ahaseurus is using to focus the spell."

"The last time I saw it, it was bonded to a sword, not a spear—but it was a sword that could manipulate time, so that makes sense. Okay, new plan: We find Ahaseurus and take the Balancer gem away from him."

"Oh, absolutely. That should prove to be immensely easier. We'll just waltz right in there and ask him, shall we? Excuse me, Mr. Immortal Wizard, sir, would you kindly give up the source of your power? We'd just like to borrow it for a bit."

"Hey, watch it, Tink. *I'm* the pessimistic, cynical half of this team, okay? You're the one in charge of goodness, lollipops, and flashing your sugarplums."

"Right. Sorry. Didn't mean to let watching my world die kill the mood."

"It's not dead yet. Besides, we have a man on the inside now, remember?"

"Tair. You really think we can rely on him?"

"Only if we make sure his own interests are at stake.

Then he'll be as reliable as a raccoon with an open garbage can."

So we go back the way we came; amazingly, the tunnel we dug hasn't collapsed yet. We retrace our steps, coming up with a rough plan as we go. Even though the last time I saw the Midnight Sword it was bonded to the Balancer gem, I'm pretty sure Tair still has the blade—he's not one to give up an advantage unless he has to. Swapping the gem for a position in Silver Blue's organization makes sense, but he would have held on to the Sword as insurance.

The fact that Ahaseurus has the Balancer bothers me, though. It's clearly the item he came to Vegas to purchase, but if what Tair told me is true, Silver Blue wouldn't have sold it to him. Which means Mr. Blue has either switched sides or been killed—unless, of course, Tair is lying to me.

And then there's Stoker.

I still have the number he gave me through his televised message. I'm a little surprised he admitted to acting irrationally, but I suppose it makes a convenient excuse for trying to paralyze every thrope and pire in the world. I doubt his goals have changed, though—and while I believe he's sincere about wanting to protect me, Ahaseurus is about to give him the planet on a platter. No way he's going to help me screw that up. Tair apparently will, so I'm going to have to trust him whether I want to or not.

When we get close, Azura casts the spell that makes us look like golems again—though we're so covered in mud we could almost pass anyway. If Tair isn't waiting for us, we'll have to find him, locate the Balancer gem, then use him to get close enough to grab it.

Sure. Easy. As a plan, it lacks the drawbacks that something more elaborate might have—things like information, preparation, equipment. Luckily, we won't have any of those pesky details hanging around to trip us up.

We exit through the concealed hatch, close it after us, step up to the tarp, and it pull it aside.

Tair isn't waiting for us.

Ahaseurus and Stoker are.

They don't give us a chance to fight back.

I have a split second to realize that Stoker's holding the Midnight Sword before he rams it through Azura's heart. Her eyes open very, very wide, and she makes a choked little gurgle. Blood seeps from the corner of her mouth.

I do my best to blow Ahaseurus's head off, but the only sound my gun makes is the click of the trigger and the dull thud of the hammer hitting the base of the shell.

"Idiot," Ahaseurus says. "The spell that banishes fire was the first one I ever learned. Here's one that's a little more recent."

He gestures and says three words that I hear clearly and immediately forget. The world goes away.

I don't lose consciousness, though. It's more like all my senses, from sight to touch, have been turned off. I'm floating in a gray void with the world's worst head cold and a full-body shot of novocaine.

Even my time sense is gone. Have I been here only a few minutes, or only a few years? I don't know. What I do know is I have plenty of time to think about how badly I've screwed up.

I underestimated Stoker. I don't know how he wound up with the sword, but I'm guessing Tair underestimated him, too. Us human types can surprise you.

I wonder who'll eventually come out on top, the terrorist or the wizard. Ahaseurus would seem to hold all the cards—but as Stoker just proved, he's not someone you should dismiss. Ever.

He's probably my best hope at this point. He told me once that killing me would be a crime against humanity,

and he meant it; he won't let Ahaseurus simply execut
me, not without a fight.

I know why I'm here. Organized serial killers are al
about control; the longer they can impose it on a victim
the more they enjoy themselves. He's put me in this limb
to emphasize the fact that he's in charge and I'm helpless

Big mistake.

My primary weapon isn't my gun, my scythes, or m'
knowledge of martial arts. It's my mind. He's left me with
access to my greatest asset—and I'm going to make sure
he regrets that.

Eventually.

I don't know how long I'm in there. When reality doe
come back, it's as sudden as a slap in the face; I'm stand
ing in a hallway, one I recognize. It's the one just outsid
my apartment, on the world I was born on.

I still can't feel my body, though, or control it. That'
because it isn't mine; even though I'm looking through it
eyes, hearing with its ears, I'm just a passenger.

And Ahaseurus is driving.

"What do you think?" his voice whispers in my mind
"Shall we pay your home another visit, see if anyone'
there?"

I try to reply, but my mouth isn't working. *Go to hell,*
think, and that seems to get through.

"Let's go together, shall we?"

He knocks on the door. He's wearing black leathe
gloves.

The door swings open. "Yes?"

It's me.

My hair's different, I might be ten pounds heavier, an
I don't recognize that T-shirt I'm wearing—but it's defi
nitely me.

He waves his hand in front of her face while murmur

ing a few soft words. Her eyes glaze over and she freezes.
He steps past her into the apartment, gently removes her
hand from the doorknob, and closes the door behind him.

He tells her to go sit down on the couch, and she does.
Then he pulls a long, curved dagger from a sheath inside
his coat.

"You know what comes next, don't you?" he says inside
my mind. "I've decided that the best punishment is for you
to witness your own death. This is you in the future, Jace;
as you can see, you've returned to your own Earth. I'm not
going to tell you how long you've been here, but I will say
this: Your murder won't come as a complete surprise. Before I let you go—and, obviously, I *do* let you go—I'm going to kill this future version of yourself, while you watch
through my eyes. I'll let you live with that horror until I
decide to let you go home, at which time I'll erase your
recollection of this murder. Mostly."

His voice is smug, self-satisfied, on the verge of laughter. This is the moment every serial killer lives for, the one
where he can feel the weight of someone's life and death in
his own two hands. He'll draw it out as long as possible.

"I'll leave just the barest echo of these events in your
memory," he continues. "A sliver of dread, a chill in your
soul. Enough to give you bad dreams, keep you nervous
and afraid. Until the day I come for you—until this very
day."

My future self's eyes suddenly flare with fear, though
she doesn't move.

And then he cuts her throat.

She bleeds out in less than a minute. He watches at-
tentively every second, and he probably has some kind of
spell in place that lets him feel my emotional reaction.

He's not going to be happy with it.

"Nice try," I subvocalize. "Good setup, decent follow-
through. A for effort."

"You don't believe this is real, do you?" he asks, staring at the lifeless body now sprawled sideways on the couch. "You're angry, a little sad, but not terrified. Not despairing."

"I know it's real. It's just not me."

He cleans the knife by wiping it on the body, then puts it back in its sheath. "I assure you, it is."

"Oh, her name is probably Jace Valchek. But she's not an FBI agent—probably not even in law enforcement—and she's never visited another reality."

He doesn't reply to that, because he knows I'm right. "Just because I'm using your eyes," I continue, "doesn't mean I have to pay attention to what you are. That graduation photo on the far wall isn't mine. I don't decorate in pastels. And that smell in the air—thanks for the use of your nose, by the way—seems to be from some kind of potpourri, which I loathe. That's not me."

"Very observant." He chuckles. "I suppose you've deduced that this is yet another alternate reality? One that has another version of you living in it? Or had, I should say."

Another version of me. One that hadn't done anything wrong, one that was killed simply for the crime of being who she was. All because of this bastard's sick fixation. I feel a surge of anger, but I can't let him get to me. My only chance is to get inside his head instead of letting him get inside mine.

"Who was she, a waitress? A librarian? Something nice and passive, I'll bet, someone *easy*. Bet you had to look pretty hard for her, too—probably aren't a lot of meek Jace Valcheks out there."

"Not anymore, no."

That chills me, even though it comes as no surprise. Yeah, this isn't the first Jace he's killed. And as much as I hate to admit it, I suddenly feel diminished—there's nothing like the knowledge that you're not unique to take

you down a peg or six. *I could kill you on a whim,* he's
telling me. *Plenty more just like you, any time I feel like
slaughtering one.*

And then, just to prove his point, he yanks me into
another reality. Same apartment, different decorator. Different Jace—so *that's* what I'd look like as a blonde—
who screams when a strange man suddenly materializes
in front of her. This one, he doesn't bother with the whole
hypnosis schtick; he just stabs her.

And then it's time for another.

And another. And another.

I know what he's doing. He's trying to overload me on
horror, show me how completely and totally beaten I am.
I can't look away, can't even close my eyes. *I can do this
to you anytime I want,* he's saying. *You're powerless.
You're nothing.*

After the fifth one, I start to laugh.

"Losing your mind already?" he says, watching a dying
Jace spasm on the floor in front of him. "I really hoped
you'd last longer."

"Oh, I still have all my marbles. I just realized something."

"How inconsequential you are?"

"Just the opposite. See, from what I understand of the
multiverse, it's infinite. And infinite possibilities times infinite realities equals infinite Jaces." I laugh again. "You
can't kill me, you moron. I'm like that whack-a-mole game;
no matter how many versions of me you ice, there are always going to be more. You're like an amoeba nibbling on
a whale and congratulating himself on how big his stomach is."

Okay, I'm not crazy about comparing myself to a whale
in *any* context, but I've got to get under his skin. Because,
honestly, he's getting under mine.

I'm bluffing. Seeing myself die is like a hard punch

to my soul every time it happens, but I can't let him
know that. I push that emotion aside and summon the
coldest, nastiest, most cynical attitude I can muster; a
my-boyfriend-broke-up-with-me-on-New-Year's-Eve, I
have-the-worst-hangover-of-my-life-and-just-finished
my-third-pot-of-coffee kind of snark, something truly
black and vile. It's the only armor I have.

"You call these *Jaces*?" I spit. "They're pathetic. Los
ers, imitations, cheap knockoffs. God, this one looks like
she has a prison tattoo."

"You're not fooling me."

"And you're not impressing me. What, you though
you could demonstrate how powerful and unstoppable
you are by killing a series of file clerks and coffee baris
tas? Ooh, what a bad, bad man. Hey, why don't we drop in
on Disneyland? You can prove your manliness by beating
up a teenager in a Goofy costume."

"You fail to see the point. Do you have any idea how
much sheer power it takes to cross even *one* dimensional
boundary?"

I do, in fact. A lot. The fact that he can casually squan-
der that kind of power is a great deal scarier than the
murders, but I can't acknowledge that—especially now
that I've got him on the defensive. Yeah, he'll be throwing
in the towel any second now.

"I don't get magic, anyway," I continue. "I mean, how
do I know any of this is real? Maybe it's all an illusion."

"I'm not an illusionist," he says, and now there's anger
in his voice. "I am a *sorcerer*. I manipulate reality itself, I
don't perform tricks for crowds of subhuman *idiots*."

Subhuman idiots? Obviously, he doesn't have the highest regard for either his former colleagues or the supernatural races; maybe I can use that against him.

"I see I'll have to be more . . . *inventive* in order to
gain your respect," he says. "Unfortunately, I don't have

ime right now. People to see, places to go, worlds to
:onquer . . ."

He makes another gesture, and the scene shifts
igain—but this time I'm back in my own body. A body
vith my wrists cuffed together, the chain running through
i metal ring in the arm of a heavy wooden chair, the kind
specifically designed to take the weight of a golem.

I'm in a throne room.

I'm pretty sure it didn't start out life as a throne room.
n fact, I'm guessing that it used to be some sort of big
:orporate boardroom, the kind that usually has a table
he size of an aircraft carrier and big windows overlooking
in impressive view. This doesn't have either, but I can see
leep impressions in the carpet where the table used to be.

And then there's the throne.

I guess Ahaseurus is a traditionalist at heart, because
ie's got an honest-to-goodness, ornately carved, gigantic
irmchair at the head of the room. It would be more impressive if I didn't recognize the corporate logo of a
nedieval-style restaurant worked into the base.

My chair is off to the side, along with about a dozen oth-
:rs. Azura is in the chair next to mine, bound with some
<ind of silvery rope and apparently unconscious. I'm not
hat surprised to see she's still alive; Stoker impaled her
vith the Midnight Sword, a blade that can manipulate
ime. One of its effects is to cause injuries that vanish af-
er a specific amount of time has passed—a weapon with
in undo option.

Ahaseurus himself lounges on the throne; standing
peside him is a woman dressed from head to toe in white,
vith a white veil that covers all of her face except her
:yes.

Eyes I know only too well. They're the same ones that
ook back at me every morning when I brush my teeth.

You're probably wondering why he seems so obsessed

with you, Stoker had said. *It's because of your counterpart—
the Jace Valchek of my world. It's why you were targeted in
the first place, why Asher brought you over.*

I'd almost forgotten about the woman Ahaseurus was
traveling with, the one that Azura had posed as over the
phone. She's another Jace, of course. And according to
Stoker, she's the one from this world.

I stare at her, at the pallor of her skin, at the emptiness
in her eyes, and realize something else.

She's dead.

That shouldn't come as much of a surprise. Ahaseurus
is from a reality with plenty of animated corpses running
around, and he used a zombie to construct the spell that
created golems in the first place. But why a dead Jace
when he has so many live ones to choose from?

Because serial killers love to keep trophies. And just
as a romantic never forgets his first love, a serial never
forgets his first kill. Why should he, when he can have it
follow him around forever?

I know, deep in my gut, that this isn't the Jace of this
world after all. She's much, much older than that—as old
as Ahaseurus himself. She's the Jace of Azura's world.
Ahaseurus must have turned her into one of the underdead
after he murdered her, so he could keep her by his side
forever. Brunt may have thought he was the last of his kind,
but he was wrong; Ahaseurus had one more in reserve, a
prized possession he just couldn't bring himself to part
with.

He studies me from his perch, looking like he should
be dressed in purple fur-lined robes instead of the black
silk suit he's wearing, a crown instead of that red turban;
even so, his bony, hawk-nosed profile still reminds me
more of an undertaker than an emperor.

"Chassinda," he says, "bring in our other guests, won't
you?"

The woman in white moves forward slowly, her gaze fixed dead ahead. She isn't lurching, but there's a certain stiffness to her gait. I can smell a strong floral fragrance as she moves past, but there's something underneath it, the merest hint of decay. I guess even sorcery can't stave off entropy forever.

When she's gone, Ahaseurus smiles at me. "My most trusted aide. More of a pet than an assistant, but I'm quite attached to her."

I'm thinking furiously. Azura's out of commission, I'm chained up and disarmed—but I still have allies. My best hope right now is that one of them will come through.

And then they do. They come right through the door, in fact: Cassius and Tair.

Too bad they're also in chains and being herded by a pair of heavily armed lems.

Cassius has been beaten, his pretty surfer-boy face looking more like a boxer after eighteen rounds in the ring with a trained sasquatch. Tair is in slightly better shape, but he's in half-were form; thropes heal quicker that way. There's a lot of blood on his fur, though.

Silver Blue is right behind them, following Chassinda. The expression on his shiny face is somewhere between fury and worry—he looks like someone who just used what he thought was a spray-on tan and is extremely upset by the results.

"Ah, Mr. Blue," says Ahaseurus. "I'm glad you're here. We need to discuss the reliability of your employees."

Blue strides right up, but stops about ten feet away. He's still a little too close for my comfort; the reek of garlic coming off him is intense. Chassinda returns to her place beside the throne. She stares straight ahead, not blinking.

"What's going on?" Blue demands. "Why is my lieutenant in chains?"

"Because he's an animal," says Ahasuerus. "Both of them are—I thought you understood that."

"What's Tair done?"

"I think one of my associates can explain it better than I. Ah, here he comes now."

Charlie stalks through the door. He doesn't meet my eyes, but he knows I'm there. He strides up to stand beside Silver Blue.

"What—" Blue says. It's all he has time to say, because Charlie draws his short sword from its scabbard and decapitates him with a single backhand blow.

"Silver and garlic do little against cold steel, I'm afraid," Ahasuerus says as the body slumps to the floor. "And what your lieutenant did wrong was to follow your orders."

So much for allies.

"And now, Miss Valchek, it's your turn." Ahasuerus gestures.

And Charlie turns in my direction.

TWENTY

Well, it's not like I didn't do it to him first.

"Stop," Cassius says. He sounds terrible, like he's barely holding on to consciousness. Pires are pretty much invulnerable—but there are definite exceptions, and silver weapons are one of them. Cassius looks like he's been worked over with a pair of very expensive candelabra.

"Why should I?" Ahaseurus asks. "Oh, wait—you think I meant he should *kill* her. No, no. Mr. Aleph?"

Charlie turns back to the sorcerer, who leans over and picks something up from beside his throne. "Here."

Charlie takes my scythes from him with one hand, sheathes his sword with the other. Tests the weight of them as if he's never held them before, as if he's never borrowed them from me and practiced until he was almost as good as I was. "A partner should be prepared," he'd said. "You should be able to handle yourself with my weapons as well as I do with yours." And then he'd given me the first of many lessons in the proper use of the *gladius*.

"I just think she needs a little *alteration*," Ahaseurus says. "Removing her vocal cords, for instance. Don't worry if you make a mess; I won't let her bleed to death or asphyxiate. Underdead magic is quite handy for stabilizing injuries."

Charlie snaps both blades open with a flick of his wrists. Looks like it's coming back to him.

But he still just stands there, staring at me. He brings his elbows in close to his body, his wrists against his belly. He holds the *eskrima* batons straight up and down, the scythe blades curving away from him at chest level. He widens his stance a little, bending his knees and moving his hips ever so slightly back and forth. He lowers his head, moving it forward and down. There's something about how he's holding his body that's strange but familiar, like I've seen it somewhere before but not on him—

A dinosaur.

I've never seen a live one, but I've seen plenty of computer simulations in big-budget movies and PBS specials. He's adjusting his weight for a nonexistent tail, getting ready to lunge forward on immense, muscular legs and bite me in half with jaws like a steam shovel. But he doesn't have any of those things; he has my scythes, which he's holding as if they were tiny little forearms jutting out in front of him. Because, at heart, that's what Charlie *is*; not a walking sandbag, not a zombie, not even a snappy-dressing, swing-dancing cop. He's a prehistoric, carnivorous dinosaur.

He's the Devouring Ghost.

I remember the story Silverado told me while we were both locked up. I remember how the shaman made the Devouring Ghost his Spirit Animal, and how the Ghost eventually devoured him, too; and I think I finally understand just what it was the old bounty hunter was trying to say.

Charlie told me once that he'd gone bowhunting and bagged himself a couple of grizzlies. "They were big," he'd said. "They just weren't big *enough*."

Not to an apex predator like *Tyrannosaurus rex*. Seven and a half tons of meat-eating hunger, he wouldn't consider something as paltry as a full-grown bear to be more than an appetizer. Taming something like that would require more than just powerful magic—you'd have to find a way to *channel* that hunger, make it something that worked for you. You'd have to impose order on raging chaos.

That was what the golem activation spell did. It imposed a bit of underdead magic on the life essence of an animal—and since the underdead were basically servants of the living, that translated into golem loyalty. It was all about balance; the Lyrastoi had used much the same process to combine underdead magic with the essence of bats, producing an immortal being with the heritage of a flying rodent—but that was imposing zombie magic on a were bat. Golems were the reverse, imposing were magic on what, I suppose, could be best described as a zombie rock. A mineral substrate with just enough underdead magic in it to let it bond with the spiritual essence of the animal being used—otherwise, you'd just have a rock that thought it was a steer, or a lion, or a snake. Strangely enough, it must be the underdead part of a lem that gave it the capacity for rational thought.

But Charlie's had his balance messed with—by the Balancer gem, of course—to make him follow Ahaseurus's orders. More order, less chaos. His *T.-rex*-iness is being suppressed—and his body language tells me he doesn't like it. Is, in fact, fighting it.

I don't need to get Charlie to see reason. I need to get him *angry*—that's how Silverado must have been able to resist, must be what he was trying to tell me in that jail cell. I have to let Charlie's inner Barney out, the one that drinks heavily in his trailer between takes and gobbles production assistants like potato chips. I have to get Charlie's goat, then refuse to let him eat it.

But I'm going to need a little help to do it. Luckily, I came prepared.

"The most important part of any illusion is preparation,"
Azura says. "Gaining access to the battleground before the
battle is worth more than a legion of troops behind you. If
we have the opportunity, I intend to infiltrate Asaheurus's
headquarters before any confrontation and leave this be-
hind." She shows me a small, bright purple egg nestled in
the middle of her palm. "This is called the Warbler's Child.
It contains a potent charm that can be activated by anyone
who knows the proper incantation, which I am now going
to teach you."

"What does it do?"

Azura smiles. "It deceives the senses. It lasts no more
than a minute and only on one person, but in that time you
can make them see and experience almost anything. It is
one of the Hidden Clan's most potent weapons; used
properly, it can convince a king that he is a pauper, a mon-
ster that he is a saint, a sane man that he is mad. We use it
rarely, for illusion is at its most useful when it is perceived
to be real."

"Is this going to let us take down a sorcerer as dan-
gerous as Ahasuerus?"

"No. But it may grant us that most elusive and power-
ful of all wishes: a second chance."

The Warbler's Child is underneath the throne. I would
have preferred something more lethal, but Azura told me
one of the big advantages of this particular charm is that
it's much harder to detect than something designed to
kill. I whisper the incantation Azura made me memorize
under my breath, and focus my will on Charlie.

Azura said I'd see the same thing that my target would,
but it's still a shock when the room abruptly transforms

into a grassy meadow. You'd think I'd be getting used to these shifts in reality; what with myths, interdimensional travel, and vivid flashbacks, I seem to be spending as much time these days in unreal places as real ones.

Everybody who was here when the meadow was a throne room is still here, but not all of us look the same. I do, Azura does, the lem guards and their two prisoners haven't changed—but Ahaseurus is now a giant rat. Kind of obvious, maybe, but I'm a little rushed.

Charlie's a dinosaur. For real.

He glares at me suspiciously and snorts. His breath stinks of rotting flesh—tyrannosaurs ate carrion as well as their own kills. Well, Azura did say the illusion would be detailed.

Charlie's hunched over, his gigantic, toothy head on the same level as mine. I wonder what would happen if he tried to eat me—would I get chomped by actual golem teeth, or would the scythes bite into my body? Either would be unpleasant, and being cuffed to this chair means I have exactly zero chance of getting out of the way. So I do the only thing I can, which fortunately I'm pretty good at.

"You overgrown, walking brick wall—what the hell do you think you're doing? You're not a dinosaur, you're a birdbath with legs—pigeons hang RESTROOM signs around your neck while you're sleeping. The only reptilian ancestor you can lay claim to is a gargoyle that fell off the corner of a building."

Who knew a tyrannosaur could squint? Or that he could convey so much hostility by doing so?

"You don't *hunt* quarry, you were *born* in a quarry. You're a walking sidewalk, the illegitimate offspring of a rolling stone and a cement mixer. The last time you sneezed the shrapnel killed a waitress!"

He takes a step toward me on those massive, scaly legs. My minute is almost up.

Ahaseurus starts to say something, but I don't let Charlie hear it. I want his full attention on me, and right now the only things he's seeing and hearing are those I want him to—

No. Not just seeing and hearing. Smelling, too.

His nostrils flare as he catches the scent I introduce. Tyrannosaurs had extremely large nasal cavities, and right now he's getting a heady whiff of delicious, decaying meat. He turns his head toward the source.

Ahaseurus isn't just a giant rat anymore. He's a giant *dead* rat.

"Forget it!" I yell. "You, you refugee from a marble factory! You don't eat meat, you're not even *made* of meat! You're a driveway that learned how to talk!" I'm seesawing him, appealing to his animal nature on one hand and reminding him of his connection to me with the other. I don't just need him angry, I need him *defiant,* and the only way to push him there is to pound on as many of his buttons as I can. "You couldn't digest a breath mint! You send a card to Mount Rushmore every Father's Day! *And you dance like a dump truck!*"

The illusion abruptly ends. Charlie still stands between Ahaseurus and me, my scythes clenched in his fists. He turns to me and raises one over his head.

It comes down, hard and fast. The tip of the scythe impacts the keyhole of the handcuffs with enough force to break off the tip, but the lock pops open.

I yank the chain free of the ring, jump to my feet, and catch the scythe Charlie tosses me. He uses the other one on the nearest lem, who's spraying gray-tinted sand all over the floor before he can even raise his sword.

I don't waste time with thanks, or even another snappy one-liner. I just dive and roll, straight at my target.

Chassinda.

Ahaseurus tries to stop me, but whatever spell or enchantment he tosses my way doesn't connect. I'm moving fast and he's rattled; he's not used to people challenging him on his own turf.

I come out of the shoulder roll and slam into Chassinda, knocking her over. She doesn't react at all; I may as well have knocked over a mannequin. I grab her body around the waist as we fall, twisting so that she lands on top, her body shielding me. An instant later I have the edge of the scythe pressed against her throat.

"No!" Ahaseurus shouts.

Charlie ignores him. Didn't catch what he did to the other lem, but both guards are now sprawled, unmoving, on the floor. Charlie's already moving toward the door; he knows we can't afford to let reinforcements arrive.

But right now, at this very second, we have the upper hand.

Because I know where the Balancer gem is.

"Let her go," Ahaseurus says, his voice low and cold.

"No." I know what I have to do, but I don't know if I can make myself do it. I shift my weight, but Chassinda puts up about as much resistance as a rag doll—or maybe I should say voodoo doll. Charlie's guarding the door, but nobody's crashed through it yet.

"This is laughable," Ahaseurus says with a sneer. "You seek to use your own corpse as a hostage? You must have lost your mind."

"This isn't me. But whoever she is, whoever she *was,* you've tormented her long enough. I'm going to end this."

"Go ahead. And when you're done, I will destroy you and your friends. Slowly."

"No, you won't. You're focusing your worldwide spell through the Balancer—but you needed a safe place to keep the gem while it's doing its work, didn't you? I'm no magician, but if you're casting a zombie-based spell it makes sense to have a zombie hold on to your focus—and who better than the zombie that's always at your side?"

He glares at me, but there's fear in it now. "Give an item of such power to one who means nothing? She owns nothing, not even the clothes I choose to dress her in. Search her and see for yourself."

"Oh, she won't be wearing it on a necklace or anything else visible and easy to steal. It's *inside* her, isn't it, you bastard? Dead flesh that doesn't decay makes an ideal hiding place. So what happens if I cut off her head?"

He stares at me stonily but says nothing.

"It ends the enchantment," a voice whispers hoarsely. Azura, barely conscious but fighting to raise her head. "Kill her . . . kill the spell."

"You can't," Ahaseurus growls. "She's already dead."

"Yeah? Then cutting off her head will make her a whole lot deader, won't it?"

"Do it and you will never see your home again," he says. "Your *real* home."

Oh, crap.

"I can see I've underestimated you," he says. "But I can admit when I've made a mistake. I have an offer for you, Jace. I think you're going to want to hear it."

I don't say a word. I don't trust myself to.

"I'll return you to your world, no less than a day from when you left it. You'll have your life back—your career, your friends, your family. All this can be no more than a bad dream."

"Sure. Until you show up in the middle of the night and yank me back here again."

"I understand you're reluctant to trust me. But as you pointed out before, there are an infinite number of yous available as replacements. Why should I bother with something poisonous when there are so many more ripe apples on the tree?"

"You want to know what the first thing is they teach a professional hostage negotiator? Don't compare your subject to a piece of toxic fruit."

He chuckles. "But you *are* poisonous—lethal, in fact. And I have no more desire to die at your hands than you have to die at mine. So here's my offer: I will not only return you to your world, I'll seal that world off forever. I won't be able to return to it, or bother you, ever again. You'll be safe—at least from me."

"You're lying."

"He isn't," a voice croaks.

Not Azura this time. Tair.

"Shut up," Cassius hisses.

Tair's reverted to human form. I can see just how injured he is now; cuts cover most of his body, his one leg is at an angle that means his kneecap has been smashed, and his face is so bruised he can barely speak. He does anyway. "S'true, Jace." It comes out more like *ss-droo, Jaysh.* "I'll make sure he does it. Go. Be safe."

That shakes me a little. Tair never does anything he isn't ultimately going to benefit from, but this is one helluva gamble. If it pays off, he might wind up going from being the disgraced lieutenant of a Judas to the new right-hand man of Emperor Ahaseurus—but the sorcerer could just as easily kill Tair as being untrustworthy once he gets what he's after.

But I still don't know if Ahaseurus is telling the truth. Or what I should do if he is.

"Jace," Cassius says. "Don't listen to him. He's lying."

"Azura," I say. "Please. *Is he telling the truth?*"

Azura lifts her head with an effort, meets my eyes. This is a woman whose entire life is based on deception, on weaving illusions that let her trick people and steal their secrets. I have no idea why I'm asking her to verify what is probably the single most important fact I'll ever have to question.

Slowly, she nods.

"Your friends can go free as well," Ahaseurus says. "They can stand at your side as I send you across the dimensional divide, to ensure no betrayal. Leave this world and all it's done to you to those who belong here."

And then, for the first time, Chassinda moves.

It's nothing violent. She doesn't try to break free or disarm me. She just lifts one arm, very slowly, to her face. I don't try to stop her.

She grabs the white veil that conceals everything but her eyes and pulls it off. In the position I'm in I can't see her face, but I can see the pain and sorrow in Azura's.

I keep my scythes highly polished, and silver makes a pretty good mirror. I move the blade away from her throat and angle it so it shows me what everyone else in the room can see.

Her lips are sewn shut. The holes where the thread goes through have pulled wider over time; her owner has kept her in good repair, but everything shows wear and tear eventually, even the underdead.

It's not her mouth that horrifies me the most, though. It's her eyes. They aren't blank anymore. Every bit of feeling left in her soul is trying to rise up, to *communicate,* through those eyes. They're actually trembling with effort.

And I know what they're trying to say.

Kill me.

TWENTY-ONE

Things happen very fast after that.

I shove Chassinda forward at the same time I cock my arm back.

The lem soldiers we were expecting finally crash through the door at the front of the room.

Ahasuerus chants the first two syllables of something that will no doubt rain nasty magic death on my head. He doesn't have the time to finish.

I bring the scythe around in a tight, fast strike. It takes Chassinda's head off cleanly. There's no blood. White light bursts from the wound instead.

Cassius leaps at Ahaseurus. His arms are still bound, but a pire's legs are just as strong as the rest of his body. He slams into the sorcerer, interrupting his spell and smashing the throne to pieces; apparently they just don't build 'em like they used to.

The mayhem at the back of the room stops as abruptly as it started. Charlie's facing down a horde of lems that suddenly look more confused than hostile.

I vault over Chassinda's body, trying to get to Ahaseurus. I have to take him out of commission before he can recover—

Too late.

Cassius comes hurtling back the way he came, and I narrowly miss being his second target.

A slit appears in midair, between me and Ahaseurus. Aristotle Stoker steps through it, the Midnight Sword in his hand. Looks like we aren't the only ones with a backup plan in place.

I'm not clear on everything the sword can do, but I know it can affect time. I'm not entirely surprised when everything seems to slow to a crawl.

And then Stoker kills every one of my allies.

It's exactly like one of those nightmares where you're running from something terrible and your legs feel like they're mired in quicksand. I can see what's happening, but I'm stuck in slow motion.

Stoker isn't.

He moves from target to target, not hesitating. He plunges the sword into Cassius's chest, Azura's throat, Tair's eye. He cuts Charlie in half. None of them react as the blade passes through them, and neither blood or sand spills onto the floor.

When he's done he whirls around and rejoins Ahaseurus at the front of the room. I have a frozen instant to wonder why he didn't use the sword on me, and then time returns to normal.

I wait for bodies to topple to the floor. Nothing happens.

"Stop," Stoker says. "Or your friends will die."

I don't know what to say to that. Didn't I just *see* them all die?

Then I get it. "You didn't kill them *now*. You killed them in the future, didn't you?"

"That's right. You're going to let Ahasuerus and me leave—or at some point, not too long from now, all your friends will simply drop dead."

"You're bluffing. That sword used to belong to a thrope, it doesn't have any silver in it. Which means it won't affect Cassius *or* Tair—"

"It doesn't have any silver in it *now*. But it did once, long ago—and I can return it to that state whenever I want."

Have I mentioned how much I hate time travel? He's saying he can kill any of the people he just stabbed by projecting a version of the sword that existed in the past—and was made of silver—into their bodies in the future. Assassination on a timer. Except—

Another slit appears in thin air, and my gun drops out of it. I catch it with my free hand and aim it at Stoker's head.

"You know," I say, "I'm starting to warm up to this whole time-travel idea."

Stoker's eyes flicker to the Midnight Sword and back to me. He's a bright guy, and understands immediately. His reaction is to grin. "So at some point in the future, you manage to take the sword from me, and then use it to rearm yourself in the past. I assume that since only one portal opened, you managed to destroy or lock away the sword immediately afterward. Smart."

"No, just good planning. I'm making a note to repay my future self with a bottle of tequila and a massage from a bodybuilder named Sven."

Standoff. I could kill either the sorcerer or the terrorist before either of them can blink—even Stoker's fast-forward trick with the sword won't work if all I have to do is twitch. I doubt he can do it twice in a row, anyway; most powerful magic needs some downtime to recharge.

I can do it. I can kill Stoker with a single shot, and capture Ahaseurus. Then I find wherever it is they've stashed my gun, use the sword to send it back in time, and lock up the sword afterward so nobody can use it again, ever—

The sword disappears from Stoker's hand.

"I've sent it through time," Stoker says. "Kill me, and it will obey my last order, to reappear and kill your friends. Let us go, and I promise I'll never use it."

The weird thing is, I believe him.

But it doesn't change the decision I have to make.

My contract is with the government. Even with Cassius dead, it will still stand. And if I hand them a live Ahaseurus and a dead Stoker, I'm pretty sure they'll live up to their end of the bargain. I can go home.

And all it will cost will be the lives of four people I care about. Well, three and a half, anyway.

I stare at Stoker for a long, long time.

"If you break your word," I say evenly, "I will make sure you live the rest of your very long life chained up in a Yakuza blood farm, paralyzed from the neck down. You understand me?"

"I do," he says. "Better than you think."

He nods at Ahaseurus. The sorcerer closes his eyes, raises his hands, and begins to mutter. He and Stoker both grow transparent, then disappear altogether.

"Outstanding," Tair says. "Yeah, I'm sure we can trust the word of a psychopathic, serial-killing terrorist. Good call."

Yeah. I guess we'll see.

Tom Omicron was on his way to Washington to negotiate terms of surrender with the president—that's how close Ahaseurus was to succeeding. When his plane touches down he's arrested instead, and taken into custody by the same lems that were supposed to greet him as an honor guard. He'll plead that he was under Ahaseurus's mystic control the entire time, of course, but Gretch and her team are putting together a fairly extensive case for his collusion beforehand. As so often happens at the end of a case, it's in the hands of the lawyers now.

Not a lot of lem lawyers that I know of.

Vegas and Night's Shining Jewel snapped back into their proper places when I killed Chassinda—or maybe *ended her existence* is a more accurate description. I wonder how long Ahaseurus had her captive; centuries, at least. If Azura's friend Brunt was the true father of the golem race, I guess that makes her, what, its aunt? Which makes me—

Nothing.

I'm just another cop. I'm not special, not some sort of linchpin in this whole mess. A different version of myself, from a different world and a different time, had the bad luck to be a killer's first victim, that's all. The consequences eventually filtered down to me, but that's not my fault.

I've seen many victims blame themselves for the horrible things that have happened to them, and I'm not going to do that. I understand the process—it's a way of imposing control, of trying to make sense of a senseless situation. To someone who's been targeted and attacked, it's actually more comforting to think they've done something wrong than to view it as random; you can fix a mistake, but you can't fix chaos.

But chaos is a part of life, just like order is a part of death. You have to accept that, adapt to it.

It's the only way to survive.

Azura disappears, too.

Not into thin air like Ahaseurus and Stoker did. No, she's still there after they've gone, a little groggy from whatever the sorcerer did to her, and the first thing she does after I untie her is to retrieve the Warbler's Child from the wreckage of the throne. Then she helps me free Cassius while the room slowly fills up with confused lems, all of whom are suddenly being very helpful. Some kind of psychic backlash, I guess.

The next time I look around, she's gone.

Makes sense, I suppose. Secret agents aren't really supposed to hang around afterward and answer questions—it detracts from the whole mysterious vibe. Plus, there's always the chance they'll get thrown in jail for the indiscriminate slaughter of henchmen. I have no doubt she's still after Ahaseurus, which means I'll probably run into her again. I'm kind of looking forward to it.

Cassius is in pretty bad shape—a pire becomes more vulnerable to damage when he's aging. He'll recover, though, as will Tair. I grab the highest-ranking lem I can find and shout at him until he finds someone who can get me a chopper. I want both my boss and my prisoner in a hospital, but their injuries aren't life threatening; I tell the pilot to take them to the nearest medical facility across the state line. Nevada still feels like a war zone, and those are never safe.

When a thrope dies, he reverts to human form, while a lem just becomes inert. A pire who expires pays off the time-debt his body owes the universe: If he's been undead for a hundred years, then a century's worth of decay sets in all at once. I expect something similar to occur with an underdead body, but to my surprise the exact opposite happens: Chassinda's corpse turns to stone. I remember something from one of the myths about sunlight affecting them that way, which makes me sad. Not only was Chassinda a possession for all those years, she never saw the sun the entire time.

I have an NSA team haul the corpse away. Eisfanger's going to have to chisel the Balancer gem out of her body.

I wrap things up in Vegas as quickly as I can, then commandeer another chopper to get the hell out of town. Turns out my instincts were right; not less than twenty-four hours later the Mantle enters into negotiations with the US government to turn the entire state into a self-governing entity, a golem country. Tom Omicron is still in prison, but that's probably just a negotiating tactic. Now that they've demonstrated they can take over the world anytime they want to, the prevailing political opinion seems to be *Let's not give them a reason to want to.* Besides, it's only Nevada—it's not like they're asking us to give up California or New York.

Chassinda's body never makes it to Eisfanger's lab. Somewhere on the road between Vegas and Seattle, it disappears; when the NSA agents who were transporting it open the back of the truck, all that's there is a full bottle of tequila and a note that reads: *You still owe me a drink. Thought I'd hold on to this in the meantime.* Well, I'd rather she had the Balancer than Ahaseurus.

I don't see Charlie for a while.

I sent him out on the chopper with Cassius and Tair, telling him to keep an eye on the thrope. He didn't argue.

I get back to Seattle. Debrief with Gretchen. Turns out the whole time-traveling stabby thing can be handled with some industrial-strength wards in place on each of the victims, preventing the blade from showing up and killing them. The news is a great relief, and I celebrate by going home, feeding my dog, and falling into bed.

The world slowly gets back to normal, or what passes for it here. Cassius spends all of a day in the hospital then comes back to work. He wants a full report, which I give him. Charlie isn't with him.

I go see Damon Eisfanger in the forensics lab. He's got an uncomfortable look on his face when I walk through his door.

"Uh, hi, Jace. Glad to see you're okay."

"Better than a lot of other Vegas tourists, anyway." After the cities snapped back into their proper places, hundreds of bodies were found inside the initial swap sites. Ahaseurus needed something to get his spell going, and apparently he used the Balancer to trade innocent lives for a mystic jump-start. I'm sure Azura's people discovered the same thing in NSJ.

"You said you had something to tell me," I say. "When I contacted you over the Internet. What was it?"

"Oh, that."

"Yeah, that."

"I don't know, I thought the situation was dire, so maybe there was something you should know. Maybe." He looks miserable.

"Please tell me you're not going to reveal you're madly in love with me."

"What? No! No, this is about Asher. Uh, Ahaseurus."

"So spill it, already."

"Do you know the legend of the Wandering Jew?"

"Vaguely. Taunted Jesus on the cross, right? Doomed to wander the Earth until Judgment Day as punishment. Always sounded kinda harsh to me; make one bad joke and pay for it forever? That's not exactly turning the other cheek. And come on, the guy was up and around three days later—apparently the only thing that stayed dead was his sense of humor."

"That's the story—more or less—from your world. Here, it's a little different." He hesitates. "You have to understand, pires and thropes weren't exactly on good terms with the human race back then. There were periodic purges, wholesale slaughters of the supernatural races. Until the Christians came along, people thought we were demons. Then, suddenly, there was one person saying maybe we weren't so bad."

"Hold up. Are you saying the early Christian church was *pro*-supernatural?"

"Not explicitly. But some people took the whole 'love thy neighbor' thing to include hemovores and lycanthropes."

"But not the Wandering Jew."

"No. In fact, it's said that what he taunted Jesus about was his support of the supernaturals—that that's what got him crucified. It split religious scholars for a long time, with people arguing that the taunter was right or wrong, or that he did or didn't exist. The Catholic Church eventually endorsed the view that yes, he did exist, and yes, his punishment was deserved. This wasn't a condemnation of the Jewish faith in general, you understand, just this one individual. In fact, he's usually just referred to as the Wanderer these days."

"It's what I'm going to call you if you don't get to the point."

"Despite what the church says, most people still consider the Wanderer a myth. But he's not. In fact, he's a powerful sorcerer who helped end World War Two."

I can see why Eisfanger was reluctant to talk about this. "You mean he was one of the shamans who crafted the Shub-Niggurath spell? The spell that sacrificed six million human beings?"

"He was in charge." Eisfanger's voice is low and ashamed. "I'm not supposed to know any of this, Jace. I did some snooping where I shouldn't. The names of all the sorcerers who worked on the project were top secret, but I managed to get the name of the top guy. It was—"

"Ahaseurus."

"Yeah."

I don't know how to respond to that. The look on my face must be telling Eisfanger volumes, though, because he blurts out, "I didn't know if the information would do you any good, but you were stranded in Vegas and there were riots breaking out everywhere and no one could get in touch with Cassius—"

"It's okay, Damon," I say. "It doesn't make any difference. I already hate the son-of-a-bitch; this just makes me hate him more."

"What are you going to do?"

"Keep on chasing him."

"And when you catch him?" I notice he doesn't make the mistake of saying *if*.

"Honestly, I don't know," I say. "Depends on whether or not I've run out of bullets by then."

I can hardly believe it. No matter how evil I thought Ahaseurus was, I still believed he was a human being. But like all sociopaths, he's a species of one; nobody other than himself is real to him. He didn't create golems to help the human race, he created them to help *him*.

And he's been alive for a long, long time. I wonder what other events in history he's manipulated, what other genocides or atrocities he's engineered.

He's responsible for the deaths of at least six million people, maybe more. Somebody has to avenge them.

Even if it means ripping up my ticket home.

On the third day, Charlie's waiting for me outside my apartment when I leave for work.

"Hey," he says. He's wearing a new suit, a plum-colored one with gray pinstripes. Gray fedora with plum hatband, polished dark gray shoes. He's leaning up against a lamppost with his hands jammed in his pockets.

"Hey." I stop, look him up and down. "Nice."

"Picked it up in Reno."

"Thought you were in California."

"I was. Stopped in Reno on the way back." He hasn't met my eyes yet. "Got a job offer."

I blink. "As what, a replacement for a cigar-store Indian? Something that doesn't show quite as much emotion?"

He doesn't take the bait. "Reno's going to be the new capital. The Mantle thought I might make a good police chief."

I don't know what to say to that, so I just nod. "Oh."

"Haven't given them an answer yet."

"Ah."

"Oh? Ah? You gonna use actual words, or just practice your vowels?"

"You'd make a great police chief, Charlie."

He rubs the back of his head with one hand. "Maybe. Thing is, I don't like to leave things unfinished. Not in my nature."

"Sure. I know what that's like."

"And you and me, we have some unfinished business."

"I guess we do."

"Which is why I'm here."

I take a deep breath. I knew this was coming, I just didn't know how I was going to handle it. "Okay. Look, I'm sorry. You didn't give me any choice."

Now he looks offended. "What, you replaced me already? I know you have the patience of a chimpanzee that's been guzzling espresso, but it's only been two days—"

"Replace you? I'm trying to *apologize* to you, you moron."

"For what?"

"Shooting you?"

"Oh, *that*." He snorts. "I've taken worse. No, what I'm saying is that I can't just quit my assignment. It wouldn't be fair. I mean, the next poor guy to get stuck with you would never forgive me."

"No, of course not."

"So I guess I'll stick around. At least until we catch Stoker."

"And Ahaseurus."

"Yeah. Him, too."

We look at each other for a moment. "Then what?" I

ask. "Going to move to Nevada, help build the new len homeland?"

"Nah. I like the home I've got."

We fall in step beside each other. It's a nice night, and the office isn't that far away.

"Yeah," I say. "Me, too."

Death definitely blows. And dying sure does bite…

Don't miss more novels from *The Bloodhound Files*

by

DD Barant

DYING BITES

ISBN: 978-0-312-94258-8

DEATH BLOWS

ISBN: 978-0-312-94258-8

Available from St. Martin's Paperbacks